Other Anthologies edited by
Dennis Pepper

For Older Readers

The Oxford Book of Animal Stories
The Oxford Book of Christmas Stories
A Book of Tall Stories
The Young Oxford Book of Ghost Stories
The New Young Oxford Book of Ghost Stories
The Young Oxford Book of Supernatural Stories
The Young Oxford Book of Nasty Endings
The Young Oxford Book of Nightmares

For Younger Readers

The Oxford Book of Scarytales
The Oxford Christmas Storybook
The *Happy Birthday* Book
(*with* David Jackson)
The Oxford Funny Story Book

The
Young Oxford Book
of
Aliens

DENNIS PEPPER

OXFORD
UNIVERSITY PRESS

OXFORD
UNIVERSITY PRESS

Great Clarendon Street, Oxford OX2 6DP

Oxford University Press is a department of the University of Oxford.
It furthers the University's objective of excellence in research, scholarship,
and education by publishing worldwide in

Oxford New York

Athens Auckland Bangkok Bogotá Buenos Aires Calcutta
Cape Town Chennai Dar es Salaam Delhi Florence Hong Kong Istanbul
Karachi Kuala Lumpur Madrid Melbourne Mexico City Mumbai
Nairobi Paris São Paulo Shanghai Singapore Taipei Tokyo Toronto Warsaw
with associated companies in Berlin Ibadan

Oxford is a registered trade mark of Oxford University Press
in the UK and in certain other countries

First published 1998
First published in paperback 2000

British Library Cataloguing in Publication Data
Data available

Cover by John Walker

ISBN 0 19 278155 3 (hardback)
ISBN 0 19 278177 4 (paperback)

Cover image reproduced by kind permission of Millennium Images Ltd.
Photograph by Herborg Pedersen

Typeset by
Mike Brain

Printed in Great Britain by Biddles Ltd, Guildford and King's Lynn

Contents

The truth is in here—somewhere

Introduction

Take another look at the dustjacket or cover of this book. Is this what you expect an alien to be like: a skinny, hairless, bug-eyed geriatric who forgot to put his false teeth in when he got up this morning? Or would he—or she—be more like Nicholas Stuart Gray's star beast? Or Barbara Paul's warlike Broghoke who glory in fighting and conquest? Or Damon Knight's Kanamit, always endeavouring to see that the human race is happy and contented? Or Ray Nelson's lizard-like Fascinators whose methods of control are very different from those of the Broghoke and Kanamit but, at least until George Nada 'wakes up', no less effective?

In fact most of the aliens who have been active on this planet over the centuries have looked more like Worden and his companions in Murray Leinster's story or Harry Harrison's Garth and Mark: white-skinned and hairy, with superior weapons and technology, seeking to control and colonize, exploit and convert. They 'discovered' the Americas, and began a bloodthirsty programme of conquest and annihilation against the people already living there. They 'opened up' Africa to colonization, exploitation, and trade, including trade in slaves. They embarked on 'voyages of discovery' through the Pacific, and in the process claimed many countries (and their peoples) for themselves, extending their colonies round the planet.

The history books we read don't put it quite like this, of course, but then they were written for the most part by historians belonging to the alien civilization. And it does depend on what we mean by 'alien'.

In the novels and stories we read, the films and television plays we watch, aliens are almost always creatures from a different planet rather than humans from a different continent, but the issues that are being explored are much the same. What happens when contact is first made, and *how* do we communicate? Are these aliens military invaders, empire builders, settlers, traders, peaceful emissaries? Do we welcome them, because if we do it may then be too late to take military action? Can we *trust* them? Do they even think like us? What do they believe in? And so on. The writers in this collection of stories are exploring these, and other, matters but although they write about aliens the issues they raise are about humans, about ourselves.

As you might expect, many of these stories take place on Earth and the aliens are from out there somewhere. They are stories about how humans receive alien visitors and how aliens treat the human population. In other stories humans are themselves aliens on distant planets and the spaceman's boot is, as it were, on the other foot, but those persistent questions—they are really questions about what it means to be human—remain much the same. Indeed, they pervade one story, specially written for this collection, which takes place on an alien planet and involves the indigenous people and alien emissaries but in which there are no humans at all.

That leads us to another question: is it *possible* for a human writer to write about anything other than the human condition? Aliens, however they may be presented, are aspects of ourselves.

Dennis Pepper
June 1998

Encounter at Dawn

ARTHUR C. CLARKE

It was in the last days of the Empire. The tiny ship was far from home, and almost a hundred light-years from the great parent vessel searching through the loosely packed stars at the rim of the Milky Way. But even here it could not escape from the shadow that lay across civilization: beneath that shadow, pausing ever and again in their work to wonder how their distant homes were faring, the scientists of the Galactic Survey still laboured at their never-ending task.

The ship held only three occupants, but among them they carried knowledge of many sciences, and the experience of half a lifetime in space. After the long interstellar night, the star ahead was warming their spirits as they dropped down towards its fires. A little more golden, a trifle more brilliant than the sun that now seemed a legend of their childhood. They knew from past experience that the chance of locating planets here was more than ninety per cent, and for the moment they forgot all else in the excitement of discovery.

They found the first planet within minutes of coming to rest. It was a giant, of a familiar type, too cold for protoplasmic life and probably possessing no stable surface. So they turned their search sunward, and presently were rewarded.

It was a world that made their hearts ache for home, a world where everything was hauntingly familiar, yet never quite the same. Two great land masses floated in blue-green seas, capped by ice at both poles. There were some desert regions, but the larger part of the planet was obviously fertile. Even from this distance, the signs of vegetation were unmistakably clear.

They gazed hungrily at the expanding landscape as they fell down into the atmosphere, heading towards noon in the sub-tropics. The ship plummeted through cloudless skies towards a great river, checked its fall with a surge of soundless power, and came to rest among the long grasses by the water's edge.

No one moved: there was nothing to be done until the automatic instruments had finished their work. Then a bell tinkled softly and the lights on the control board flashed in a pattern of meaningful chaos. Captain Altman rose to his feet with a sigh of relief.

'We're in luck,' he said. 'We can go outside without protection, if the pathogenic tests are satisfactory. What did you make of the place as we came in, Bertrond?'

'Geologically stable—no active volcanoes, at least. I didn't see any trace of cities, but that proves nothing. If there's a civiliza-tion here, it may have passed that stage.'

'Or not reached it yet?'

Bertrond shrugged. 'Either's just as likely. It may take us some time to find out on a planet this size.'

'More time than we've got,' said Clindar, glancing at the com-munications panel that linked them to the mother ship and thence to the Galaxy's threatened heart. For a moment there was a gloomy silence. Then Clindar walked to the control board and pressed a pattern of keys with automatic skill.

With a slight jar, a section of the hull slid aside and the fourth member of the crew stepped out on to the new planet, flexing metal limbs and adjusting servomotors to the unaccustomed gravity. Inside the ship, a television screen glimmered into life, revealing a long vista of waving grasses, some trees in the middle distance, and a glimpse of the great river. Clindar punched a button, and the picture flowed steadily across the screen as the robot turned its head.

'Which way shall we go?' Clindar asked.

'Let's have a look at those trees,' Altman replied. 'If there's any animal life we'll find it there.'

'Look!' cried Bertrond. 'A bird!'

Clindar's fingers flew over the keyboard: the picture centred on the tiny speck that had suddenly appeared on the left of the screen, and expanded rapidly as the robot's telephoto lens came into action.

'You're right,' he said. 'Feather—beak—well up the evolutionary ladder. This place looks promising. I'll start the camera.'

The swaying motion of the picture as the robot walked forward did not distract them: they had grown accustomed to it long ago. But they had never become reconciled to this exploration by proxy when all their impulses cried out to them to leave the ship, to run through the grass and to feel the wind blowing against their faces. Yet it was too great a risk to take, even on a world that seemed as fair as this. There was always a skull hidden behind Nature's most smiling face. Wild beasts, poisonous reptiles, quagmires—death could come to the unwary explorer in a thousand disguises. And worst of all were the invisible enemies, the bacteria and viruses against which the only defence might often be a thousand light-years away.

A robot could laugh at all these dangers and even if, as sometimes happened, it encountered a beast powerful enough to destroy it—well, machines could always be replaced.

They met nothing on the walk across the grasslands. If any small animals were disturbed by the robot's passage, they kept outside its field of vision. Clindar slowed the machine as it approached the trees, and the watchers in the spaceship flinched involuntarily at the branches that appeared to slash across their eyes. The picture dimmed for a moment before the controls readjusted themselves to the weaker illumination; then it came back to normal.

The forest was full of life. It lurked in the undergrowth, clambered among the branches, flew through the air. It fled chattering and gibbering through the trees as the robot advanced. And all the while the automatic cameras were recording the pictures that formed on the screen, gathering material for the biologists to analyse when the ship returned to base.

Clindar breathed a sigh of relief when the trees suddenly thinned. It was exhausting work, keeping the robot from smashing into obstacles as it moved through the forest, but on open ground it could take care of itself. Then the picture trembled as if beneath a hammer blow, there was a grinding metallic thud, and the whole scene swept vertiginously upward as the robot toppled and fell.

'What's that?' cried Altman. 'Did you trip?'

'No,' said Clindar grimly, his fingers flying over the keyboard. 'Something attacked from the rear. I hope . . . ah . . . I've still got control.'

He brought the robot to a sitting position and swivelled its head. It did not take long to find the cause of the trouble. Standing a few feet away, and lashing its tail angrily, was a large quadruped with a most ferocious set of teeth. At the moment it was, fairly obviously, trying to decide whether to attack again.

Slowly, the robot rose to its feet, and as it did so the great beast crouched to spring. A smile flitted across Clindar's face: he knew how to deal with this situation. His thumb felt for the seldom-used key labelled 'Siren'.

The forest echoed with a hideous undulating scream from the robot's concealed speaker, and the machine advanced to meet its adversary, arms flailing in front of it. The startled beast almost fell over backwards in its effort to turn, and in seconds was gone from sight.

'Now I suppose we'll have to wait a couple of hours until everything comes out of hiding again,' said Bertrond ruefully.

'I don't know much about animal psychology,' interjected Altman, 'but is it usual for them to attack something completely unfamiliar?'

'Some will attack anything that moves, but that's unusual. Normally they attack only for food, or if they've already been threatened. What are you driving at? Do you suggest that there are other robots on this planet?'

'Certainly not. But our carnivorous friend may have mistaken our machine for a more edible biped. Don't you think that this opening in the jungle is rather unnatural? It could easily be a path.'

'In that case,' said Clindar promptly, 'we'll follow it and find out. I'm tired of dodging trees, but I hope nothing jumps on us again: it's bad for my nerves.'

'You were right, Altman,' said Bertrond a little later. 'It's certainly a path. But that doesn't mean intelligence. After all, animals—'

He stopped in mid-sentence, and at the same instant Clindar brought the advancing robot to a halt. The path had suddenly opened out into a wide clearing, almost completely occupied by a village of flimsy huts. It was ringed by a wooden palisade, obviously defence against an enemy who at the moment presented no threat. For the gates were wide open, and beyond them the inhabitants were going peacefully about their ways.

For many minutes the three explorers stared in silence at the screen. Then Clindar shivered a little and remarked: 'It's uncanny. It might be our own planet, a hundred thousand years ago. I feel as if I've gone back in time.'

'There's nothing weird about it,' said the practical Altman. 'After all, we've discovered nearly a hundred planets with our type of life on them.'

'Yes,' retorted Clindar. 'A hundred in the whole Galaxy! I still think it's strange it had to happen to us.'

'Well, it had to happen to *somebody*,' said Bertrond philosophically. 'Meanwhile, we must work out our contact procedure. If we send the robot into the village it will start a panic.'

'That,' said Altman, 'is a masterly understatement. What we'll have to do is catch a native by himself and prove that we're friendly. Hide the robot, Clindar. Somewhere in the woods where it can watch the village without being spotted. We've a week's practical anthropology ahead of us!'

It was three days before the biological tests showed that it would be safe to leave the ship. Even then Bertrond insisted on going alone—alone, that is, if one ignored the substantial company of the robot. With such an ally he was not afraid of this planet's larger beasts, and his body's natural defences could take care of the micro-organisms. So, at least, the analysers had assured him; and considering the complexity of the problem, they made remarkably few mistakes . . .

He stayed outside for an hour, enjoying himself cautiously, while his companions watched with envy. It would be another three days before they could be quite certain that it was safe to follow Bertrond's example. Meanwhile, they kept busy enough watching the village through the lenses of the robot, and recording everything they could with the cameras. They had moved the spaceship at night so that it was hidden in the depths of the forest, for they did not wish to be discovered until they were ready.

And all the while the news from home grew worse. Though their remoteness here at the edge of the Universe deadened its impact, it lay heavily on their minds and sometimes overwhelmed them with a sense of futility. At any moment, they knew, the signal for recall might come as the Empire summoned up its last resources in its extremity. But until then they would continue their work as though pure knowledge were the only thing that mattered.

Seven days after landing, they were ready to make the experiment. They knew now what paths the villagers used when going hunting, and Bertrond chose one of the less frequented ways. Then he placed a chair firmly in the middle of the path and settled down to read a book.

It was not, of course, quite as simple as that: Bertrond had taken all imaginable precautions. Hidden in the undergrowth fifty yards away, the robot was watching through its telescopic lenses, and in its hand it held a small but deadly weapon. Controlling it from the spaceship, his fingers poised over the keyboard, Clindar waited to do what might be necessary.

That was the negative side of the plan: the positive side was more obvious. Lying at Bertrond's feet was the carcass of a small, horned animal which he hoped would be an acceptable gift to any hunter passing this way.

Two hours later the radio in his suit harness whispered a warning. Quite calmly, though the blood was pounding in his veins, Bertrond laid aside his book and looked down the trail. The savage was walking forward confidently enough, swinging a spear in his right hand. He paused for a moment when he saw

Bertrond, then advanced more cautiously. He could tell that there was nothing to fear, for the stranger was slightly built and obviously unarmed.

When only twenty feet separated them, Bertrond gave a re-assuring smile and rose slowly to his feet. He bent down, picked up the carcass, and carried it forward as an offering. The gesture would have been understood by any creature on any world, and it was understood here. The savage reached forward, took the animal, and threw it effortlessly over his shoulder. For an instant he stared into Bertrond's eyes with a fathomless expression; then he turned and walked back towards the village. Three times he glanced round to see if Bertrond was following, and each time Bertrond smiled and waved reassurance. The whole episode lasted little more than a minute. As the first contact between two races it was completely without drama, though not without dignity.

Bertrond did not move until the other had vanished from sight. Then he relaxed and spoke into his suit microphone.

'That was a pretty good beginning,' he said jubilantly. 'He wasn't in the least frightened, or even suspicious. I think he'll be back.'

'It still seems too good to be true,' said Altman's voice in his ear. 'I should have thought he'd have been either scared or hostile. Would *you* have accepted a lavish gift from a peculiar stranger with such little fuss?'

Bertrond was slowly walking back to the ship. The robot had now come out of cover and was keeping guard a few paces behind him.

'*I* wouldn't,' he replied, 'but I belong to a civilized community. Complete savages may react to strangers in many different ways, according to their past experience. Suppose this tribe has never had any enemies. That's quite possible on a large but sparsely populated planet. Then we may expect curiosity, but no fear at all.'

'If these people have no enemies,' put in Clindar, no longer fully occupied in controlling the robot, 'why have they got a stockade round the village?'

'I meant no *human* enemies,' replied Bertrond. 'If that's true, it simplifies our task immensely.'

'Do you think he'll come back?'

'Of course. If he's as human as I think, curiosity and greed will make him return. In a couple of days we'll be bosom friends.'

Looked at dispassionately, it became a fantastic routine. Every morning the robot would go hunting under Clindar's direction, until it was now the deadliest killer in the jungle. Then Bertrond would wait until Yaan—which was the nearest they could get to his name—came striding confidently along the path. He came at the same time every day, and he always came alone. They wondered about this: did he wish to keep his great discovery to himself and thus get all the credit for his hunting prowess? If so, it showed unexpected foresight and cunning.

At first Yaan had departed at once with his prize, as if afraid that the donor of such a generous gift might change his mind. Soon, however, as Bertrond had hoped, he could be induced to stay for a while by simple conjuring tricks and a display of brightly coloured fabrics and crystals, in which he took a child-like delight. At last Bertrond was able to engage him in lengthy conversations, all of which were recorded as well as being filmed through the eyes of the hidden robot.

One day the philologists might be able to analyse this material; the best that Bertrond could do was to discover the meanings of a few simple verbs and nouns. This was made more difficult by the fact that Yaan not only used different words for the same thing, but sometimes the same word for different things.

Between these daily interviews, the ship travelled far, surveying the planet from the air and sometimes landing for more detailed examinations. Although several other human settlements were observed, Bertrond made no attempt to get in touch with them, for it was easy to see that they were all at much the same cultural level as Yaan's people.

It was, Bertrond often thought, a particularly bad joke on the part of Fate that one of the Galaxy's very few truly human races should have been discovered at this moment of time. Not long ago this would have been an event of supreme importance; now civilization was too hard-pressed to concern itself with these savage cousins waiting at the dawn of history.

Not until Bertrond was sure he had become part of Yaan's everyday life did he introduce him to the robot. He was showing Yaan the patterns in a kaleidoscope when Clindar brought the machine striding through the grass with its latest victim dangling across one metal arm. For the first time Yaan showed something akin to fear; but he relaxed at Bertrond's soothing words, though he continued to watch the advancing monster. It halted some distance away, and Bertrond walked forward to meet it. As he did so, the robot raised its arms and handed him the dead beast. He took it solemnly and carried it back to Yaan, staggering a little under the unaccustomed load.

Bertrond would have given a great deal to know just what Yaan was thinking as he accepted the gift. Was he trying to decide whether the robot was master or slave? Perhaps such conceptions as this were beyond his grasp: to him the robot might be merely another man, a hunter who was a friend of Bertrond.

Clindar's voice, slightly larger than life, came from the robot's speaker.

'It's astonishing how calmly he accepts us. Won't anything scare him?'

'You will keep judging him by your own standards,' replied Bertrond. 'Remember, his psychology is completely different, and much simpler. Now that he has confidence in me, anything that I accept won't worry him.'

'I wonder if that will be true of all his race?' queried Altman. 'It's hardly safe to judge by a single specimen. I want to see what happens when we send the robot into the village.'

'Hello!' exclaimed Bertrond. '*That* surprised him. He's never met a person who could speak with two voices before.'

'Do you think he'll guess the truth when he meets us?' said Clindar.

'No. The robot will be pure magic to him—but it won't be any more wonderful than fire and lightning and all the other forces he must already take for granted.'

'Well, what's the next move?' asked Altman, a little impatiently. 'Are you going to bring him to the ship, or will you go into the village first?'

Bertrond hesitated. 'I'm anxious not to do too much too quickly. You know the accidents that have happened with strange races when that's been tried. I'll let him think this over, and when we get back tomorrow I'll try to persuade him to take the robot back to the village.'

In the hidden ship, Clindar reactivated the robot and started it moving again. Like Altman, he was growing a little impatient of this excessive caution, but on all matters relating to alien life-forms Bertrond was the expert, and they had to obey his orders.

There were times now when he almost wished he were a robot himself, devoid of feelings or emotions, able to watch the fall of a leaf or the death agonies of a world with equal detachment . . .

The sun was low when Yaan heard the great voice crying from the jungle. He recognized it at once, despite its inhuman volume: it was the voice of his friend, and it was calling him.

In the echoing silence, the life of the village came to a stop. Even the children ceased to play: the only sound was the thin cry of a baby frightened by the sudden silence.

All eyes were upon Yaan as he walked swiftly to his hut and grasped the spear that lay beside the entrance. The stockade would soon be closed against the prowlers of the night, but he did not hesitate as he stepped out into the lengthening shadows. He was passing through the gates when once again that mighty voice summoned him, and now it held a note of urgency that came clearly across all the barriers of language and culture.

The shining giant who spoke with many voices met him a little way from the village and beckoned him to follow. There was no sign of Bertrond. They walked for almost a mile before they saw him in the distance, standing not far from the river's edge and staring out across the dark, slowly moving waters.

He turned as Yaan approached, yet for a moment seemed unaware of his presence. Then he gave a gesture of dismissal to the shining one, who withdrew into the distance.

Yaan waited. He was patient and, though he could never have expressed it in words, contented. When he was with Bertrond he felt the first intimations of that selfless, utterly irrational devotion his race would not fully achieve for many ages.

It was a strange tableau. Here at the river's brink two men were standing. One was dressed in a closely fitting uniform equipped with tiny, intricate mechanisms. The other was wearing the skin of an animal and was carrying a flint-tipped spear. Ten thousand generations lay between them, ten thousand generations and an immeasurable gulf of space. Yet they were both human. As she must do often in Eternity, Nature had repeated one of her basic patterns.

Presently Bertrond began to speak, walking to and fro in short, quick steps as he did, and in his voice there was a trace of madness.

'It's all over, Yaan. I'd hoped that with our knowledge we could have brought you out of barbarism in a dozen generations, but now you will have to fight your way up from the jungle alone, and it may take you a million years to do so. I'm sorry—there's so much we could have done. Even now I wanted to stay here, but Altman and Clindar talk of duty, and I suppose that they are right. There is little enough that we can do, but our world is calling and we must not forsake it.

'I wish you could understand me, Yaan. I wish you knew what I was saying. I'm leaving you these tools: some of them you will discover how to use, though as likely as not in a generation they'll be lost or forgotten. See how this blade cuts: it will be ages before your world can make its like. And guard this well: when you press the button—look! If you use it sparingly, it will give you light for years, though sooner or later it will die. As for these other things—find what use for them you can.

'Here come the first stars, up there in the east. Do you ever look at the stars, Yaan? I wonder how long it will be before you have discovered what they are, and I wonder what will have happened to us by then. Those stars are our homes, Yaan, and we cannot save them. Many have died already, in explosions so vast that I can imagine them no more than you. In a hundred thousand of your years, the light of those funeral pyres will reach your world and set its people wondering. By then, perhaps, your race will be reaching for the stars. I wish I could warn you against the mistakes we made, and which now will cost us all that we have won.

'It is well for your people, Yaan, that your world is here at the frontier of the Universe. You may escape the doom that waits for us. One day, perhaps, your ships will go searching among the stars as we have done, and they may come upon the ruins of our worlds and wonder who we were. But they will never know that we met here by this river when your race was young.

'Here come my friends; they would give me no more time. Goodbye, Yaan—use well the things I have left you. They are your world's greatest treasures.'

Something huge, something that glittered in the starlight, was sliding down from the sky. It did not reach the ground, but came to rest a little way above the surface, and in utter silence a rectangle of light opened in its side. The shining giant appeared out of the night and stepped through the golden door. Bertrond followed, pausing for a moment at the threshold to wave back at Yaan. Then the darkness closed behind him.

No more swiftly than smoke drifts upward from a fire, the ship lifted away. When it was so small that Yaan felt he could hold it in his hands, it seemed to blur into a long line of light slanting upwards into the stars. From the empty sky a peal of thunder echoed over the sleeping land; and Yaan knew at last that the gods were gone and would never come again.

For a long time he stood by the gently moving waters, and into his soul there came a sense of loss he was never to forget and never to understand. Then, carefully and reverently, he collected together the gifts that Bertrond had left.

Under the stars, the lonely figure walked homeward across a nameless land. Behind him the river flowed softly to the sea, winding through the fertile plains on which, more than a thousand centuries ahead, Yaan's descendants would build the great city they were to call Babylon.

Day of Succession

THEODORE L. THOMAS

General Paul T. Tredway was an arrogant man with the unforgivable gift of being always right. When the object came out of the sky in the late spring of 1979, it was General Tredway who made all of the decisions concerning it.

Sweeping in over the northern tip of Greenland, coming on a dead line from the Yamal Peninsula, the object alerted every warning unit from the Dew Line to the radar operator at the Philadelphia National Airport. Based on the earliest reports, General Tredway concluded that the object was acting in an anomalous fashion; its altitude was too low too long. Accordingly, acting with a colossal confidence, he called off the manned interceptor units and forbade the launching of interceptor missiles. The object came in low over the Pocono Mountains and crashed in south-eastern Pennsylvania two miles due west of Terre Hill.

The object still glowed a dull red, and the fire of the smashed house still smouldered when General Tredway arrived with the troops. He threw a cordon around it and made a swift investigation. The object: fifty feet long, thirty feet in diameter, football-shaped, metallic, too hot to inspect closely. Visualizing immediately what had to be done, the general set up a command headquarters and began ordering the items he needed. With no wasted word or motion he built towards the finished plan as he saw it.

Scientists arrived at the same time as the asbestos clothing needed for them to get close. Tanks and other matériel flowed towards the impact site. Radios and oscillators scanned all frequencies seeking—what? No man there knew what to expect, but no man cared. General Tredway was on the ground personally, and no one had time for anything but his job. The gunners sat with eyes glued to sights, mindful of the firing pattern in which they had been instructed. Handlers poised over their ammunition. Drivers waited with hands on the wheel, motors idling.

Behind this ring of steel a more permanent bulwark sprang up. Spotted back further were the technical shacks for housing the scientific equipment. Behind the shacks the reporters gathered, held firmly in check by armed troops. The site itself was a strange mixture of taut men in frozen immobility and casual men in bustling activity.

In an hour the fact emerged which General Tredway had suspected all along: the object was not of earthly origin. The alloy of which it was made was a known high-temperature alloy, but no technology on Earth could cast it in seamless form in that size and shape. Mass determinations and ultrasonic probes showed that the object was hollow but was crammed inside with a material different from the shell. It was then that General Tredway completely reorganized his fire power and mapped out a plan of action that widened the eyes of those who were to carry it out.

On the general's instructions, everything said at the site was said into radio transmitters and thus recorded a safe fifty miles away. And it was the broadcasting of the general's latest plan of action that brought in the first waves of mild protest. But the general went ahead.

The object had lost its dull hot glow when the first indications of activity inside could be heard. General Tredway immediately removed all personnel to positions of safety outside the ring of steel. The ring itself buttoned up; when a circle of men fire towards a common centre, someone can get hurt.

With the sound of tearing, protesting metal, a three-foot circle appeared at the top of the object, and the circle began to turn. As it turned it began to lift away from the main body of the object, and soon screw threads could be seen. The hatch rose silently, looking like a bung being unscrewed from a barrel. The time came when there was a gentle click, and the hatch dropped back a fraction of an inch; the last thread had become disengaged. There was a pause. The heavy silence was broken by a throbbing sound from the object that continued for forty-five seconds and then stopped. Then, without further sound, the hatch began to lift back on its northernmost rim.

In casual tones, as if he were speaking in a classroom, General Tredway ordered the northern, north-eastern and north-western regions of the ring into complete cover. The hatch lifted until finally its underside could be seen; it was coloured a dull, nonreflecting black. Higher the hatch lifted, and immediately following it was a bulbous mass that looked like a half-opened rose blossom. Deep within the mass there glowed a soft violet light, clearly apparent to the eye even in the sharp Pennsylvania sunshine.

The machine-gun bullets struck the mass first, and the tracers could be seen glancing off. But an instant later the shaped charges in the rockets struck the mass and shattered it. The 105s, the 101 rifles, the rocket launchers, poured a hail of steel onto the canted hatch, ricocheting much of the steel into the interior of the object. Delay-timed high-explosive shells went inside and detonated.

A flame tank left the ring of steel and lumbered forward, followed by two armoured trucks. At twenty-five yards a thin stream of fire leaped from the nozzle of the tank and splashed off the hatch in a Niagara of flame. A slight correction, and the Niagara poured down into the opening. The tank moved in close, and the guns fell suddenly silent. Left in the air was a high-pitched shrieking wail, abruptly cut off.

Flames leaped from the opening, so the tank turned off its igniter and simply shot fuel into the object. Asbestos-clad men jumped from the trucks and fed a metal hose through the opening and forced it deep into the object. The compressors started, and a blast of high-pressure air passed through the hose, insuring complete combustion of everything inside. For three minutes the men fed fuel and air to the interior of the object, paying in the metal hose as the end fused off. Flames shot skyward with the roar of a blast furnace. The heat was so great that the men at work were saved only by the constant streams of water that played on them. Then it was over.

General Tredway placed the burned-out cinder in charge of the scientists and then regrouped his men for resupply and criticism. These were in progress when the report of the second object came in.

The trackers were waiting for it. General Tredway had reasoned that when one object arrived, another might follow, and so he had ordered the trackers to look for it. It hit twenty-five miles west of the first one, near Florin. General Tredway and his men were on their way even before impact. They arrived twenty minutes after it hit.

The preparations were the same, only more streamlined now. The soldiers and the scientists moved more surely, with less wasted motion than before. But as the cooling period progressed, the waves of protest came out of Washington and reached towards General Tredway. 'Terrible.' 'First contact . . .' 'Exterminating them like vermin . . .' 'Peaceful relationship . . .' '. . . military mind.'

The protests took on an official character just before the hatch on the second object opened. An actual countermanding of General Tredway's authority came through just as the rockets opened fire on the half-opened rose blossom. The burning out proceeded on schedule. Before it was complete, General Tredway climbed into a helicopter to fly the hundred miles to Washington, DC. In half an hour he was there.

It is one of the circumstances of a democracy that in an emergency half a dozen men can speak for the entire country. General Tredway stalked into a White House conference room where waited the President, the Vice-President, the Speaker of the House, the President Pro Tempore of the Senate, the House Minority Leader, and a cabinet member. No sooner had he entered than the storm broke.

'Sit down, General, and explain to us if you can the meaning of your reprehensible conduct.'

'What are you trying to do, make butchers of us all?'

'You didn't give those . . . those persons a chance.'

'Here we had a chance to learn something, to learn a lot, and you killed them and destroyed their equipment.'

General Tredway sat immobile until the hot flood of words subsided. Then he said, 'Do any of you gentlemen have any evidence that their intentions were peaceable? Any evidence at all?'

There was silence for a moment as they stared at him. The President said, 'What evidence have you got they meant harm? You killed them before there was any evidence of anything.'

General Tredway shook his head, and a familiar supercilious tone crept unbidden into his voice. '*They* were the ones who landed on *our* planet. It was incumbent on them to find a way to convince us of their friendliness. Instead they landed with no warning at all, and with a complete disregard of human life. The first missile shattered a house, killed a man. There is ample evidence of their hostility,' and he could not help adding, 'if you care to look for it.'

The President flushed and snapped, 'That's not the way I see it. You could have kept them covered; you had enough fire power there to cover an army. If they made any hostile move, that would have been time enough for you to have opened up on them.'

The House Speaker leaned forward and plunked a sheaf of telegrams on the table. He tapped the pile with a forefinger and said, 'These are some of thousands that have come in. I picked out the ones from some of our outstanding citizens—educators, scientists, statesmen. All of them agree that this is a foolhardy thing you have done. You've destroyed a mighty source of knowledge for the human race.'

'None of them is a soldier,' said the general. 'I would not expect them to know anything about attack and defence.'

The Speaker nodded and drew one more telegram from an inner pocket. General Tredway, seeing what was coming, had to admire his tactics; this man was not Speaker for nothing. 'Here,' said the Speaker, 'is a reply to my telegram. It is from the Joint Chiefs. Care to read it?'

They all stared at the general, and he shook his head coldly. 'No. I take it that they do not understand the problem, either.'

'Now just a min—' A colonel entered the room and whispered softly to the President. The President pushed his chair back, but he did not get up. Nodding, he said, 'Good. Have Barnes take over. And see that he holds his fire until something happens. Hear? Make certain of that. I'll not tolerate any more of this unnecessary slaughter.' The colonel left.

The President turned and noted the understanding in the faces of the men at the table. He nodded and said, 'Yes, another one. And this time we'll do it right. I only hope the other two haven't got word to the third one that we're a bunch of killers.'

'There could be no communication of any kind emanating from the first two,' said General Tredway. 'I watched for that.'

'Yes. Well, it's the only thing you did right. I want you to watch to see the proper way to handle this.'

In the intervening hours General Tredway tried to persuade the others to adopt his point of view. He succeeded only in infuriating them. When the time came for the third object to open, the group of men were trembling in anger. They gathered around the television screen to watch General Barnes's handling of the situation.

General Tredway stood to the rear of the others, watching the hatch unscrew. General Barnes was using the same formation as that developed by General Tredway; the ring of steel was as tight as ever.

The familiar black at the bottom of the hatch came into view, followed closely by the top of the gleaming rose blossom. General Tredway snapped his fingers, the sound cracking loud in the still room. The men close to the set jumped and looked back at Tredway in annoyance. It was plain that the general had announced in his own way the proper moment to fire. Their eyes had hardly got back to the screen when it happened.

A thin beam of delicate violet light danced from the heart of the rose to the front of the steel ring. The beam rotated like a lighthouse beacon, only far, far faster. Whatever it touched, it sliced. Through tanks and trucks and guns and men it sliced, over and over again as the swift circular path of the beam spun in ever widening circles. Explosions rocked the site as high explosives detonated under the touch of the beam. The hatch of the object itself, neatly cut near the bottom, rolled ponderously down the side of the object to the ground. The beam bit into the ground and left seething ribbons of slag.

In three seconds the area was a mass of fused metal and molten rock and minced bodies and flame and smoke and thunder. In another two seconds the beam reached the television cameras, and the screen went blank.

The men near the screen stared speechless. At that moment the colonel returned and announced that a fourth object was on its way, and that its probable impact point was two miles due east of Harrisburg.

The group turned as one man to General Tredway, but he paid no attention. He was pacing back and forth, pulling at his lower lip, frowning in concentration.

'General,' said the President, 'I . . . I guess you had the right idea. These things are monsters. Will you handle this next one?'

General Tredway stopped and said, 'Yes, but I had better explain what is now involved. I want every vehicle that can move to converge on the fourth object; the one that is now loose will attempt to protect it. I want every plane and copter that can fly to launch a continuing attack on it. I want every available missile zeroed in and launched at it immediately. I want every fusion and fission bomb we've got directed at the fourth object by means of artillery, missiles and planes; one of them might get through. I want a request made to Canada, Brazil, Great Britain, France, Germany, Russia, and Italy to launch fusion-headed missiles at the site of the fourth object immediately. In this way we might have a chance to stop them. Let us proceed.'

The President stared at him and said, 'Have you gone crazy? I will give no such orders. What you ask for will destroy our middle eastern seaboard.'

The general nodded. 'Yes, everything from Richmond to Pittsburgh to Syracuse, I think, possibly more. Fallout will cover a wider area. There's no help for it.'

'You're insane. I will do no such thing.'

The Speaker stepped forward and said, 'Mr President, I think you should reconsider this. You saw what that thing could do; think of two of them loose. I am very much afraid the general may be right.'

'Don't be ridiculous.'

The Vice-President stepped to the President's side and said, 'I agree with the President. I never heard of such an absurd suggestion.'

The moment froze into silence. The general stared at the three men. Then, moving slowly and deliberately, he undid his holster flap and pulled out his pistol. He snapped the slide back and fired once at point-blank range, shifted the gun, and fired again. He walked over to the table and carefully placed the gun on it. Then he turned to the Speaker and said, 'Mr President, there is very little time. Will you give the necessary orders?'

Not Yet the End

FREDRIC BROWN

There was a greenish, hellish tinge to the light within the metal cube. It was a light that made the dead-white skin of the creature seated at the controls seem faintly green.

A single, faceted eye, front centre in the head, watched the seven dials unwinkingly. Since they had left Xandor that eye had never once wavered from the dials. Sleep was unknown to the race to which Kar-388Y belonged. Mercy, too, was unknown. A single glance at the sharp, cruel features below the faceted eye would have proved that.

The pointers on the fourth and seventh dials came to a stop. That meant the cube itself had stopped in space relative to its immediate objective. Kar reached forward with his upper right arm, and threw the stabilizer switch. Then he rose and stretched his cramped muscles.

Kar turned to face his companion in the cube, a being like himself. 'We are here,' he said. 'The first stop, Star Z-5689. It has nine planets, but only the third is habitable. Let us hope we find creatures here who will make suitable slaves for Xandor.'

Lal-16B, who had sat in rigid immobility during the journey, rose and stretched also. 'Let us hope so, yes. Then we can return to Xandor and be honoured while the fleet comes to get them. But let's not hope too strongly. To meet with success at the first place we stop would be a miracle. We'll probably have to look a thousand places.'

Kar shrugged. 'Then we'll look a thousand places. With the Lounacs dying off we must have slaves else our mines must close and our race will die.'

He sat down at the controls again and threw a switch that activated a visiplate that would show what was beneath them. He said, 'We are above the night side of the third planet. There is a cloud layer below us. I'll use the manuals from here.'

He began to press buttons. A few minutes later he said, 'Look, Lal, at the visiplate. Regularly spaced lights—a city! The planet *is* inhabited.'

Lal had taken his place at the other switchboard, the fighting controls. Now he too was examining dials. 'There is nothing for us to fear. There is not even the vestige of a forcefield around the city. The scientific knowledge of the race is crude. We can wipe the city out with one blast if we are attacked.'

'Good,' Kar said. 'But let me remind you that destruction is not our purpose—yet. We want specimens. If they prove satisfactory and the fleet comes and takes as many thousand slaves as we need, then will be time to destroy not a city but the whole planet. So that their civilization will never progress to the point where they'll be able to launch reprisal raids.'

Lal adjusted a knob. 'All right. I'll put on the megrafield and we'll be invisible to them unless they see far into the ultraviolet, and, from the spectrum of their sun, I doubt that they do.'

As the cube descended the light within it changed from green to violet and beyond. It came to a gentle rest. Kar manipulated the mechanism that operated the airlock.

He stepped outside, Lal just behind him. 'Look,' Kar said, 'two bipeds. Two arms, two eyes—not dissimilar to the Lounacs, although smaller. Well, here are our specimens.'

He raised his lower left arm, whose three-fingered hands held a thin rod wound with wire. He pointed it first at one of the creatures, then at the other. Nothing visible emanated from the end of the rod, but they both froze instantly into statuelike figures.

'They're not large, Kar,' Lal said. 'I'll carry one back, you carry the other. We can study them better inside the cube, after we're back in space.'

Kar looked about him in the dim light. 'All right, two are enough, and one seems to be male and the other female. Let's get going.'

A minute later the cube was ascending and as soon as they were well out of the atmosphere, Kar threw the stabilizer switch and joined Lal, who had been starting a study of the specimens during the brief ascent.

'Viviparous,' said Lal. 'Five-fingered, with hands suited to reasonably delicate work. But—let's try the most important test, intelligence.'

Kar got the paired headsets. He handed one pair to Lal, who put one on his own head, one on the head of one of the specimens. Kar did the same with the other specimen.

After a few minutes, Kar and Lal stared at each other bleakly.

'Seven points below minimum,' Kar said. 'They could not be trained even for the crudest labour in the mines. Incapable of understanding the most simple instructions. Well, we'll take them back to the Xandor museum.'

'Shall I destroy the planet?'

'No,' Kar said. 'Maybe a million years from now—if our race lasts that long—they'll have evolved enough to become suitable for our purpose. Let us move on to the next star with planets.'

The make-up editor of the *Milwaukee Star* was in the composing room, supervising the closing of the local page. Jenkins, the head make-up compositor, was pushing in leads to tighten the second-to-last column.

'Room for one more story in the eight column, Pete,' he said. 'About thirty-six picas. There are two there in the overset that will fit. Which one shall I use?'

The make-up editor glanced at the type in the galleys lying on the stone beside the chase. Long practice enabled him to read the headlines upside down at a glance. 'The convention story and the zoo story, huh? Oh, hell, run the convention story. Who cares if the zoo director thinks two monkeys disappeared off Monkey Island last night?'

The Star Beast

NICHOLAS STUART GRAY

Soon upon a time, and not so far ahead, there was a long streak of light down the night sky, a flicker of fire, and a terrible bang that startled all who heard it, even those who were normally inured to noise. When day came, the matter was discussed, argued, and finally dismissed. For no one could discover any cause at all for the disturbance.

Shortly afterwards, at a farm, there was heard a scrabbling at the door, and a crying. When the people went to see what was there, they found a creature. It was not easy to tell what sort of creature, but far too easy to tell that it was hurt and hungry and afraid. Only its pain and hunger had brought it to the door for help.

Being used to beasts, the farmer and his wife tended the thing. They put it in a loose-box and tended it. They brought water in a big basin and it drank thirstily, but with some difficulty—for it seemed to want to lift it to its mouth instead of lapping, and the basin was too big, and it was too weak. So it lapped. The farmer dressed the great burn that seared its thigh and shoulder and arm. He was kind enough, in a rough way, but the creature moaned, and set its teeth, and muttered strange sounds, and clenched its front paws . . .

Those front paws . . . ! They were so like human hands that it was quite startling to see them. Even with their soft covering of grey fur they were slender, long-fingered, with the fine nails of a girl. And its body was like that of a boy—a half-grown lad—though it was as tall as a man. Its head was man-shaped. The long and slanting eyes were as yellow as topaz, and shone from inside with their own light. And the lashes were thick and silvery.

'It's a monkey of some kind,' decided the farmer.

'But so beautiful,' said his wife. 'I've never heard of a monkey like this. They're charming—pretty—amusing—all in their own way. But not beautiful, as a real person might be.'

They were concerned when the creature refused to eat. It turned away its furry face, with those wonderful eyes, the straight nose, and curving fine lips, and would not touch the best of the season's hay. It would not touch the dog biscuits or the bones. Even the boiled cod-head that was meant for the cats' supper, it refused. In the end, it settled for milk. It lapped it delicately out of the big basin, making small movements of its hands—its forepaws—as though it would have preferred some smaller utensil that it could lift to its mouth.

Word went round. People came to look at the strange and injured creature in the barn. Many people came. From the village, the town, and the city. They prodded it, and examined it, turning it this way and that. But no one could decide just what it was. A beast for sure. A monkey, most likely. Escaped from a circus or menagerie. Yet whoever had lost it made no attempt to retrieve it, made no offer of reward for its return.

Its injuries healed. The soft fur grew again over the bare grey skin. Experts from the city came and took it away for more detailed examination. The wife of the farmer was sad to see it go. She had grown quite attached to it.

'It was getting to know me,' said she. 'And it talked to me—in its fashion.'

The farmer nodded slowly and thoughtfully.

'It was odd,' he said, 'the way it would imitate what one said. You know, like a parrot does. Not real talking, of course, just imitation.'

'Of course,' said his wife. 'I never thought it was real talk. I'm not so silly.'

It was good at imitating speech, the creature. Very soon, it had learned many words and phrases, and began to string them together quite quickly, and with surprising sense. One might have thought it knew what it meant—if one was silly.

The professors and elders and priests who now took the creature in hand were far from silly. They were puzzled, and amused, and interested—at first. They looked at it, in the disused monkey-cage at the city's menagerie, where it was kept. And it stood upright, on finely-furred feet as arched and perfect as the feet of an ancient statue.

'It is oddly human,' said the learned men.

They amused themselves by bringing it a chair and watching it sit down gracefully, though not very comfortably, as if it was used to furniture of better shape and construction. They gave it a plate and a cup, and it ate with its hands most daintily, looking round as though for some sort of cutlery. But it was not thought safe to trust it with a knife.

'It is only a beast,' said everyone. 'However clever at imitation.'

'It's so quick to learn,' said some.

'But not in any way human.'

'No,' said the creature, 'I am not human. But, in my own place, I am a man.'

'Parrot-talk!' laughed the elders, uneasily.

The professors of living and dead languages taught it simple speech.

After a week, it said to them:

'I understand all the words you use. They are very easy. And you cannot quite express what you mean, in any of your tongues. A child of my race—' It stopped, for it had no wish to seem impolite, and then it said, 'There is a language that is spoken throughout the universe. If you will allow me—'

And softly and musically it began to utter a babble of meaningless nonsense at which all the professors laughed loudly.

'Parrot-talk!' they jeered. 'Pretty Polly! Pretty Polly!'

For they were much annoyed. And they mocked the creature into cowering silence.

The professors of logic came to the same conclusions as the others.

'Your logic is at fault,' the creature had told them, despairingly. 'I have disproved your conclusions again and again. You will not listen or try to understand.'

'Who could understand parrot-talk?'

'I am no parrot, but a man in my own place. Define a man. I walk upright. I think. I collate facts. I imagine. I anticipate. I learn. I speak. What is a man by your definition?'

'Pretty Polly!' said the professors.

They were very angry. One of them hit the creature with his walking-cane. No one likes to be set on a level with a beast. And the beast covered its face with its hands, and was silent.

It was warier when the mathematicians came. It added two and two together for them. They were amazed. It subtracted eight from ten. They wondered at it. It divided twenty by five. They marvelled. It took courage. It said:

'But you have reached a point where your formulae and calculuses fail. There is a simple law—one by which you reached the earth long ago—one by which you can leave it at will—'

The professors were furious.

'Parrot! Parrot!' they shouted.

'No! In my own place—'

The beast fell silent.

Then came the priests, smiling kindly—except to one another. For with each other they argued furiously and loathingly regarding their own views on rule and theory.

'Oh, stop!' said the creature, pleadingly.

It lifted its hands towards them and its golden eyes were full of pity.

'You make everything petty and meaningless,' it said. 'Let me tell you of the Master-Plan of the Universe. It is so simple and nothing to do with gods or rules, myths or superstition. Nothing to do with fear.'

The priests were so outraged that they forgot to hate one another. They screamed wildly with one voice:

'Wicked!'

They fled from the creature, jamming in the cage door in their haste to escape and forget the soul-less, evil thing. And the beast sighed and hid its sorrowful face, and took refuge in increasing silence.

The elders grew to hate it. They disliked the imitating and the parrot-talk, the golden eyes, the sorrow, the pity. They took away its chair, its table, its plate and cup. They ordered it to walk properly—on all fours, like any other beast.

'But in my own place—'

It broke off there. Yet some sort of pride, or stubbornness, or courage, made it refuse to crawl, no matter what they threatened or did.

They sold it to a circus.

A small sum was sent to the farmer who had first found the thing, and the rest of its price went into the state coffers for making weapons for a pending war.

The man who owned the circus was not especially brutal, as such men go. He was used to training beasts, for he was himself the chief attraction of the show, with his lions and tigers, half-drugged and toothless as they were. He said it was no use being too easy on animals.

'They don't understand over-kindness,' said he. 'They get to despising you. You have to show who's master.'

He showed the creature who was master.

He made it jump through hoops and do simple sums on a blackboard. At first it also tried to speak to the people who came to look at it. It would say, in its soft and bell-clear tones:

'Oh, listen—I can tell you things—'

Everyone was amazed at its cleverness and most entertained by the eager way it spoke. And such parrot-nonsense it talked!

'Hark at it!' they cried. 'It wants to tell us things, bless it!'

'About the other side of the moon!'

'The far side of Saturn!'

'Who taught it to say all this stuff?'

'It's saying something about the block in mathematics now!'

'And the language of infinity!'

'Logic!'

'And the Master-Plan!'

They rolled about, helpless with laughter in their ringside seats.

It was even more entertaining to watch the creature doing its sums on the big blackboard, which two attendants would turn so that everyone could admire the cleverness: 2 and 2, and the beautifully-formed 4 that it wrote beneath. $10 - 8 = 2$. Five into 20. 11 from 12.

'How clever it is,' said a small girl, admiringly.

Her father smiled.

'It's the trainer who's clever,' he said. 'The animal knows nothing of what it does. Only what it has been taught. By kindness, of course,' he added quickly, as the child looked sad.

'Oh, good,' said she, brightening. 'I wouldn't like it hurt. It's so sweet.'

But even she had to laugh when it came to the hoop-jumping. For the creature hated doing it. And, although the long whip of the trainer never actually touched its grey fur, yet it cowered at the cracking sound. Surprising, if anyone had wondered why. And it ran, upright on its fine furred feet, and graceful in spite of the red and yellow clothes it was wearing, and it jumped through the hoops. And then more hoops were brought. And these were surrounded by inflammable material and set on fire.

The audience was enthralled. For the beast was terrified of fire, for some reason. It would shrink back and clutch at its shoulder, its arm, its thigh. It would stare up wildly into the roof of the great circus canopy—as if it could see through it and out to the sky beyond—as though it sought desperately for help that would not come. And it shook and trembled. And the whip cracked. And it cried aloud as it came to each flaming hoop. But it jumped.

And it stopped talking to the people. Sometimes it would almost speak, but then it would give a hunted glance towards the ring-master, and lapse into silence. Yet always it walked and ran and jumped as a man would do these things—upright. Not on all fours, like a proper beast.

And soon a particularly dangerous tightrope dance took the fancy of the people. The beast was sold to a small touring animal-show. It was getting very poor in entertainment value, anyway. It moved sluggishly. Its fur was draggled and dull. It had even stopped screaming at the fiery hoops. And—it was such an eerie, man-like thing to have around. Everyone was glad to see it go.

In the dreary little show where it went, no one even pretended to understand animals. They just showed them in their cages. Their small, fetid cages. To begin with, the keeper would bring the strange creature out to perform for the onlookers. But it was a boring performance. Whip or no whip, hunger or less hunger, the beast could no longer run or jump properly. It shambled round and round, dull-eyed and silent. People merely wondered what sort of animal it was, but not with any great interest. It could hardly even be made to flinch at fire, not even when sparks touched its fur. It was sold to a collector of rare beasts. And he took it to his little menagerie on the edge of his estate near a forest.

He was not really very interested in his creatures. It was a passing hobby for a very rich man. Something to talk about among his friends. Only once he came to inspect his new acquisition. He prodded it with a stick. He thought it rather an ugly, dreary animal.

'I heard that you used to talk, parrot-fashion,' said he. 'Go on, then, say something.'

It only cowered. He prodded it some more.

'I read about you when they had you in the city,' said the man, prodding harder. 'You used to talk, I know you did. So talk now. You used to say all sorts of clever things. That you were a man in your own place. Go on, tell me you're a man.'

'Pretty Polly,' mumbled the creature, almost inaudibly.

Nothing would make it speak again.

It was so boring that no one took much notice or care of it. And one night it escaped from its cage.

The last glimpse that anyone saw of it was by a hunter in the deeps of the forest.

It was going slowly looking in terror at rabbits and squirrels. It was weeping aloud and trying desperately to walk on all fours.

Judgement Day

FRANCIS BECKETT

M'rek materialized in London's West End. At once, an uncomfortable feeling at the base of his spine told him that his unfamiliar human body wanted to dispose of its waste products. Those fools in Technical Section! He'd told them: make sure you drain the body before I use it.

Of course, they'd not had much time. There was a panic on. Earth-based agents had come up with an alarming report. Any moment the dominant Earth species was expected to develop a Doomsday Bomb. M'rek had to gauge whether the species was mature enough never to use it. Otherwise the planet would have to be eliminated. Technical Section gave him the best equipment they could come up with in a hurry. Research Section gave him a list of words and phrases which they thought would get him by in London in the late 1990s.

Among the crowds, M'rek spotted a short, stout, youngish woman in a dark blue uniform. He dodged through the dense crowd, towered over her and said:

'I say, old bean, where's the nearest khasi?'

The traffic warden's small, round face stared up at him. Surely, thought M'rek, every Londoner knew a khasi was a toilet. He himself remembered the word from the last time he had used a human body, in 1945. He also remembered the human body's warning signs. Any minute, the one he was wear-ing was going to spill its contents over the pavement. He badly wanted the woman to help him out, and not just for his own comfort. If the first human he met saw a fellow creature in M'rek's sort of distress and refused to help him, the Intergalactic Federation would certainly draw some sinister conclusions.

She took in the shoulder length hair, the bottle green crushed velvet trousers, narrow at the top, which spread out into huge flares just above the bright green sandals; the wild beard; the flowered shirt open halfway down to reveal a huge silver medallion over a hairy chest. She could see beads of sweat on his forehead, his legs going backwards and forwards in a kind of agitated dance.

'Khasi!' The man was bending over her now. She remembered

how her father, a regular soldier, used the word, and hoped she remembered correctly what it meant. She pointed a trembling hand and whispered 'Leicester Square'.

'Takes all sorts!' shouted the old man selling evening newspapers in front of a hoarding which read ENGLAND LOSES THE ASHES TO AUSTRALIA, as the strange man walked awkwardly but rapidly down Regent Street. Meanwhile M'rek, with that part of his mind which he could spare from clenching his bowel muscles, was recalling his last visit to this city.

Back in 1945, there had been a sudden panic at Federation HQ. The dominant Earth species had dropped an atomic bomb, and the head of Planning Section sent for M'rek and told him: 'They're only at Emotional Level 2.' And M'rek knew that was serious. Generally, when a species has advanced to Technology Level 5, and can destroy its planet, it has also advanced at least to Emotional Level 3, which means it can be trusted never to use it.

M'rek had had to decide whether humans were going to reach Emotional Level 3 before they reached Technology Level 6 and could destroy solar systems. He was to decide whether the planet lived or died. He had spent a week in London. He learned that a great and terrible war had just ended. He listened to talk of creating a better world. He reported back that this race would soon be safe. But had he been wrong? Alarm bells were ringing again, this time more urgently.

He ran into Leicester Square, his human body in acute discomfort, but his Federation brain clearly remembering the grim words of the Head of Planning Section. 'You have one Earth day. If you bring evidence that they're emotionally near Level 3, fine. If you don't, we eliminate the place five minutes after your return.' A few minutes of fire and terror, and it would be as though Earth had never existed. Demolition Section avoided unnecessary suffering, but M'rek knew that during those few minutes, all living creatures on the planet would suffer indescribable terror and agony.

'Please let there be evidence of emotional development,' he muttered, as he ran down the narrow staircase to the gentleman's lavatory.

The automatic doors were shut. M'rek stared round wildly as he searched his pockets for a coin, but Technical Section had only given him banknotes. Two young, thick-set men in T-shirts, with close-cropped hair and tattoos on their muscular arms, pushed past him as they came out of the toilet. M'rek chose another of Research Section's speech options. 'G'day, cobber, strewth, could you lend a bloke a buck for the dunny?'

Could this species be so lost to compassion that the men would refuse to help him? As they advanced towards him, their fists rolled into menacing balls, M'rek started to feel that there might be no hope: Demolition Section would have to do its worst. The bigger of the two put his face close to M'rek's and said: 'You Ozzies make me sick. Just because you win a lousy game of cricket.' And M'rek felt his arms suddenly pinioned behind his back, while the squat, brutal looking man in front prepared to punch him. M'rek threw a thought stunner at them, paralysing them for the few minutes it took to rummage through their pockets and find the necessary coin.

When he came out, relieved in body but more perturbed in mind, they were still there, frozen for a few more seconds in aggressive attitudes. There was little evidence there that this species could reach Emotional Level 3, he thought. But perhaps he was looking in the wrong place. He would go to one of his old haunts, where in 1945 he had found the care and the friendship he sought.

A few minutes walk from Leicester Square, there is a big old pub with sawdust on the floor. In 1945 M'rek had found both the beer and the company good. At the end of the evening, every-one had linked arms and sung. The song seemed mostly to consist of the words 'We'll meet again, don't know where, don't know when' endlessly repeated, but they sang it with such affection for each other that M'rek was convinced the species was growing up.

He marched to the bar. The young barman was dressed, not in the homely sleeveless jersey which he remembered, but in some sort of sinister black uniform. M'rek thought for a moment and said:

'Eee bah gum, lad, pint o' mild, reet bonny lad.' The pub fell silent. Then, slowly, the few drinkers—men in grey suits with jugs of beer, women in black suits with padded shoulders and glasses of wine—returned to their own drinks and their own talk. Except for one—a young man seated by the bar, sipping a glass of sparkling water and looking at M'rek with bright, keen eyes. A young man whose gaze, M'rek now realized, was frank and steady, whose smile, when he caught M'rek's eye, was mischievous and knowing, whose suit seemed clean and pressed, as though he looked after himself, and whose face seemed open and honest, as though he cared for others.

M'rek remembered another young man, half a century ago, in that very spot. A young man who had bought him beer for his thirst, and showed him a wall, away from prying eyes, against which they companionably disposed of their liquid waste. A young man who had talked about how they were going to make society better, and who had convinced M'rek that this planet must be spared.

Now, fifty years later, another young man beckoned M'rek on to the bar stool beside him and said: 'What part of the world are you from, my friend?'

M'rek took a deep draught of his beer and remembered, just for a moment, the strange feeling you get in a human body when you give it alcohol. He said: 'Cornwall. 'Appen.'

'Don't sound like Cornwall to me.' The young man's eyes rested briefly on M'rek's medallion. Then he said: 'In our trade you don't want everyone to know where you're from.' The wide smile twinkled and the perfect teeth gleamed. He bought M'rek a new glass of beer. M'rek felt almost overcome with gratitude, sure now that he had found the good man who could prove the emotional maturity of the species.

The man said, quietly and confidentially: 'What do your punters want? E? Tammys? Jellies? Crack? Tabs? Say the word. Look, you're not being set up and I'm not Old Bill. You've got the capital—that medallion's worth thousands. Ten thousand K buys all your punters enough drugs to make you very rich.'

'Drugs?' In his sudden passion, M'rek forgot what accent to use. 'I don't want drugs. I want food, and drink, and love.'

'Right.' The young man looked as though a lifetime's search was over. 'Stick with me and you can have food and drink coming out of your ears. You can have new clothes for every hour in the day. Even love, you can even afford that.'

M'rek poured his new pint of beer over the man's head and walked unsteadily out of the door. The young man tried to smirk at the barman, but for a few seconds found himself unaccountably unable to move.

A light rain had started, and the reflections of dozens of dancing signs jumped out at M'rek from the wet pavement. He shivered, took from his bag Technical Section's great black cape, and threw the empty bag into the nearest shopfront. A sudden movement from the shopfront made him turn back quickly. An old woman dressed in rags was on her hands and knees, running her hands hopefully over every part of the bag's interior.

He watched her for an hour. Men and women walked past, talking and laughing, sheltering from the rain under umbrellas, and every so often the old woman called out, in a flat, featureless voice: 'Spare some change?' They pretended not to hear her. Midnight passed, fewer people walked by, and the old woman lay down in the shopfront. She rolled M'rek's soft bag into a pillow, pulled a tattered overcoat around her, and slept.

The intergalactic agent walked the streets of central London, shivering beneath his flowing black cape and slowly soaking to the skin from the light but cold and persistent rain. Most shopfronts contained at least one derelict like the old lady, and often more than one. The occasional gleaming car sped down the street, spraying water over him, its windows wound tight to keep the rain out and the pounding music in, as remote from the humanity on those streets as if they were at Intergalactic HQ. At first light he took a bus to one of the city's suburbs.

Molly was late. She arrived at the supermarket as she arrived at most places, breathless because running didn't suit her. Tall, slim and elegant she wasn't.

'Is the promotion still on?' she said to the man who stood outside.

He turned slowly and watched her. At last he said: 'I dinna ken.'

'I beg your pardon?'

'Sorry. I mean, I've no idea at all. Is it important?' From his accent she knew he was a Londoner.

'Up to 9.30 you get two packets of cereal for the price of one. Want an apple?' She dredged to the bottom of an enormous carrier bag and produced two apples.

'That's very kind,' said the stranger, and he seemed to mean it. 'You're here to buy food?'

'No, I'm too late, look. They're taking the sign down. Ah, well. It's on to the other supermarket.'

It seemed natural to her that the strange man should fall into step beside her.

'Seb—that's my oldest, he's 14—his mates have all got this special sort of bike, and they're laughing at him because he hasn't, but I can't send my old man to ask for a rise again. Last time, the boss gave him such a rocket, he was shaking for a week.' She burst into hearty, contented laughter.

'So,' the man persisted. 'You are going to buy food.'

'Well,' said Molly, 'I've got this loyalty card. If I spend £25 I get 50 points on my loyalty card, and 450 points are worth £2 off any own-brand purchases. Now, at the other supermarket, my £25 only gets me 30 points and 500 points gets you £1.50 off whatever's on special offer any Thursday. So unless there's a special promotion, like the cereals, I'm better off where we're going now.'

'I don't understand.'

'Except for the scratchcards.'

'Scratchcards?'

'So long as you have the loyalty card and you spend more than £25 in any month, you get a free scratchcard, and if you have the right combination of symbols your name goes into a draw for a new car. But you have to ring this number and give them the name and address of one friend who might like to receive their promotional material.'

The man looked at her, and for the first time she noticed the medallion on his chest. She didn't mind. She never had been fashionable, and she liked men with hairy chests.

'Is that how shopping for food works here?' he asked.

'Well, it does if you're poor.'

For a moment she thought she saw a look of infinite sadness pass over his hairy face. Then, suddenly and disconcertingly, he faded away. The last thing to disappear was the medallion. A minute later she heard a deep rumble, coming, it seemed, from hundreds of miles beneath her, but she took no notice. No point in being late.

The Holiday-Makers

ROGER MALISSON

S tuart Blake awoke slowly as the summer sun streamed into
his bedroom. He yawned and stretched luxuriously, then
turned over and closed his eyes. He didn't have to get up,
because this was the first day of his school holidays.

Presently a scent of bacon and eggs wafted up to him from
the kitchen, and the radio began to play. Stuart lay for a while
longer, savouring the thought of six weeks' freedom, two of
which were to be spent on an Italian beach with his mum and
dad and baby sister.

On the frame of his open window a small spider was busy
making a web. Stuart got up lazily, flicked it outside and closed
the window. He wandered down to breakfast and was greeted
with great delight by little Alison, who was making free with a
soft-boiled egg. Blobs of the stuff decorated her plump face and
her high chair, and she generously thrust a soggy soldier in the
general direction of his mouth.

'No thanks, Alison, it's all for you,' he said, laughing as he ruffled her blonde hair.

'Any plans for today, Stuart?' his mother asked as she brought in his breakfast.

'Not really. I thought I'd laze around, read for a while . . .'

'Oh. Well, if you get bored, you might think about shifting some of the junk out of the attic,' she suggested, giving the baby a quick clean-up with one hand while eating a piece of toast with the other.

Stuart always admired the way his mum seemed to be able to do two things at once. She was brisk and sprightly; he tended to be quiet and easy-going, like his dad.

'The attic? Yes, I'll do that. Any particular reason?'

'Well, we'll be moving later this year, you know,' she replied. 'This house is far too big and isolated. I think it would be a good idea if we started clearing out some of the useless stuff. I hate going up there, it's so dark and cobwebby; but I know you don't mind that, and it could even be fun. There's some interesting stuff your gran left us—you never know what you might find.'

'Undiscovered treasure?' Stuart teased. 'A van Gogh sketch, a few Penny Blacks, Anne Hathaway's diary . . . ?'

'Don't be cheeky,' smiled his mother, hauling Alison out of her high chair. 'You've too much imagination, my lad, that's your trouble. Of course, you are on holiday, and if you'd *rather* do nothing at all . . .'

Stuart grinned and finished his coffee. He knew when he was beaten. 'OK, Mum, you've talked me into it.'

Later in the morning he took his little sister out, but their walk was cut short by a sudden summer shower which settled to a miserable and persistent drizzle. Alison fell asleep after lunch, and Mrs Blake decided on a nap, too. When they had gone upstairs Stuart read for a while, then stared out at the misty, pattering rain and dreamed of hot golden beaches, cool blue seas and large amounts of Italian ice cream. There's not long to go now, he thought; oh, well, I suppose I'd better tackle the attic.

He climbed three flights of stairs and opened the attic door. It was a large room, meagrely lit by one small window set into the sloping roof. Fourteen years' accumulated lumber lived there—unwanted presents still packed in their boxes, forgotten toys, inherited bric-a-brac that someone had been too sentimental to throw away.

There were no cobwebs.

Stuart sighed and switched on the light, and at once there was a dry scuttering sound, as if small creatures were hurrying into dark corners, and then silence. He shivered in spite of himself, though he wasn't scared of mice and such, and set to work. He cleared a space near the door and worked steadily inwards, sorting the junk into three piles—Definitely Out, Ask Mum, and Probably Keep.

Under the skylight there was a cardboard box which had contained their spin dryer. Stuart tried to lift it and couldn't. He walked round it to the open end, curious to see what was making it so heavy, and then became suddenly and horribly aware that, inside it, things were *moving*. He steadied his nerves and approached the opening cautiously. What could be in there? Some sort of nest? He peered inside; eyes stared back at him.

Eight eyes, set in one greyish face the size of a large rat's.

Stuart leapt back, stifling a cry, unable to wrench his gaze from the creature which had begun, very slowly, to emerge from the box. It resembled a huge spider; others moved restlessly behind it, myriad eyes glinting in the dim light. *I must move*, thought Stuart, his legs inert with terror. As soon as the thought entered his mind a soft, heavy body plopped on to his shoulder and scurried across him to the ground; another ran across his feet.

The spiderlike thing halted at the edge of the box, and its jaw fell open.

'But you *cannot* move,' said a low, metallic voice. 'Try, if you will.'

Stuart twisted and turned, but silvery strands, thin as string and strong as chain, fastened him to the wall behind him.

'And if you call out,' continued the hideous voice, 'something unpleasant will happen. I will show you.'

The creature lifted its front legs, which ended in claws like a crab's. There was a flash, and Stuart felt an electric shock from the material which bound him. He shrank back against the wall, unable to believe that this was happening. Surely he was dreaming?

The spider's jaw drooped again, revealing sharp, yellowish fangs. 'No, we are real, not figments. We do not mean you harm.

We simply wish to question you, and I think that you have questions for us.'

Could these things read his mind? Stuart licked his dry lips.

'Who are you?' he said, and his voice sounded high and frightened. 'What are you doing here? Why—'

'One question at a time,' murmured the voice. 'We are what you would call Arachnids, from a galaxy of which you have no knowledge.'

A planet inhabited by spiders! Stuart couldn't believe it.

'But you—you're *intelligent*,' he said.

'Quite. Spiders have existed on your planet for three hundred million years, and mankind only four million; yet spiders here have only instinctive behaviour. In a word, they are dim.'

There was a strange, tinny crackle which might have been laughter.

'As to the reason for our being here—why, we are on holiday.'

'Holiday . . . ?' said Stuart faintly. His sense of nightmare was increasing.

'Yes, indeed. We are the Holiday Site Investigation Section of our planet's Personnel Department,' explained the Arachnid. 'We have explored Earth and found that it would make a splendid recreation centre for our people. You have nothing to fear. If we let you go, will you co-operate?'

Stuart nodded and closed his eyes, shuddering violently as thin black legs scurried over him and a hairy body brushed his cheek. When he opened his eyes he was free of his bonds. The web had been dismantled, but the whole attic seemed to be crowded with Arachnids, suspended from the ceiling, motionless on the walls, crouching in corners.

Stuart's knees were trembling, and he sank gratefully on to an old chair.

'You find us repulsive, do you not?' The Arachnid's voice sounded faintly mocking. 'And yet our technology is thousands of years ahead of yours. We have mastered space flight, brain reading, miniaturization . . . such sciences as your species is only just beginning to study.'

While it talked, Stuart examined the thing closely. Two eyes were set in the front of its head, with six smaller ones ranged below them and above the thin, fanged mouth. The body was round and distended, greyish skin covered, like its eight legs, with sparse black hair. Its voice seemed to come from a tiny box hung below its head which, Stuart assumed, was a device which converted its own language into English.

'Miniaturization . . . ?' quavered Stuart, as the creature paused. 'How big are you naturally?' He was trying desperately to remember all he had read about spiders, and he was sure that they could not survive if they grew large—it was something to do with their method of breathing.

His question provoked more of their horrible laughter, but no reply; instead, the Arachnid began to explain how they had come to dominate their planet. It said that creatures like man had ruled their world a million years ago, and had destroyed themselves in a nuclear war. But the Arachnids had easily survived the radiation the terrible weapons had caused, though it had affected their genetic structure—their lungs had grown, their size increased and their brains had developed a far greater capacity than those of the anthropoids who had foolishly blown themselves up.

'We have conquered space,' the Arachnid continued boastfully, 'and we are now looking for entertainment centres on other worlds.'

Stuart couldn't believe his ears.

'Do you mean that you want Earth as a . . . a sort of enormous holiday camp?'

'Correct,' said the Arachnid. 'We are looking forward to our holidays here.'

'But that's impossible!' Stuart cried. 'You don't really think you could just land here and take over, do you? Just as if we'd let you!'

'Just as if you had a choice,' sneered the Arachnid.

Stuart could see that he had angered the creature. Its claws twitched menacingly.

'Why this planet?' he asked desperately. 'Why do you want to come here?'

'Because it interests us,' replied the Arachnid, calming down a little. 'There is so much to see and enjoy here because the climate and land are so varied; unlike our world, which is bare and rocky. Earth's atmosphere is similar to ours, and as for food—well, we are able to eat almost anything . . . and then there is your culture. We have learned a great deal about mankind by watching television.'

Stuart shivered at the thought of the Arachnids, having shrunk themselves to the size of normal spiders, lurking unseen in living-rooms and silently spying on the human race.

'We have seen your surgeons performing operations on television,' continued the Arachnid, 'and our scientists would be very interested in studying the brain of a primitive life form such as mankind. And your sports are wonderful! Human-racing and fighting are most exciting. I wish to know, though, why you do not pursue humans when hunting. Dull as he is, Man is so much more ingenious than the stag or the fox.'

Stuart stared at the creature in disbelief.

'Ah, I think I know the answer to my own question,' the Arachnid went on. 'You think that you are a superior species!'

Again there was a ratchety cackle of laughter, and the sound of it suddenly infuriated Stuart.

'Well, we're superior to *you*, anyway!' he cried. 'You're just—heartless, hideous insects. I'm not staying here to listen to you! I'm going, right now, to phone the police!'

He rose and kicked over his chair, hearing a satisfying, panicky scuttling as the Arachnids which had been crouching near his feet got out of its way, and rushed to the door before they could stop him. He ran down the stairs to his parents' room, flung open the door—and froze. His mother was lying on her bed, sleeping, with Alison in the cot beside her. Across them both lay a huge, glistening cobweb, and half-covering one wall was an enormous Arachnid, staring at him with shiny, soulless eyes.

Choking with terror, Stuart ran downstairs. He could not wait to telephone. He wrenched open the back door and ran into the garden, almost tripping over a furry object which lay in his path. He reached the gate, which was set into the high wall surrounding the garden, and saw that the bolt was covered over with cobweb. Two tiny Arachnids were crawling over it. Stuart did not dare to touch the web; he was sure it was sufficiently electrified to kill anyone who did.

He was equally sure that the front door would be similarly guarded. The Arachnids were not fools. But perhaps if he threw something at the web, he could fuse it, and get out to raise the alarm. It was no use shouting, for the nearest house was much too far away.

He looked frantically round the neat lawn for something to throw, and his eye fell on the hairy object which had almost tripped him on his dash outside. It looked like a glove puppet, but, with a growing sense of horror, he recognized it as one of the neighbourhood dogs.

It was then that Stuart remembered how spiders killed. They sank their fangs into their victim, injecting a fluid which paralysed the creature and eventually liquefied all its internal organs. They waited until their dreadful venom had worked, and then . . . they *sucked*. Only the husk remained.

Stuart felt unnaturally calm. He turned and went indoors, back to the attic. The Arachnid's words rang in his ears—

'We are able to eat almost anything . . .'

They had not moved. They could read his mind; they'd known exactly what was going to happen. And what was the use of trying to raise the alarm? Who would ever believe this, especially coming from a dreamy, imaginative kid like him?

Stuart sank, exhausted, into the chair opposite the Arachnid leader, or spokesman . . . no, spokescreature—spokespider? —and stifled a hysterical giggle.

'There's nothing I can do, is there?' he said. 'You've trapped me and you're threatening my family. My father won't be home from work for hours yet. Are you going to destroy me? Or simply go on telling me how clever you are? Get on with it, can't you. I don't care any more.'

'All in good time,' said the Arachnid. 'As I was about to say before you tried to leave, I believe that Earth is going to be the favourite of our holiday centres. But you needn't worry—we don't plan to wipe out the human race. Well, not entirely. Some carefully chosen humans will remain to wait upon us and provide us with entertainment, and so forth—specially bred and trained, you understand. In fact, you were among the few whom we selected for survival, but I see from your brain readings that you would probably not be suitable . . .'

Stuart felt his nerves giving way.

'You won't succeed!' he burst out. 'You want to enslave mankind, to use us; it's a ghastly plan! You might think us an inferior species, but it will never work!'

'Why ever not?' murmured the Arachnid. 'It worked for you for centuries. Try to see our point of view. I mean, what do *you* expect from your forthcoming holiday abroad? Nice new surroundings, good food, plenty of fun and reliable service? Well, so do we. That's not too much to ask, surely.'

It paused a moment, as if listening to something Stuart couldn't hear, then continued: 'But I can't stay talking to you all day, pleasant though it's been . . .'

As it spoke, the creature seemed to shrink before his eyes. Stuart realized all the other Arachnids were diminishing, too, almost to the size of money spiders. They dropped from the ceiling and walls, running silently towards the centre of the attic, swarming over and around each other like some tiny, grotesque army. Were they planning to leave?

Stuart's skin itched with repulsion at the sight, and then, with a surge of exultation, he realized this was an opportunity to crush them—literally, to stamp them out—while they were still small enough to destroy. He started towards them, but a sudden stabbing, agonizing pain at the back of his neck stopped him dead.

His arms and legs felt like solid rubber; his throat closed on a scream, and he sank, paralysed, to the ground. Above him loomed the dark, throbbing bulk of an immense Arachnid, the eyes above its bloodstained fangs glaring and hungry.

It retreated into a corner . . . and waited.

The Father-Thing

PHILIP K. DICK

D inner's ready,' commanded Mrs Walton. 'Go get your
father and tell him to wash his hands. The same applies
to you, young man.' She carried a steaming casserole to
the neatly set table. 'You'll find him out in the garage.'

Charles hesitated. He was only eight years old, and the
problem bothering him would have confounded anyone. 'I . . .'
he began uncertainly.

'What's wrong?' June Walton caught the uneasy tone in her
son's voice and her matronly bosom fluttered with sudden
alarm. 'Isn't Ted out in the garage? For heaven's sake, he was
sharpening the hedge shears a minute ago. He didn't go over to
the Andersons', did he? I told him dinner was practically on the
table.'

'He's in the garage,' Charles said. 'But, he's . . . talking to
himself.'

'Talking to himself!' Mrs Walton removed her bright plastic apron and hung it over the doorknob. 'Ted? Why, he never talks to himself. Go tell him to come in here.' She poured boiling black coffee in the little blue-and-white china cups and began ladling out creamed corn. 'What's wrong with you? Go tell him!'

'I don't know which of them to tell,' Charles blurted out desperately. 'They both look alike.'

June Walton's fingers lost their hold on the aluminium pan; for a moment the creamed corn slushed dangerously. 'Young man—' she began angrily, but at that moment Ted Walton came striding into the kitchen, inhaling and sniffing and rubbing his hands together.

'Ah,' he cried happily. 'Lamb stew.'

'Beef stew,' June murmured. 'Ted, what were you doing out there?'

Ted threw himself down at his place and unfolded his napkin. 'I got the shears sharpened like a razor. Oiled and sharpened. Better not touch them—they'll cut your hand off.' He was a good-looking man in his early thirties; thick blond hair, strong arms, competent hands, square face, and flashing brown eyes. 'Man, this stew looks good. Hard day at the office—Friday, you know. Stuff piles up and we have to get all the accounts out by five. Al McKinley claims the department could handle twenty per cent more stuff if we organized our lunch hours; staggered them so somebody was there all the time.' He beckoned Charles over. 'Sit down and let's go.'

Mrs Walton served the frozen peas. 'Ted,' she said, as she slowly took her seat, 'is there anything on your mind?'

'On my mind?' He blinked. 'No, nothing unusual. Just the regular stuff. Why?'

Uneasily June Walton glanced over at her son. Charles was sitting bolt-upright at his place, face expressionless, white as chalk. He hadn't moved, hadn't unfolded his napkin or even touched his milk. A tension was in the air; she could feel it. Charles had pulled his chair away from his father's; he was huddled in a tense little bundle as far from his father as possible. His lips were moving, but she couldn't catch what he was saying.

'What is it?' she demanded, leaning towards him.

'*The other one*,' Charles was muttering under his breath. 'The other one came in.'

'What do you mean, dear?' June Walton asked out loud. 'What other one?'

Ted jerked. A strange expression flitted across his face. It vanished at once; but in the brief instant Ted Walton's face lost all familiarity. Something alien and cold gleamed out, a twisting, wriggling mass. The eyes blurred and receded, as an archaic sheen filmed over them. The ordinary look of a tired, middle-aged husband was gone.

And then it was back—or nearly back. Ted grinned and began to wolf down his stew and frozen peas and creamed corn. He laughed, stirred his coffee, and ate. But something terrible was wrong.

'The other one,' Charles muttered, face white, hands beginning to tremble. Suddenly he leaped up and backed away from the table. 'Get away!' he shouted. 'Get out of here!'

'Hey,' Ted rumbled ominously. 'What's got into you?' He pointed sternly at the boy's chair. 'You sit down there and eat your dinner, young man. Your mother didn't fix it for nothing.'

Charles turned and ran out of the kitchen, upstairs to his room. June Walton gasped and fluttered in dismay. 'What in the world—'

Ted went on eating. His face was grim; his eyes were hard and dark. 'That kid,' he grated, 'is going to have to learn a few things. Maybe he and I need to have a little private conference together.'

Charles crouched and listened.

The father-thing was coming up the stairs, nearer and nearer. 'Charles!' it shouted angrily. 'Are you up there?'

He didn't answer. Soundlessly he moved back into his room and pulled the door shut. His heart was pounding heavily. The father-thing had reached the landing; in a moment it would come in his room.

He hurried to the window. He was terrified; it was already fumbling in the dark hall for the knob. He lifted the window and climbed out on the roof. With a grunt he dropped into the flower garden that ran by the front door, staggered and gasped, then leaped to his feet and ran from the light that streamed out of the window, a patch of yellow in the evening darkness.

He found the garage; it loomed up ahead, a black square against the skyline. Breathing quickly, he fumbled in his pocket for his flashlight, then cautiously slid the door up and entered.

The garage was empty. The car was parked out front. To the left was his father's workbench. Hammers and saws on the wooden walls. In the back were the lawnmower, rake, shovel, hoe. A drum of kerosene. Licence plates nailed up everywhere. Floor was concrete and dirt; a great oil slick stained the centre, tufts of weeds greasy and black in the flickering beam of the flashlight.

Just inside the door was a big trash barrel. On top of the barrel were stacks of soggy newspapers and magazines, mouldy and damp. A thick stench of decay issued from them as Charles began to move them around. Spiders dropped to the cement and scampered off; he crushed them with his foot and went on looking.

The sight made him shriek. He dropped the flashlight and leaped wildly back. The garage was plunged into instant gloom. He forced himself to kneel down, and for an ageless moment, he groped in the darkness for the light, among the spiders and greasy weeds. Finally he had it again. He managed to turn the beam down into the barrel, down the well he had made by pushing back the piles of magazines.

The father-thing had stuffed it down in the very bottom of the barrel. Among the old leaves and torn-up cardboard, the rotting remains of magazines and curtains, rubbish from the attic his mother had lugged down here with the idea of burning someday. It still looked a little like his father, enough for him to recognize. He had found it—and the sight made him sick at his stomach. He hung onto the barrel and shut his eyes until finally he was able to look again. In the barrel were the remains of his father, his real father. Bits the father-thing had no use for. Bits it had discarded.

He got the rake and pushed it down to stir the remains. They were dry. They cracked and broke at the touch of the rake. They were like a discarded snake skin, flaky and crumbling, rustling at the touch. *An empty skin.* The insides were gone. The important part. This was all that remained, just the brittle, cracking skin, wadded down at the bottom of the trash barrel in a little heap. This was all the father-thing had left; it had eaten the rest. Taken the insides—and his father's place.

A sound.

He dropped the rake and hurried to the door. The father-thing was coming down the path, towards the garage. Its shoes crushed the gravel; it felt its way along uncertainly. 'Charles!' it called angrily. 'Are you in there? Wait'll I get my hands on you, young man!'

His mother's ample, nervous shape was outlined in the bright doorway of the house. 'Ted, please don't hurt him. He's all upset about something.'

'I'm not going to hurt him,' the father-thing rasped; it halted to strike a match. 'I'm just going to have a little talk with him. He needs to learn better manners. Leaving the table like that and running out at night, climbing down the roof—'

Charles slipped from the garage; the glare of the match caught his moving shape, and with a bellow the father-thing lunged forward. '*Come here!*'

Charles ran. He knew the ground better than the father-thing; it knew a lot, had taken a lot when it got his father's insides, but nobody knew the way like *he* did. He reached the fence, climbed it, leaped into the Andersons' yard, raced past their clothesline, down the path around the side of their house, and out on Maple Street.

He listened, crouched down and not breathing. The father-thing hadn't come after him. It had gone back. Or it was coming around the sidewalk.

He took a deep, shuddering breath. He had to keep moving. Sooner or later it would find him. He glanced right and left, made sure it wasn't watching, and then started off at a rapid dog-trot.

'What do you want?' Tony Peretti demanded belligerently. Tony was fourteen. He was sitting at the table in the oak-panelled Peretti dining room, books and pencils scattered around him, half a ham-and-peanut-butter sandwich and a coke beside him. 'You're Walton, aren't you?'

Tony Peretti had a job uncrating stoves and refrigerators after school at Johnson's Appliance Shop, downtown. He was big and blunt-faced. Black hair, olive skin, white teeth. A couple of times he had beaten up Charles; he had beaten up every kid in the neighbourhood.

Charles twisted. 'Say, Peretti. Do me a favour?'

'What do you want?' Peretti was annoyed. 'You looking for a bruise?'

Gazing unhappily down, his fists clenched, Charles explained what had happened in short, mumbled words.

When he had finished, Peretti let out a low whistle. 'No kidding.'

'It's true.' He nodded quickly. 'I'll show you. Come on and I'll show you.'

Peretti got slowly to his feet. 'Yeah, show me. I want to see.'

He got his b.b. gun from his room, and the two of them walked silently up the dark street, towards Charles's house. Neither of them said much. Peretti was deep in thought, serious and solemn-faced. Charles was still dazed; his mind was completely blank.

They turned down the Anderson driveway, cut through the backyard, climbed the fence, and lowered themselves cautiously into Charles's backyard. There was no movement. The yard was silent. The front door of the house was closed.

They peered through the living room window. The shades were down, but a narrow crack of yellow streamed out. Sitting on the couch was Mrs Walton, sewing a cotton T-shirt. There was a sad, troubled look on her large face. She worked listlessly, without interest.

Opposite her was the father-thing. Leaning back in his father's easy chair, its shoes off, reading the evening newspaper. The TV was on, playing to itself in the corner. A can of beer rested on the arm of the easy chair. The father-thing sat exactly as his own father had sat; it had learned a lot.

'Looks just like him,' Peretti whispered suspiciously. 'You sure you're not bulling me?'

Charles led him to the garage and showed him the trash barrel. Peretti reached his long tanned arms down and carefully pulled up the dry, flaking remains. They spread out, unfolded, until the whole figure of his father was outlined. Peretti laid the remains on the floor and pieced broken parts back into place. The remains were colourless. Almost transparent. An amber yellow, thin as paper. Dry and utterly lifeless.

'That's all,' Charles said. Tears welled up in his eyes. 'That's all that's left of him. The thing has the insides.'

Peretti had turned pale. Shakily he crammed the remains back in the trash barrel. 'This is really something,' he muttered. 'You say you saw the two of them together?'

'Talking. They looked exactly alike. I ran inside.' Charles wiped the tears away and snivelled; he couldn't hold it back any longer. 'It ate him while I was inside. Then it came in the house. It pretended it was him. But it isn't. It killed him and ate his insides.'

For a moment Peretti was silent. 'I'll tell you something,' he said suddenly. 'I've heard about this sort of thing. It's a bad business. You have to use your head and not get scared. You're not scared, are you?'

'No,' Charles managed to mutter.

'The first thing we have to do is figure out how to kill it.' He rattled his b.b. gun. 'I don't know if this'll work. It must be plenty tough to get hold of your father. He was a big man.' Peretti considered. 'Let's get out of here. It might come back. They say that's what a murderer does.'

They left the garage. Peretti crouched down and peeked through the window again. Mrs Walton had got to her feet. She was talking anxiously. Vague sounds filtered out. The father-thing threw down its newspaper. They were arguing.

'For God's sake!' the father-thing shouted. 'Don't do anything stupid like that.'

'Something's wrong,' Mrs Walton moaned. 'Something terrible. Just let me call the hospital and see.'

'Don't call anybody. He's all right. Probably up the street playing.'

'He's never out this late. He never disobeys. He was terribly upset—afraid of you! I don't blame him.' Her voice broke with misery. 'What's wrong with you? You're so strange.' She moved out of the room, into the hall. 'I'm going to call some of the neighbours.'

The father-thing glared after her until she had disappeared. Then a terrifying thing happened. Charles gasped; even Peretti grunted under his breath.

'Look,' Charles muttered. 'What—'

'Golly,' Peretti said, black eyes wide.

As soon as Mrs Walton was gone from the room, the father-thing sagged in its chair. It became limp. Its mouth fell open. Its eyes peered vacantly. Its head fell forward, like a discarded rag doll.

Peretti moved away from the window. 'That's it,' he whispered. 'That's the whole thing.'

'What is it?' Charles demanded. He was shocked and bewildered. 'It looked like somebody turned off its power.'

'Exactly.' Peretti nodded slowly, grim and shaken. 'It's controlled from outside.'

Horror settled over Charles. 'You mean, something outside our world?'

Peretti shook his head with disgust. 'Outside the house! In the yard. You know how to find?'

'Not very well.' Charles pulled his mind together. 'But I know somebody who's good at finding.' He forced his mind to summon the name. 'Bobby Daniels.'

'That little black kid? Is he good at finding?'

'The best.'

'All right,' Peretti said. 'Let's go get him. We have to find the thing that's outside. That made *it* in there, and keeps it going . . .'

'It's near the garage,' Peretti said to the small, thin-faced black boy who crouched beside them in the darkness. 'When it got him, he was in the garage. So look there.'

'In the garage?' Daniels asked.

'*Around* the garage. Walton's already gone over the garage, inside. Look around outside. Nearby.'

There was a small bed of flowers growing by the garage, and a great tangle of bamboo and discarded debris between the garage and the back of the house. The moon had come out; a cold, misty light filtered down over everything. 'If we don't find it pretty soon,' Daniels said, 'I got to go back home. I can't stay up much later.' He wasn't any older than Charles. Perhaps nine.

'All right,' Peretti agreed. 'Then get looking.'

The three of them spread out and began to go over the ground with care. Daniels worked with incredible speed; his thin little body moved in a blur of motion as he crawled among the flowers, turned over rocks, peered under the house, separated stalks of plants, ran his expert hands over leaves and stems, in tangles of compost and weeds. No inch was missed.

Peretti halted after a short time. 'I'll guard. It might be dangerous. The father-thing might come and try to stop us.' He posted himself on the back step with his b.b. gun while Charles and Bobby Daniels searched. Charles worked slowly. He was tired, and his body was cold and numb. It seemed impossible, the father-thing and what had happened to his own father, his real father. But terror spurred him on; what if it happened to his mother, or to him? Or to everyone? Maybe the whole world.

'I found it!' Daniels called in a thin, high voice. 'You all come around here quick!'

Peretti raised his gun and got up cautiously. Charles hurried over; he turned the flickering yellow beam of his flashlight where Daniels stood.

Daniels had raised a concrete stone. In the moist, rotting soil the light gleamed on a metallic body. A thin, jointed thing with endless crooked legs was digging frantically. Plated, like an ant; a red-brown bug that rapidly disappeared before their eyes. Its rows of legs scrabbled and clutched. The ground gave rapidly under it. Its wicked-looking tail twisted furiously as it struggled down the tunnel it had made.

Peretti ran into the garage and grabbed up the rake. He pinned down the tail of the bug with it. 'Quick! Shoot it with the b.b. gun!'

Daniels snatched the gun and took aim. The first shot tore the tail of the bug loose. It writhed and twisted frantically; its tail dragged uselessly and some of its legs broke off. It was a foot long, like a great millipede. It struggled desperately to escape down its hole.

'Shoot again,' Peretti ordered.

Daniels fumbled with the gun. The bug slithered and hissed. Its head jerked back and forth; it twisted and bit at the rake holding it down. Its wicked specks of eyes gleamed with hatred. For a moment it struck futilely at the rake; then abruptly, without warning, it thrashed in a frantic convulsion that made them all draw away in fear.

Something buzzed through Charles's brain. A loud humming, metallic and harsh, a billion metal wires dancing and vibrating at once. He was tossed about violently by the force; the banging crash of metal made him deaf and confused. He stumbled to his feet and backed off; the others were doing the same, white-faced and shaken.

'If we can't kill it with the gun,' Peretti gasped, 'we can drown it. Or burn it. Or stick a pin through its brain.' He fought to hold on to the rake, to keep the bug pinned down.

'I have a jar of formaldehyde,' Daniels muttered. His fingers fumbled nervously with the b.b. gun. 'How does this thing work? I can't seem to—'

Charles grabbed the gun from him. 'I'll kill it.' He squatted down, one eye to the sight, and gripped the trigger. The bug lashed and struggled. Its force-field hammered in his ears, but he hung on to the gun. His finger tightened . . .

'All right, Charles,' the father-thing said. Powerful fingers gripped him, a paralysing pressure around his wrists. The gun fell to the ground as he struggled futilely. The father-thing shoved against Peretti. The boy leaped away and the bug, free of the rake, slithered triumphantly down its tunnel.

'You have a spanking coming, Charles,' the father-thing droned on. 'What got into you? Your poor mother's out of her mind with worry.'

It had been there, hiding in the shadows. Crouched in the darkness watching them. Its calm, emotionless voice, a dreadful parody of his father's, rumbled close to his ear as it pulled him relentlessly towards the garage. Its cold breath blew in his face, an icy-sweet odour, like decaying soil. Its strength was immense; there was nothing he could do.

'Don't fight me,' it said calmly. 'Come along, into the garage. This is for your own good. I know best, Charles.'

'Did you find him?' his mother called anxiously, opening the back door.

'Yes, I found him.'

'What are you going to do?'

'A little spanking.' The father-thing pushed up the garage door. 'In the garage.' In the half-light a faint smile, humourless and utterly without emotion, touched its lips. 'You go back in the living room, June. I'll take care of this. It's more in my line. You never did like punishing him.'

The back door reluctantly closed. As the light cut off, Peretti bent down and groped for the b.b. gun. The father-thing instantly froze.

'Go on home, boys,' it rasped.

Peretti stood undecided, gripping the b.b. gun.

'Get going,' the father-thing repeated. 'Put down that toy and get out of here.' It moved slowly towards Peretti, gripping Charles with one hand, reaching towards Peretti with the other. 'No b.b. guns allowed in town, sonny. Your father know you have that? There's a city ordinance. I think you better give me that before—'

Peretti shot it in the eye.

The father-thing grunted and pawed at its ruined eye. Abruptly it slashed out at Peretti. Peretti moved down the driveway, trying to cock the gun. The father-thing lunged. Its powerful fingers snatched the gun from Peretti's hands. Silently the father-thing mashed the gun against the wall of the house.

Charles broke away and ran numbly off. Where could he hide? It was between him and the house. Already, it was coming back towards him, a black shape creeping carefully, peering into the darkness, trying to make him out. Charles retreated. If there were only some place he could hide . . .

The bamboo.

He crept quickly into the bamboo. The stalks were huge and old. They closed after him with a faint rustle. The father-thing was fumbling in its pocket; it lit a match, then the whole pack flared up. 'Charles,' it said, 'I know you're here, someplace. There's no use hiding. You're only making it more difficult.'

His heart hammering, Charles crouched among the bamboo. Here, debris and filth rotted. Weeds, garbage, papers, boxes, old clothing, boards, tin cans, bottles. Spiders and salamanders squirmed around him. The bamboo swayed with the night wind. Insects and filth.

And something else.

A shape, a silent, unmoving shape that grew up from the mound of filth like some nocturnal mushroom. A white column, a pulpy mass that glistened moistly in the moonlight. Webs covered it, a mouldy cocoon. It had vague arms and legs. An indistinct half-shaped head. As yet, the features hadn't formed. But he could tell what it was.

A mother-thing. Growing here in the filth and dampness, between the garage and the house. Behind the towering bamboo.

It was almost ready. Another few days and it would reach maturity. It was still a larva, white and soft and pulpy. But the sun would dry and warm it. Harden its shell. Turn it dark and strong. It would emerge from its cocoon, and one day when his mother came by the garage . . .

Behind the mother-thing were other pulpy white larvae, recently laid by the bug. Small. Just coming into existence. He could see where the father-thing had broken off; the place where it had grown. It had matured here. And in the garage, his father had met it.

Charles began to move numbly away, past the rotting boards, the filth and debris, the pulpy mushroom larvae. Weakly he reached out to take hold of the fence—and scrambled back.

Another one. Another larva. He hadn't seen this one, at first. It wasn't white. It had already turned dark. The web, the pulpy softness, the moistness, were gone. It was ready. It stirred a little, moved its arm feebly.

The Charles-thing.

The bamboo separated, and the father-thing's hand clamped firmly around the boy's wrist. 'You stay right here,' it said. 'This is exactly the place for you. Don't move.' With its other hand it tore at the remains of the cocoon binding the Charles-thing. 'I'll help it out—it's still a little weak.'

The last shred of moist grey was stripped back, and the Charles-thing tottered out. It floundered uncertainly, as the father-thing cleared a path for it towards Charles.

'This way,' the father-thing grunted. 'I'll hold him for you. When you're fed you'll be stronger.'

The Charles-thing's mouth opened and closed. It reached greedily towards Charles. The boy struggled wildly, but the father-thing's immense hand held him down.

'Stop that, young man,' the father-thing commanded. 'It'll be a lot easier for you if you—'

It screamed and convulsed. It let go of Charles and staggered back. Its body twitched violently. It crashed against the garage, limbs jerking. For a time it rolled and flopped in a dance of agony. It whimpered, moaned, tried to crawl away. Gradually it became quiet. The Charles-thing settled down in a silent heap. It lay stupidly among the bamboo and rotting debris, body slack, face empty and blank.

At last the father-thing ceased to stir. There was only the faint rustle of the bamboo in the night wind.

Charles got up awkwardly. He stepped down onto the cement driveway. Peretti and Daniels approached, wide-eyed and cautious. 'Don't go near it,' Daniels ordered sharply. 'It ain't dead yet. Takes a little while.'

'What did you do?' Charles muttered.

Daniels set down the drum of kerosene with a gasp of relief. 'Found this in the garage. We Daniels always used kerosene on our mosquitoes, back in Virginia.'

'Daniels poured kerosene down the bug's tunnel,' Peretti explained, still awed. 'It was his idea.'

Daniels kicked cautiously at the contorted body of the father-thing. 'It's dead, now. Died as soon as the bug died.'

'I guess the others'll die too,' Peretti said. He pushed aside the bamboo to examine the larvae growing here and there among the debris. The Charles-thing didn't move at all, as Peretti jabbed the end of a stick into its chest. 'This one's dead.'

'We better make sure,' Daniels said grimly. He picked up the heavy drum of kerosene and lugged it to the edge of the bamboo. 'It dropped some matches in the driveway. You get them, Peretti.'

They looked at each other.

'Sure,' Peretti said softly.

'We better turn on the hose,' Charles said. 'To make sure it doesn't spread.'

'Let's get going,' Peretti said impatiently. He was already moving off. Charles quickly followed him and they began searching for the matches, in the moonlit darkness.

Space-Born

ROBERT BLOCH

The probe-mission ship locked into orbit and began its
sensor-scan of the planet Echo.

Seated at his post on the bridge, Mission Commander
Richard Tasman, United States Navy, checked out the data
processed by the technical teams of his crew. Beside him
Lieutenant Ted Gilbey, his second in command, nodded
approvingly.

'Looks good,' Gilbey said. 'Looks very good.'

And it did.

According to the computerized data fed back through the
tapes, Echo was indeed an Earth-type planet, just as had been
suspected. Photoscopes confirmed the presence of running
water, surface soil, and abundant vegetation. The bacterial life
analysis indicated nothing harmful or unfamiliar. Echo's
planetary profile was that of a miniature world—alive and
unpolluted, unspoiled by the presence of man.

Then the tapes began running wild.

Tasman stared at Gilbey. Gilbey stared at Tasman. And both
men turned to stare at the photoscope.

The confirming data coming in told the story, but one picture
is always worth ten thousand words, even though for a moment
this particular picture left them both speechless.

Clearly and unmistakably it showed the boulder-strewn
hillside and what rested on the sloping surface—landing gear
crumpled against the looming rocks. The scope moved in for a
close shot, panning across the hull, picking up the insignia and
legible lettering: USS *Orion*.

There on the face of a minor planet near the edge of the galaxy, unexplored and unvisited by man, was a spacecraft from Earth.

Tasman took over the landing party himself, leaving Gilbey behind in command.

There were five members in the task force, counting Tasman, as the auxiliary launch settled safely on target. When the spacemen emerged from the hatch, they were less than a thousand yards from the hulk of the USS *Orion* on the hillside.

Even before they forced their way inside, all doubts had vanished. Weber, the chief petty officer of the party, spoke for them all. 'This is it, sir. Kevin's ship.'

Tasman shook his head grimly. 'Our ship,' he said. 'Kevin stole it.'

There was no answer to that, not from Weber or any of the others, because all of them knew Tasman spoke the truth.

Senior Commander Kevin Nichols, USN—veteran astronaut, hero of the space programme, next in line for appointment to head the entire space project itself—had stolen the ship.

A year ago, almost to the day by Earth calendar, Nichols and the *Orion* had vanished. No advance warning, no clearance, nothing. And no telltale traces left behind; even his wife had disappeared. It took almost six months of intensive investigation to unravel the tangle of red tape surrounding the flight, and even now there were a thousand loose ends. All the evidence added up to the fact that Kevin Nichols had moved swiftly and secretly, according to a well-prepared plan.

Forged orders for a security-sealed mission had been used to get the *Orion* equipped and on the launching pad without a leak. One of the very latest miniaturized spacecraft, *Orion* required only the services of a pilot, with all flight functions self-powered, self-contained, and computer-directed. It was a top secret test model, designed for future exploration projects, and put through its trial runs by Kevin Nichols himself. So when he ordered it supplied and readied for take-off, no one had questioned him or broken security regulations to reveal its departure.

Not until the *Orion* soared into space did the scandal rise in its wake—and even that was secret, hushed up by the space programme itself before the news could break to the public.

Then came the investigation, and the eventual discovery of Kevin's probable destination—not Echo itself, but Sector XXIII, the same area of the space chart.

It was then that Commander Tasman had been assigned to go after the missing ship and the missing man. Tasman knew Kevin Nichols—they had been classmates at the Cape years ago—and perhaps that's why he was chosen for the mission. But knowing Kevin hadn't made the job of locating him any easier. They had touched down at a dozen points before the process of elimination zeroed them in on Echo. It was only now, months after the start of the expedition, that they had caught up with the fugitive.

Or had they?

Kevin wasn't on the ship.

Neither were its supplies and portable instruments.

'Now what?' Tasman muttered.

Weber, the CPO, suggested scouting the surrounding terrain, and it was he who discovered the cave set in the rocks.

Tasman was the first to enter, and what he found there in the dark depths brought the others to his side on the run.

Living in a cave is not an ideal existence at best, and when one's supplies are exhausted and the battery-powered light sources fail, there's nothing left but shadows—shadows looming up everywhere from the twisted tunnels which wind on down endlessly beyond the outer chamber. And when one cries out, the shadows do not answer—there is only the sound of echoes screaming through the darkness. Echo; the planet was well named.

Had Kevin Nichols thought of that while he screamed, or when he grew too weak for screaming? Had he stared at the shapeless shadows which seemed to seethe and stir in the tunnel mouths beyond?

It didn't matter now. The tunnel mouths were open, but Kevin's mouth was closed; closed and set in the grim grin of death. One look at the gaunt face and emaciated body brought one word to Weber's lips.

'Starvation.'

Commander Tasman nodded without comment, then stooped to examine the other body.

For there *was* another body lying there, some little distance away—lying face downward, arms outstretched as though attempting to crawl towards the tunnels when death halted her.

Her.

Tasman turned the body over, staring in recognition at the wasted form.

'Kevin's wife,' he murmured. 'He took her with him.'

Kevin took her with him, and death took them both. Here, in a remote cave on a distant planet, surrounded by shadows, the fugitives had died in darkness, and now only echoes lingered, wailing in the depths. If you listened closely, you could almost hear them now, faint and faraway.

And then they *did* hear the sound, all of them, and recognized it for what it was—issuing from the shadows beyond, impossibly but unmistakably.

A baby had cried.

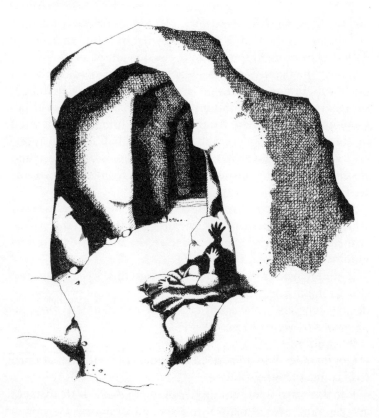

There were problems, many problems.

The first was physical—how to transport a newborn infant back to Earth on a probe-mission ship lacking the facilities and even the feeding formula necessary to sustain its fragile hold on life.

Surprisingly enough, the little one survived and even flourished on the hastily improvised diet of powdered milk and juices. The infant girl seemed to have inherited some of Kevin Nichols's toughness and tenacity as well as his features. Indeed, the resemblance was so close between father and daughter that it was decided to name her after him. They called her Keva.

It wasn't until after splashdown on Earth that the other problems arose. Then Space Control took charge of Keva and inherited the dilemma she brought with her.

There was no publicity, of course, but that in itself solved nothing. Sooner or later the news would inevitably leak out. An honoured and acclaimed astronaut had succeeded in violating top security, had foiled all interplanetary precautions, and had stolen the latest and most advanced spacecraft.

Waves of panic rose and spread behind the locked doors of Space Command. Top brass and top government officials floundered, engulfed in those waves, spluttering in confusion, choking in consternation.

'Do you know what this means? When the story gets out, the whole programme will be discredited. Stealing a prototype ship right out from under our noses—we're going to be the laughing-stock of the world, the whole galaxy!'

Those words were shouted by a senior spokesman for the space project, and a senior spokesman for the government answered him.

'Then why not tell the truth? Tell them that we had our eye on Kevin Nichols all along, knew he was cracking up. Sure, he was next in line for the big promotion, but he wasn't going to make it. Not after what our investigation uncovered—the drug thing, the embezzlement of project funds. He must have realized we were going to blow the whistle on him and that's why he got out, taking his wife with him. Let the public know what happened, that we were the victims of a conspiracy—'

'You're crazy!' Psychiatrists usually disapprove of using such language, but it was a senior member of the psychiatric advisory staff who spoke. 'We can't afford to be laughed at, and we can't afford to be pitied, either. Right now we can't afford anything, period. I don't need to remind you gentlemen that the vote on new appropriations for the entire space project is coming up next week. There couldn't possibly be a worse time to tell the world that the largest and most important programme in all history has been victimized by one man—and that the biggest hero of that programme was a psychotic, a thief, and a traitor. There's got to be another answer.'

There was.

Exactly who gave it is not known—probably some minor member of the staff. It is the fate of junior officers to come up with the right suggestion, and their reward is to be forgotten even while the suggestion is remembered.

'Keva is our answer,' said the nameless junior officer.

Everyone looked at him, everyone listened, and everyone understood.

'Don't you realize what Nichols has done for the programme? He's given us the biggest public-relations hook anyone could wish for. His daughter, Keva. The first child ever to be born in outer space! Not on Mars or Venus or a colony, but on a new frontier, the farthermost outpost of all interplanetary exploration known to man!

'You don't have to say that her father was flipping out, that the ship was stolen. Make the whole thing part of a top security mission, a secret programme to test human survival on an earth-type world. Nichols and his wife volunteered to take the ship off to Echo and have their child there. A heroic experiment that turned into a heroic sacrifice when they emerged from the crash unharmed but unable to return or communicate with the project back on Earth. Let it be known that Nichols kept a complete record of his stay on Echo, up to and including the actual birth of the infant, but that the data are still classified information. That should put an end to any further embarrassing questions about the affair. But there won't be any trouble about the appropriation—not if you concentrate publicity where it belongs and keep it there. You're sitting on the greatest story of all time, the greatest celebrity ever known—Keva, the spacechild!'

They didn't sit much longer.

Within a matter of hours the well-oiled machinery of the space programme's Information Unit started to function. The wheels began to turn, and the end product of the manufacturing process appeared. Instant heroes.

Kevin Nichols, heroic astronaut who piloted an untested ship to an uncharted world. His wife, who risked her unborn baby in the unknown. The space programme itself, bravely breaking through all barriers to prove, once and for all, that humanity could move forward without fear and perpetuate itself on other planets.

Nichols and his wife were dead, but the space programme survived. Just as predicted, the appropriation passed.

And as for young Keva herself, she lived and thrived. Keva, the new symbol of the Age of Space. Publicized, photographed, promoted, praised; in a matter of days, her name was known throughout the solar system and beyond. Child of space, heir to the future.

And ward of the space programme.

Jealously guarded, possessively protected, little Keva was withdrawn from public scrutiny shortly after she had served her primary purpose, and was placed in a private—very private—nursery. While Keva dolls and Keva toys flooded the market, and Keva songs and Keva pictures kept her image bright, the object of all this adulation was being carefully nursed and tended by a team of medical specialists. Paediatricians and psychologists alike agreed; Keva was a very special baby. Not just because of her value as a living symbol, but for what she was—exceptionally sturdy, bright, alert, healthy, and precocious.

Yet, in spite of security, rumours poured out of the nursery-laboratory where young Keva was hidden.

Standing alone at five months. Walking at seven months. Only nine months old and seems to understand everything you say to her. One year old and she's already talking—complete sentences! Did you hear the latest about Keva? Two and a half, going on three, and they say she already is reading! Can you imagine that?

The public could imagine it very easily. As a matter of fact, they were beginning to imagine a little too much. No matter how much a genius was praised, nobody really loved one.

A genius was too hard to understand. And the whole point of the plan was plain; Keva *had* to be loved.

So, after much consideration, Keva was placed in an exclusive private school—in first-phase classes, or what used to be called kindergarten. Good thinking, everyone said; give her a chance to grow up with other youngsters, learn to be like the rest of the kids.

But Keva wasn't like the rest of the kids. She grew faster and learned more quickly. She seemed immune to childhood diseases and she was never ill. Perhaps this was a result of the antiseptic care of the medical team, but even so it was highly unusual. The doctors took notes.

The psychologists took notes, too. Keva did not relate to her peer group—that was the way *they* phrased it. In plainer words, she didn't want to have anything to do with the other children. And what she did not want to do she did not bother with. She read. She asked questions—intelligent, penetrating questions—and she was impatient with stupid answers.

Keva had no interest in nursery rhymes or fairy tales or bedtime stories. Facts and figures, those were the things that fascinated her. She never played with toys, and she refused to learn any games.

The other youngsters didn't understand her, and what children can't understand they usually dislike—a trait often carried over into adult life.

Two of the children never got to carry that or any other trait into adult life. They took to teasing Keva, calling her names, but only for a few days. Then they died.

One of them fell out of an upstairs window while walking in his sleep. The other went into convulsions—an epileptic seizure, the doctors decided.

Of course, Keva had nothing to do with it; she was nowhere near either of the youngsters at the time. But there was bound to be talk, so the medical team took her out of the school.

To put an end to any possible rumours, a thorough check-up was programmed for the prodigy. And prodigy she was—a beautiful, healthy child, without functional defect. The results of the battery of mental tests indicated genius.

What Keva needed, the medical team decided, was a chance to lead a normal existence, an opportunity to relate to ordinary people in ordinary surroundings. As a celebrity such a life was, of course, impossible.

So they changed her name, took her clear across the country, and put her up for adoption.

The world at large was told that Keva had been sent abroad for further education under governmental supervision. Even the couple who took her into their home didn't realize that their bright, good-looking new daughter was the famous spacechild.

To George and Elaine Rutherford, Keva was an orphan named Robin. A quiet girl but well-behaved, quick in her studies, sailing through high school and into college at fifteen. There were no problems.

At least, the security reports didn't indicate any. The space programme had her under observation, of course, monitoring her progress in school.

Perhaps they should have spent more time monitoring her foster parents. As it was, they didn't seem to notice the change in Mr and Mrs Rutherford. Maybe the Rutherfords weren't even aware of it themselves. It wasn't anything dramatic.

But as Keva grew, they dwindled.

Keva's growth was physically apparent. At seventeen, already a senior in college, she seemed completely mature—enough of an adult, in fact, to enter into the management of her foster father's prosperous ranch during the summer months.

Rutherford, the bluff, hearty rancher with the booming voice, made no objection. It was as though he secretly welcomed the idea of taking things easy, of not having to bawl out orders, of sitting quietly on the big screened porch and rocking away. After a time people began to notice how he mumbled and muttered, talking to himself.

Elaine Rutherford didn't say anything—she gradually stopped entertaining or going out, and never saw any of their old friends. While the girl ran the ranch, she was content just to keep house and spend her spare time resting upstairs. Then she began to talk to herself, too.

It was just about a year later—after Keva had graduated and gone into advanced work in astrophysics—that the authorities came and took the Rutherfords away.

There was a hearing and the ranch hands testified. So did the girl. Everyone agreed there had been no violence, no real crisis.

It was only that the Rutherfords had gone from talking to babbling, and from babbling to screaming.

Shadows were what they feared. Shadows, or a single shadow —apparently they never saw more than one at a given moment. A shadow moving at midnight in the corrals, making the cattle bellow in terror—but why should cattle be afraid of something that cannot be seen? A shadow creeping through the long dark ranch house hall, while the floorboards creaked—but how can there be sound without substance? A shadow glimpsed in the girl's room, stretched sleeping in the bed where the girl should be—but shadows do not sleep, and the girl testified she had seen nothing.

It was a sad affair, and the ending was inevitable. The Rutherfords were obviously incompetent and they had to be committed. Both of them died within a matter of months.

The space programme people stayed out of the affair, of course; at least, they didn't interfere publicly. But they followed the hearing and they had the data and they took charge of Keva once more.

Taking charge was a mere formality now, for they weren't dealing with a child any longer. Keva was physically adult and mentally she was—

Worthy of further study.

That's what the medical team decided.

Keva was happy to co-operate, even though it meant temporarily abandoning her research project on methods of communicating with distant planetary bodies through the use of ultrasonic frequencies.

On the appointed day she appeared before an international panel of scientific authorities at Space Command headquarters, prepared to submit to a thorough examination and check-up. But she was not prepared to meet the head of that panel—an elderly, stoop-shouldered man who was introduced to her as Mission Commander Richard Tasman, USN, Ret.

The foreign scientists noted that Keva didn't seem to react to the introduction. Perhaps she didn't recognize the name, but, of course, there was no reason that she should.

At least, there was no reason until Tasman began asking questions. The questions were polite, formally phrased, and simple. But their content was disturbing.

Tasman wanted Keva to tell him about the shadows.

Keva frowned, and then sighed. 'Surely you've read the reports of the hearing. The shadows my poor foster parents claim to have seen were nonexistent—paranoid delusions—'

Commander Tasman nodded. 'But it's the other shadows I'm interested in. The shadows that I saw with my own eyes twenty years ago when I found you in that cave on Echo.'

The listening scientists leaned forward as Keva shook her head. They turned up the earphones to hear what their translators were reporting as the conversation continued.

Keva shrugged. 'I was a baby. How do you expect me to remember anything? And if I could, why should I notice shadows?'

'Why, indeed?' Tasman smiled. 'I saw them plainly enough but at the time I had no reason to pay attention to them. Now I'm not so sure.'

'What do you mean?'

Tasman smiled again. 'I'm not so sure of *that*, either. In fact, I'm not sure of anything any more. It occurs to me that we should have followed up our findings on Echo. Somehow, in all the excitement of your discovery and rescue, certain unusual bits of data were neglected. An Earth-type planet exists within a certain range of prescribed conditions—this we know because we've located and studied others within the galaxy. Like Echo, they all contain life-forms. Micro-organisms, algae, plant life in infinite variety. And all of them, in this phase of evolution, contain animal life, too. All except Echo.'

Tasman fixed his eyes on Keva. 'I understand you have a background in space research.'

'I'm only a novice—'

'But you have studied available information?'

'Yes.'

'Then let me ask this: doesn't it seem strange to you that Echo, and Echo alone, is the only Earth-type body ever discovered that is capable of supporting higher and more complicated life-forms, yet contains none?'

'Perhaps there were such forms at one time, and they failed to survive.'

'For what reason? There's no indication of natural disaster or recent geologic upheaval.'

'Maybe the evolutionary cycle came to a natural end. Whatever might have existed there merely died out,' Keva said.

'Suppose it didn't die out? Suppose it merely developed along different lines, advanced to a point where life was no longer dependent upon a physical body of the type we're familiar with.'

'You mean something like pure thought?' It was Keva's turn to smile.

Tasman shook his head and he wasn't smiling. 'Something like shadows,' he said.

Keva stared. They were all staring now.

'Shadows,' Tasman repeated. 'Consider a life-form that may once have been human like ourselves—very much like ourselves in many ways—but had reached a turning point in the evolutionary road. Instead of continuing to evolve in terms of brawn, the emphasis became spiritual.'

'Pure thought again?' Keva gestured. 'Impossible.'

'Of course, it's impossible,' Tasman said. 'Life is energy, and energy has form. But on Echo, which seems to have existed for countless years in an idyllic state, there was no need for a sturdy body to withstand the elements. And who knows—upon reaching a certain stage of mental development, there may no longer be any dependency upon ordinary nourishment.'

'You're saying these creatures turned into shadows?'

'*Creatures?* Hardly the term I'd use to describe so advanced an organism. As for shadows, how do we know what they really are? Possibly what we saw as shadows are merely visual projections of mental energy contained in the minimum possible shape. A shape that no longer requires sensory organs for perception or communication. A shape that doesn't need the complex of mechanical aids we call civilization, that can live without our concept of comfort and shelter—'

'In caves?'

Keva rose as she spoke, and faced the assemblage around the long table. She talked and the others listened. Exactly what she said is a matter of debate—afterwards, opinions seemed to differ. But her words made sense, and everyone got the point.

Carefully, courteously, but concisely, she took Tasman's theories apart, demolishing each premiss in turn. There was no precedent, not in biology or physics or the most advanced observations of science, for sentient shadows. One might as well argue the reality of ghosts. A shadow, by definition, is merely a shade cast upon a surface by a body that intercepts rays of light. It is the body that exists. Shadows are merely illusions—like the apparitions Keva's foster parents had babbled about, or like Commander Tasman's strange beliefs.

The speech was effective. And after Tasman, cold but controlled, excused Keva from the hearing and had her escorted from the room, there was a general buzz of conversation from the scientists gathered there.

Obviously they were impressed by what they had heard. They were even more impressed when an apologetic sound engineer buzzed the chamber on intercom to report the sudden power failure that had cut off the mikes and had made translation of Keva's speech impossible.

'Amazing, the young woman!' The Italian scientist groped for words in his heavily accented English. 'Such presence, to realize this—and continue speaking in Italian.'

'*Nein.*' The guttural rejoinder came swiftly. 'It was in German she spoke.'

'*Français!*'

Dissension rose in Japanese, Russian, Spanish, and Mandarin. All had heard Keva and all had understood.

Tasman understood, too.

He raced out of the door and down the corridor. At the entrance to a small side office he found Keva's security guards stationed and waiting.

'Keva—where is she?'

The senior officer blinked and gestured. 'Inside.'

Tasman brushed past him and opened the door.

The room beyond had no windows, no other exit.

But it was empty.

There was no official report of Keva's disappearance. Even the medical team wasn't informed. But Tasman knew, and went straight to Top Security. A directive was issued.

Find Keva.

'She's bound to slip up,' Tasman said. 'What happened at the hearing proves she's not infallible. When the mikes went dead she unconsciously continued to communicate by means of direct-thought transmission. That explains why each foreign delegate believed he was hearing Keva speak to him in his own language. When Keva realized she was giving herself away, it was too late. She had to flee.'

The security officers nodded uneasily. How do you find a person who can transmit thoughts at will, hypnotize guards, and pass them by without being seen or remembered?

'If she made one mistake she'll make others,' Tasman assured them.

But Tasman himself didn't wait for mistakes. While security personnel searched for Keva in the present, Tasman sought her in the past. He talked to people who had known her at the ranch, to schoolmates, to the surviving members of the original relief mission, men such as Gilbey and Weber. What he learned he kept to himself, but the word spread.

Eventually, it reached back to a man who had known Keva's true parents.

Dr Hans Diedrich, living in retirement in the Virgin Islands, contacted Space Command with an urgent message. He had, he said, certain information which might be of vital importance in this affair.

Within twenty-four hours Diedrich was visited at his cottage home by an elderly, stoop-shouldered man who identified himself as Mission Commander Richard Tasman, USN, Ret.

'I'm glad you came,' Diedrich said. 'I have followed the reports with great interest—my nephew is in the space programme and it was he who informed me of what happened.'

His visitor frowned. 'A security leak?'

'Do not be alarmed. It is for the best that I was told, and in a moment you will understand why I say that. You see, I know what you are thinking.'

'You do?'

Diedrich frowned. 'You have a theory, haven't you? That Kevin Nichols's child was left alone in that cave on Echo when her parents died, left alone with the shadow creatures. And that somehow, before your relief expedition arrived, these beings took possession of her, so that when she was rescued she was no longer an ordinary infant but something more. Because they infused her with their powers, established a mental contact, a link with themselves which was not broken when she returned to earth. And that all through her childhood and youth, she was really acting as their pawn. A human being under alien control. Is that it?'

His visitor nodded.

'Well, you are wrong,' said Dr Diedrich. 'I was the Nichols's family physician. I have their medical records. Two years before the journey to Echo, I had to perform surgery on Mrs Nichols.'

'So?'

'That is what I wanted to tell you. The surgery made it impossible for Mrs Nichols to have a child. The infant you found in the cave was not their daughter.'

Dr Diedrich leaned forward. 'These beings must have the power to receive thoughts as well as to transmit them. They absorbed the contents of Nichols's mind as he lay dying in the cave—his wife's mind, too. And using what they learned, they created the illusion of an infant, one of their own kind disguised in a mental projection, programmed to live and grow as a child.'

'Why send it back to earth?'

Diedrich shrugged. 'I cannot say.'

'And you have no proof.'

'Only of the surgery. Here, my own medical records—'

He handed a bulky envelope to his visitor.

His visitor smiled, thanked him, pulled out a revolver, and shot Dr Diedrich through the head.

'I told you she'd make a mistake,' Tasman muttered. 'Going down there, getting the information, then deliberately using a clumsy, old-fashioned weapon to kill Diedrich—it was a clever idea. And there are half a dozen people who can testify to seeing me escape from the cottage.

'Fortunately, you know I was here at headquarters all the time. Keva didn't anticipate I'd have such an airtight alibi. And she didn't anticipate that Diedrich had taken the precaution of taping a statement of his beliefs beforehand and sending it here to Space Command. So, we understand how all this happened—and why.'

'We know something else now, too.' The Chief of Operations himself answered Tasman, and his voice was grim. 'The life-form we're dealing with has greater powers than we imagined. The ability to transmit thought and to receive it. The ability to appear in the form we identify as Keva, or to change that form at will.

'Do you realize what we're up against? A creature that can read our minds, walk unseen among us as a shadow, and alter its appearance whenever it chooses.'

'Mimicry,' Tasman said. 'Insects use it for protection, taking on the look of the plant or tree branch where they rest. The being we know as Keva has this same faculty, developed to its ultimate extent.'

The Chief of Operations frowned. 'Then why did it even bother to appear as Keva in the first place?'

'Again we can look to the insect world for a parallel,' Tasman said. 'Some insects begin in a larval state. It's only later that they emerge in new forms, with the power of disguising their shapes. Perhaps it was necessary for Keva to go through certain stages in a single body while she grew to maturity and learned our ways. Only now, as an adult, is she capable of functioning fully.'

'And just what is her function? Why did a shadow creature come to earth in human disguise?'

Tasman shrugged. 'Maybe the shadows grew tired of being shadows. Perhaps an existence of pure thought was no longer enough for them and they yearned for the sensations and satisfactions of solid physical shapes. In which case Keva was sent here as a scout, to study our ways and see if we could be taken over.'

The Chief of Operations shook his head. 'You think that is a possibility?'

'I think that is what actually happened.'

'Then what do you propose?'

'Another expedition to Echo. Give me the command, and a task force. Keep it under sealed orders, call it an exploratory operation if you like. But you and I know the real purpose of the mission.'

'Seek and destroy?'

Tasman nodded. 'It's our only chance. And we've got to move fast, before Keva suspects.'

Commander Tasman lifted off for Echo under top security, but that didn't stop the rumours.

Whether or not Keva suspected was no longer the problem. The search for her went on, but how do you find a shadow? It could be anywhere now.

It was the spread of the rumours that really caused the trouble—and the panic.

Somehow the word was out, and the world trembled. People had forgotten about the spacechild through the years, but now they remembered as the whispers grew.

There was a monster in our midst, the rumour-mongers said. An alien unlike any humanoid form on planets known to man—an invisible creature, murdering at will. True, a mission had been mounted against Echo, but it would never return.

The whispers rose to angry shouts, and there was only one way to silence them.

The President of the United States went on Emergency Band and addressed the world. Standing before the cameras and microphones in the tower at Communications Centre, he delivered his message.

The rumours were partially true, the President admitted. The spacechild was indeed an alien, but there was no longer any reason to fear her. Because Keva was dead. She had been discovered and trapped only this afternoon in a secret hideaway—a mountain cave near Pocatello, Idaho. Full details would be available on an international newscast following the President's message.

Meanwhile, it was time to put an end to the vicious falsehoods spread by our enemies, the President declared. All this wild talk of alien invasion was part of a plot, designed to prevent the opening up of free space travel and communication—but the plot had failed. After all, Commander Tasman had been sent into space for exploratory purposes and had not encountered any resistance.

It was his privilege, the President said, to announce the final expansion of the space programme. From this time forward there would be no restrictions on further flights. Every area of the galaxy was now officially declared to be open to the ships of any government or any private concern or individual. No more secrecy, no more security, no more fear. If new alien life-forms were encountered they would be met with friendship. If they chose to visit our solar system or even our own Earth, let them be welcomed. For this was the start of the true Age of Space—founded firmly in freedom and friendship.

The world listened to its leader and breathed a collective sigh of relief.

The President joined in that sigh as the broadcast ended. He watched the technical crews gather up their equipment and depart, leaving him alone in the tower room with its single window opening on the night sky and the stars.

Then the President of the United States melted into a shadow and slithered across the floor to the window, as she waited for her alien brothers to arrive.

Earth Surrenders

BARBARA PAUL

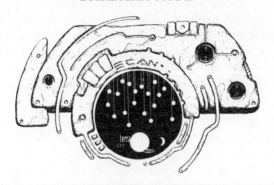

We'd had little warning; a blip on a screen splintered into a thousand blips, so large a fleet for our one small planet. We assumed we weren't the only one, merely one of the last, perched out here in the galactic suburbs. Perhaps they needed a refuelling station on their way to Andromeda. They'd destroyed our toehold colony on Mars, casually, in passing—like a slap on the wrist. There was no mistaking their intent.

We didn't even know who 'they' were; our communication had all been us-to-them. Does a man introduce himself to a bug before he steps on it? Once the ships were in range, President Brigham didn't hesitate to launch every weapon we had, as did our counterparts in their own domains around the world. We didn't get one ship. The combined firepower of the entire world was insufficient to bring down *one* ship.

It took a while; this was no six-minute war. Most of us just watched while the military tried first this, then that. Long after the rest of the world had exhausted its resources, France finally got its act together and launched an attack. It made no difference. Their superweapons had no more effect than our superweapons.

President Brigham aged twenty years before my eyes as the reports came in; I think she understood before any of us that there was no stopping these invaders. She took a few minutes to marshal her thoughts and called us all together—her advisers, both civilian and military, as well as certain scientists who so far had been able to contribute nothing. Nor, indeed, had any of us.

'Since we don't know what the invaders are going to do next,' President Brigham said, 'we need to plan for every possibility we can think of. General Schumacher, are you ready with the Joint Chiefs' contingency plans?'

'I am, Madam President,' Schumacher replied, looking un-naturally calm in the face of what was happening to us. 'We've never seen the invaders, so we don't know what will work against them. But there are things we can do.'

He started a show-and-tell with graphs, maps, computer simulations. What to do if the invaders don't destroy us but keep us alive for whatever purposes they have in mind. What to do if they kill most but not all of the people in the world in order to retain a manageable population. What to do if they have no need for the Earth but plan to destroy it simply because it is their nature to do so, like the scorpion in the story. The plans even took in the possibility that the invaders would never leave their ships . . . which meant we had no way of fighting back at all.

They were all survival plans, predicated on an assumption that we'd lost all our defences and were at the mercy of whatever force had descended upon us. In every scenario, some form of the military was proposed as the authority that would bring a measure of order out of chaos. I made no mention of this; I knew the President had caught it. Besides, I had no official standing in the underground Command Centre. But the role of First Husband did carry its perks, or I wouldn't have been there at all.

The President was frowning. 'We can't have much time. What are they doing now?'

'Still circling,' someone said.

The ships had entered the Earth's atmosphere, great silvery things that our telemetry said were loaded with armament. They had not returned our fire, other than blasting the Mars colony out of existence on their way here. The ships were positioning themselves . . . for what?

An hour later they were still circling, with no change in the orbital pattern of any of the ships. Round and round. We'd given up trying to contact them. They'd received our messages, we were assured; they just didn't bother to answer. Round and round.

'What are they waiting for?' the Secretary of the Interior finally cried out.

General Schumacher glared at the man. 'They're trying to psych us out. Make us nervous so we'll do something stupid.'

The Interior man accepted the reprimand and said no more. We all avoided looking at one another. So far there'd been no screaming or yelling, no top-of-the-voice arguing, no name-calling; we were all controlling our fear. So far.

The President was practically dead on her feet; she'd been awake for nearly forty hours. 'Use this time,' I said in her ear. 'Sleep whenever you can.'

She started to object but then changed her mind. We went into our quarters. 'I sleep better when the First Lord is warming my back,' she said. Our old joke.

We curled up together and drifted into a fitful sleep that lasted a couple of hours; then she was awake again and checking on the invaders' ships. No change in the circling patterns.

The public news channels brought us pictures of burning buildings, the inevitable looting, interviews with people who believed it was all a hoax. For those who didn't: hysteria, many suicides. The subways in New York had stopped running because the tunnels were packed with people seeking to get as far underground as they could, probably the smartest thing they could do.

It was our worst nightmare come true, the xenophobic build-up that began with the first venture into space now proving itself justified with a vengeance. The world reacted as it has always done to anything new and dangerous: with panic. The invaders were destroying us by letting us destroy ourselves.

She stood before one of the screens, sadly watching the terrified populace. 'Time to run another reassurance speech, I think. Not that it'll do any good.' She'd taped a number of them before we descended to the underground Command Centre, all of them saying basically the same thing. *We're attempting to make contact, they haven't attacked the Earth yet, stay calm.*

I was watching a different channel. 'Leila, listen to this.'

A newsman (and self-appointed pundit) was speculating that the invaders hadn't attacked the Earth because they couldn't. The newsman's theory was that the invaders had the capacity to wipe out a colony of a couple of thousand people, but not enough to annihilate the entire population of the world. The destruction of the Mars colony had been a scare tactic, an act of intimidation.

'It's all a bluff?' She laughed shortly. 'We should show him our telemetry readings. *One* of those ships could take out the Earth.'

'Are they waiting for us to make a move?' I wondered.

Leila didn't answer, but said, 'Interesting that all the contingency plans are strategic withdrawals.'

Uh-oh. 'You're not still looking for a way to fight back? All those contingency plans were based on an assumption of defeat.'

'I know.' She sighed. 'General Schumacher is a realist. He knows when to attack, when to withdraw. His guns and rockets didn't do what they were supposed to do, so the next step in his rule book is to pull back and cut your losses. I can't argue with that.'

I smiled. 'But.'

'But while I agree with Schumacher, on some level I feel we haven't done enough to resist.'

'Resist how? After what they did to Mars?'

'They have some use for us, Peter,' she argued, 'or they would have done the same to Earth by now. We know nothing about those . . . people. What are they doing right now? For all we know, they might need to go into some sort of stasis periodically to recharge their batteries. And then when they wake up, they'll blow us to smithereens. Or not. We just don't know.'

'Their ships are impregnable,' I said, 'but are they? The thing to do is get them to leave their ships. So we'll have a better shot at them.'

'Won't work. We kill some of them, they'll use the ships to retaliate. No, we need to make them go away.'

'But how?'

She tapped a fingernail against her teeth. 'Our use of force failed. What if we do a complete turnabout? What if we ask them for help?'

We discarded the idea of presenting ourselves as a plague-ridden planet in desperate need of medical aid, since what was lethal to us might prove harmless to the invaders. Besides, the invaders would see right through that; it was too transparent a ploy.

The Secretary of the Treasury suggested we fake some readings that would make the invaders think our sun was about to go nova. The scientists quickly explained to her why that was not possible.

But that gave General Schumacher an idea. 'How about faking readings that would suggest we're in for the biggest damn earthquake known to mankind? Some giant rift developing in the Earth, one that'll move continental plates, level cities . . . and just, in general, wreck the place?'

The President said, 'And then ask the invaders to evacuate as many of us as possible? It might work.'

The technicians and engineers and seismologists conferred and agreed they could produce fake readings that would fool *our* detectors. But since the invaders had already demonstrated superior technology, they couldn't promise that our unwanted visitors would be taken in.

Put that one on hold.

I cleared my throat. 'Whatever we do, the invaders are going to be suspicious—because the first thing we tried to do was shoot them out of the sky. We lost our credibility with the first rocket we fired.'

'Thank you, Peter,' Schumacher said with a touch of sarcasm. 'We'll just have to be damned convincing, that's all.'

That's all?

It was the President herself who finally made the suggestion that we ultimately adopted. 'Let's invite them to dinner,' she said.

First came the messages to the other heads of state requesting that they not attempt further contact with the invaders; we could only pray they would comply. That done, we turned back to the invaders themselves.

We surrendered. We acknowledged that the invaders occupied the dominant position and pledged to refrain from any further military action. Not that there was anything more we could have done along that line anyway. We asked the invaders what they wanted.

No response.

Then we offered to evacuate and leave the planet and all its riches to them. We were *giving* them our world. The only problem was that we did not have an interstellar drive. Did the invaders have any suggestions?

No response.

So we requested that the invaders assign us a few of their ships, so we could begin evacuating our people.

That brought a response. **Not acceptable**.

A gasping sort of cheer arose in the Command Centre; the first words we'd had from them. And confirmation that they were indeed receiving our messages and were able to understand our language. Did they have translator machines? The pronunciation was a bit odd, but the two words were perfectly understandable. I wondered how many of Earth's languages the invaders (or their machines) had mastered. But we had established communication now; the first hurdle was over.

'Good,' said the President. 'Now we step it up.'

We sent a three-part clarifying message. One: The requested ships would still be crewed and guarded by the owners of the ships. Two: We would go wherever they directed us to go. Three: If they needed a work force on Earth, we would leave part of our people behind.

There was a long silence. Then: **Not acceptable**.

'Still suspicious,' Schumacher said, showing signs of nervousness for the first time. 'I hope this isn't the stupid thing they're trying to psych us into doing.'

'It's the reply we expected, General,' said the President. 'Send the next message.'

The next message told the invaders to name their terms. We did not say please.

The next response finally told us what the invaders wanted. **Evacuate northern hemisphere. All those remaining north of equator after one lunar cycle will be destroyed**.

'*Lebensraum?*' a voice said unbelievingly. 'They want living space for themselves?'

'Not necessarily,' the President said. 'They might want a way station where they don't have to worry about controlling the local population.'

'Then why not just gas the planet? That would leave the structures intact.'

Schumacher snorted. 'It would also leave them with five billion corpses to dispose of. That's why they haven't attacked. The dead they left behind on Mars don't matter—they won't be using the colony. No, this is the best move, from their point of view. And you can bet that the equator is going to be the most heavily guarded boundary line we've ever seen.'

'At least they seem willing to coexist,' another voice suggested nervously.

'But we're not,' the President replied firmly. 'You're talking as if we've really surrendered.' She frowned. 'What would they expect us to reply?'

'More time,' I said.

'Right. Let's ask for a year.' The message was sent.

One lunar cycle.

This time we did not respond.

The President turned to Schumacher. 'I'd like film clips, news reports, still shots—everything visual that the military has on the fighting in Central America, Bosnia, Vietnam, anywhere, no matter how old.' We hadn't had a real war on Earth for twenty-five years, so she had to dip into recent history. 'And get it ready to transmit to the invaders.'

Schumacher gave her a rueful smile and shook his head. 'I don't think we're going to scare those creatures away.'

'Not scare them, General. Make them think we're more trouble than we're worth. And we don't have much time.'

He was dubious that even that would work, but he was in favour of trying almost anything. When Schumacher was ready, we requested visual contact with the invaders.

To our surprise, they agreed. There was a mutter of worried excitement in the Command Centre; no one knew what to expect. A scientist named Pellegrino, of whom I'd never heard before the invaders arrived, was set up in a small sound-proofed room so his instant analysis wouldn't be carried by our transmissions to the invaders. Miniature receivers in our ears would pick up his words.

But it seemed we were expected to go first. When the technicians had everything in place, the President stood alone before the camera and allowed her image to be transmitted to the invaders.

You are called what?

'My name is Leila Brigham. I am President of the United States of America. To whom am I speaking?'

A screen that had been showing a map of now-depleted missile sites flickered once, twice—and we had our first view of the invaders.

We were looking at a man. No question of that, he *was* a man. One head, two eyes, two arms. Very thick and squat, possibly shorter than we were—impossible to tell without a visual point of reference. Almost no neck. Flattened-out facial features.

From a heavy-gravity planet, Dr Pellegrino's voice said in our ears.

The invader was black—not black like the Earth's black races, but a glittering black that was almost blue. No facial hair, not even eyebrows.

High melanin, said Dr Pellegrino, *or their equivalent of melanin. Hot sun—hot enough to drive them away? Their home star might be an old one starting its final expansion. But they can't have a DNA radically different from ours.*

So the invaders weren't monsters, not even bugs or lizards. I wondered if they came in a variety of colours, the way we did. Somewhere else in the galaxy—perhaps in more than one place?—a life cycle like our own had begun. And produced an aggressive race that took what it wanted by force. Not too different from us.

The invader spoke. **Commander of the Broghoke.**

Ah, so that was their name . . . at least it sounded something like *Broghoke*, the second syllable more aspirated than spoken. This was not the voice we'd heard before; the Commander's tones were rougher, his accent thicker. He was waiting for the President to speak.

She said, 'Commander, it's impossible for us to move half the Earth's population in only one month's time. Our best estimate is that it would take two or three months simply to launch a successful invasion of the southern hemisphere. Then the transportation problem alone would—' She broke off when the invader raised a hand abruptly in a commanding gesture.

Note the six fingers, said Dr Pellegrino.

You do not understand well, said the Commander's rough tones. **You are not required to conquer. You are required only to vacate.**

'Vacating is impossible without conquering first. The entire southern hemisphere is in constant tumult, one war after another.' That would come as a surprise to the inhabitants of Rio and Sydney. 'Let me show you something. This is what's going on right now.' She signalled for the transmission of our old war pictures to start.

There hadn't been enough time to do any sorting or organizing, so we watched Nicaragua and Sarajevo and

Rommel's tanks in North Africa, all jumbled up together. We watched children armed with automatic weapons they could barely lift firing at soldiers. We saw emasculations and hangings. We watched explosions and bombings. People on fire ran from a burning building only to be shot down by the guerrillas waiting for them. We saw an entire Asian village lined up against a wall and shot; after the fusillade ended, only the sound of a crying baby could be heard. One more shot rang out, and then silence.

The Commander of the Broghoke had disappeared from the screen—watching elsewhere, we hoped. We finally stopped transmission when *we* couldn't take any more. Any invaders worth their salt ought to think twice about sharing a planet with that kind of turmoil. Even General Schumacher looked affected by what we'd seen, as did the other military bigwigs in the Command Centre.

The invaders' Commander reappeared. **Is this fighting confined to the southern hemisphere?**

Schumacher shot to his feet and drew one finger across his throat. The technicians cut the transmission.

'What?' the President demanded.

'Let's think this through,' the General said. 'Is the fighting all in the south? Do we say yes or no? If we say yes, the Broghokers or whatever the hell they call themselves will just drive us down across the equator and that'll be the end of it—may the most vicious survive. They don't give a hoot about us. All they want is a place for themselves, here, on half of our world, where they don't have to bother keeping an eye on us. And it's *our* half they want. We have to tell them the fighting is everywhere—it's the only weapon we've got.'

'But if we say the fighting is worldwide,' the Vice President said, 'how will that stop them?'

'Isn't the point to make ourselves look like more trouble than the invaders care to handle?' Schumacher asked. 'They just want us out of their way.'

'One sure way of handling *that*,' the Secretary of Defence said. 'The fact that they haven't killed us all yet doesn't mean they won't still do it.'

'Schumacher's right,' said Admiral Somethingorother. 'It's the only weapon we've got. We'd be fools not to use it.'

Then the loud arguing that had been absent earlier started in earnest. Everyone had an opinion which could evidently be expressed only at the top of one's lungs. I glanced at the screen; the Commander of the Broghoke had disappeared again. How long would they wait?

Leila put her hand on my arm and drew me aside. She kept licking her lips, a mannerism that appeared only when she had to make a decision she didn't want to make—and, until now, one that she indulged in only when we were alone. 'Peter, what's your take?'

'It *is* the only weapon we have,' I said. 'If they try to kill us all, they'd have to tie up half their troops on permanent burial detail . . . or whatever it is they do with dead bodies. Burn them, perhaps. And it would be a tedious, time-eating process, since they seem not to want to destroy the cities.'

She nodded. 'Most of the industry is in the north, but the mining opportunities in the southern hemisphere—why don't they want those?'

'Perhaps they don't know about them. They can't have been monitoring our transmissions very long.'

'So you agree with Schumacher?'

'I never thought I'd be saying this, but yes, I do. Confound the enemy and he is yours, as I think somebody once said.'

She stopped being Leila and went back to being the President again, calling for quiet and getting it. 'Are you agreed?'

General Schumacher looked around. 'Most of us are, I think. The invaders will believe that we're quarrelsome, violent, unruly—because the first thing we did was try to shoot them out of the sky.' He shot a self-satisfied glance in my direction. 'Anything we can do to add to that impression can only help.' There was a mutter of reservations expressed by a couple of the Cabinet members, but no one openly challenged the General's conclusions. 'And Madam President,' he went on, 'maybe you don't have to be so polite?'

She nodded slowly. 'Point taken. All right, let's restore transmission.'

Another voice spoke up. 'You're all taking a lot for granted.' Dr Pellegrino was standing in the doorway to his sound-proofed cubicle. 'Because they look like us doesn't mean they think like us. You might be provoking a reaction totally different from the one you're looking for.'

'I'm sure that's already occurred to everyone here,' the President answered with a touch of impatience. 'But since there's no way of finding out, it's a risk we're forced to take, isn't it? Unless you have an alternate course of action in mind?'

The scientist looked at his feet. 'No.'

'Then we'll proceed.' She stepped back in front of the camera. 'Commander?'

He reappeared wordlessly.

'Sorry about the interruption. We're having technical difficulties down here, but it had _better_ not happen again.' She glanced angrily off camera at an empty chair, a little bit of theatrical byplay that may have been lost on the Broghoke. 'You were asking a question about the fighting?'

Is the fighting confined to the southern hemisphere?

'The fighting is worse in the south,' she said with stagy evasiveness.

Unacceptable answer.

'The fighting is worldwide, if you have to know.' A nice touch of resentment there. 'But it's more under control in the northern hemisphere. Still, we could use some help. If your ships' weapons could clear some space for us in the southern hemisphere, we could vacate a lot sooner. Can you help us?'

No response. The Commander's facial expression didn't even change.

The President ploughed on. 'Er, we made a little mistake when we transmitted those pictures of the fighting. That last series of scenes was from a European war. Northern hemisphere, not southern.'

Our instruments detect no signs of warfare in either hemisphere.

The President made a _huh_ sound. 'Well, that's your doing, Commander. No one on Earth has ever fought an opponent like you before. None of our weapons work against you. Hostilities pretty much ground to a halt when we realized we have a common enemy now.' She let a note of sarcasm creep into her voice. 'I suppose I should thank you. You've brought us global peace.'

Whether the Broghoke caught the nuance of her last two sentences or not, I couldn't tell. The Commander conducted a brief conversation with someone off camera; their language was muted and gutteral, and was even then being analyzed by our linguistic programs. Not much to work with, though.

The Commander turned back to the camera. **You have additional images of the fighting in both hemispheres?**

They wanted more? 'Tons of it,' the President said without batting an eye.

Resume transmission.

The old war pictures started again. The President ordered that this time transmission would continue until the Broghoke themselves called a halt. She instructed Schumacher to make sure they didn't run out of film, but one of his aides was already on the phone making the arrangements. The screen was showing two young boys throwing gasoline bombs at a convoy truck in a place that looked like Ireland.

Another problem had appeared. Other nations had picked up our transmissions to the invaders and were angrily demanding to know what was going on. Interestingly, none of them had been able to intercept the Broghoke's tight-beam transmissions to us. We couldn't risk the invaders monitoring any explanation we might give, so the White House Chief of Staff was given the dirty job of asking the rest of the world to be patient and trust us. Poor man.

Leila had a pinched look on her face that I recognized; I followed her into our quarters and found her taking her headache medicine. 'You need something to eat,' I said. 'I'll be right back.'

I went to the mess area and returned with two mugs of soup and a plate of cheese, crackers, and fruit. We took our time eating; the Broghoke were evidently fascinated by our moving picture show and sent no signal that they'd seen enough. We tried sleeping again; but Leila was too restless and kept pacing back and forth in our small quarters.

'What else can we show them, Peter?' she said, more thinking out loud than actually asking. 'Floods, other natural disasters? More problems for them to deal with. Volcanoes erupting?'

'Do you think you can perch for five minutes?' She sat down, and I started massaging her neck and shoulders. 'He didn't answer you when you asked them to help invade the southern hemisphere.'

'He probably didn't believe what he was hearing. I doubt that the Broghoke are used to being asked for help. Traffic accidents—we must have some footage of gory traffic accidents. Shuttle crashes.'

'Schumacher is handling all that—leave it to him, Leila. There's nothing more you can do now.'

'I know,' she said tightly. 'That's what scares me.' She jumped up and started pacing again. 'All that armament those ships are carrying. It would take us forever to outfit a war fleet like that, even if we had an interstellar drive. They must have been planning this excursion for years. And we're hoping to trick them with a few elderly newsreels?'

'You go with what you've got,' I said inanely. It was a long shot; we all knew that. I stopped Leila in her pacing and wrapped my arms around her. We leaned against each other without speaking, both of us thinking the same thing: this could be our last night.

It was another three hours before the Broghoke had seen their fill. They'd asked for certain bits to be replayed; the invaders were interested not so much in big explosions and tell-all views of our weaponry as they were in close shots of the actual participants engaged in combat. Maybe they just enjoyed seeing blood spilled.

When the Commander appeared on the screen, the President took the initiative. 'Well? Are you going to help us invade the southern hemisphere?'

Invasion is not necessary. You are no longer required to vacate the northern hemisphere.

Aha, a change in plans; something had got through to them. 'Well, that's a relief,' said the President. 'I don't know that we could have managed it anyway.' A pause. 'Does this mean you're leaving?'

We did not know what fearless warriors the people of Earth are. Even your children show courage and valour in battle. We have never before encountered a species of natural fighters such as you. Your soldiers are your greatest treasure.

Good God in heaven, they *liked* what they'd seen! All that carnage . . . The President looked taken aback but tried to find an advantage in this unexpected response. 'Yes, I'm afraid we're always quarrelling about something. A number of our countries have gone bankrupt just from the cost of maintaining a war.'

The Broghoke weren't interested in that. **We breed our warriors through controlled mating, but for you that is not necessary. You produce soldiers naturally without planning. The Earth is an even greater resource than we had thought**.

'Resource? For . . . ?'

For warriors. We always need brave warriors.

The temperature in the Command Centre dropped twenty degrees.

'Let me understand this,' the President said, shaken. 'You want to *recruit* soldiers from the human race? From Earth?'

Your own wars must cease. Fighting among yourselves will not be tolerated. A force of Broghoke will be stationed permanently on Earth to protect the resource—this is a mandatory term of your surrender. The commander leaned towards the camera. **We don't want to lose you**.

The transmission ended.

We all stared at one another speechlessly. We'd just condemned humanity to an eternity of warfare? This was our destiny, to breed killers for a killer race? Warriors watching war, they'd seen what they wanted to see. They admired us for the very thing we'd been trying so hard all these years to suppress: human aggression. I went over to take Leila's hands, but she didn't look at me; she was staring beyond my shoulder at General Schumacher.

His eyes were gleaming.

'Look,' said Dr Pellegrino, pointing to the screen. We watched as shuttles began dropping from the warships, a dozen from each of fifty or so of the ships. Shining silver needles pointed straight at Earth.

They were coming.

The Underdweller

WILLIAM F. NOLAN

In the waiting, windless dark, Lewis Stillman pressed into the building-front shadows along Wilshire Boulevard. Breathing softly, the automatic poised and ready in his hand, he advanced with animal stealth towards Western Avenue, gliding over the night-cool concrete past ravaged clothing shops, drug and ten-cent stores, their windows shattered, their doors ajar and swinging. The city of Los Angeles, painted in cold moonlight, was an immense graveyard; the tall, white tombstone buildings thrust up from the silent pavement, shadow-carved and lonely. Overturned metal corpses of trucks, buses, and automobiles littered the streets.

He paused under the wide marquee of the Fox Wiltern. Above his head, rows of splintered display bulbs gaped—sharp glass teeth in wooden jaws. Lewis Stillman felt as though they might drop at any moment to pierce his body.

Four more blocks to cover. His destination: a small corner delicatessen four blocks south of Wilshire, on Western. Tonight he intended bypassing the larger stores like Safeway and Thriftimart, with their available supplies of exotic foods; a smaller grocery was far more likely to have what he needed. He was finding it more and more difficult to locate basic foodstuffs. In the big supermarkets, only the more exotic and highly spiced canned and bottled goods remained—and he was sick of caviare and oysters!

Crossing Western, as he almost reached the far kerb, he saw some of *them*. He dropped immediately to his knees behind the rusting bulk of an Oldsmobile. The rear door on his side was open, and he cautiously eased himself into the back seat of the deserted car.

Releasing the safety catch on the automatic, he peered through the cracked window at six or seven of them, as they moved towards him along the street. God! Had he been seen? He couldn't be sure. Perhaps they were aware of his position! He should have remained on the open street, where he'd have a running chance. Perhaps, if his aim were true, he could kill most of them; but, even with its silencer, the gun might be heard and more of them would come. He dared not fire until he was certain they had discovered him.

They came closer, their small dark bodies crowding the walk, six of them, chattering, leaping, cruel mouths open, eyes glittering under the moon. Closer. Their shrill pipings increased, rose in volume. Closer. Now he could make out their sharp teeth and matted hair. Only a few feet from the car . . . His hand was moist on the handle of the automatic; his heart thundered against his chest. Seconds away . . . Now!

Lewis Stillman fell heavily back against the dusty seat cushion, the gun loose in his trembling hand. They had passed by; they had missed him. Their thin pipings diminished, grew faint with distance.

The tomb silence of late night settled around him.

The delicatessen proved a real windfall. The shelves were relatively untouched and he had a wide choice of tinned goods. He found an empty cardboard box and hastily began to transfer the cans from the shelf nearest him.

A noise from behind—a padding, scraping sound.

Lewis Stillman whirled about, the automatic ready.

A huge mongrel dog faced him, growling deep in its throat, four legs braced for assault. The blunt ears were laid flat along the short-haired skull and a thin trickle of saliva seeped from the killing jaws. The beast's powerful chest muscles were bunched for the spring when Stillman acted.

His gun, he knew, was useless; the shots might be heard. Therefore, with the full strength of his left arm, he hurled a heavy can at the dog's head. The stunned animal staggered under the blow, legs buckling. Hurriedly, Stillman gathered his supplies and made his way back to the street.

How much longer can my luck hold? Lewis Stillman wondered, as he bolted the door. He placed the box of tinned goods on a wooden table and lit the tall lamp nearby. Its flickering orange glow illuminated the narrow, low-ceilinged room.

Twice tonight, his mind told him, twice you've escaped them—and they could have seen you easily on both occasions if they had been watching for you. They don't know you're alive. But when they find out . . .

He forced his thoughts away from the scene in his mind, away from the horror; quickly he began to unload the box, placing the cans on a long shelf along the far side of the room.

He began to think of women, of a girl named Joan, and of how much he had loved her . . .

The world of Lewis Stillman was damp and lightless; it was narrow and its cold stone walls pressed in upon him as he moved. He had been walking for several hours; sometimes he would run, because he knew his leg muscles must be kept strong, but he was walking now, following the thin yellow beam of his hooded lantern. He was searching.

Tonight, he thought, I might find another like myself. Surely, *someone* is down here; I'll find someone if I keep searching. I *must* find someone!

But he knew he would not. He knew he would find only chill emptiness ahead of him in the long tunnels.

For three years, he had been searching for another man or woman down here in this world under the city. For three years, he had prowled the seven hundred miles of storm drains which threaded their way under the skin of Los Angeles like the veins in a giant's body—and he had found nothing. *Nothing.*

Even now, after all the days and nights of search, he could not really accept the fact that he was alone, that he was the last man alive in a city of seven million . . .

The beautiful woman stood silently above him. Her eyes burned softly in the darkness; her fine red lips were smiling. The foam-white gown she wore continually swirled and billowed around her motionless figure.

'Who are you?' he asked, his voice far off, unreal.

'Does it matter, Lewis?'

Her words, like four dropped stones in a quiet pool, stirred him, rippled down the length of his body.

'No,' he said. 'Nothing matters, now, except that we've found each other. God, after all these lonely months and years of waiting! I thought I was the last, that I'd never live to see—'

'Hush, my darling.' She leaned to kiss him. Her lips were moist and yielding. 'I'm here now.'

He reached up to touch her cheek, but already she was fading, blending into darkness. Crying out, he clawed desperately for her extended hand. But she was gone, and his fingers rested on a rough wall of damp concrete.

A swirl of milk-fog drifted away in slow rollings down the tunnel.

Rain. Days of rain. The drains had been designed to handle floods, so Lewis Stillman was not particularly worried. He had built high, a good three feet above the tunnel floor, and the water had never yet risen to this level. But he didn't like the sound of the rain down here: an orchestrated thunder through the tunnels, a trap-drumming amplified and continuous.

Since he had been unable to make his daily runs, he had been reading more than usual. Short stories by Welty, Gordimer, Aiken, Irwin Shaw, Hemingway; poems by Frost, Lorca, Sandburg, Millay, Dylan Thomas. Strange, how unreal this present day world seemed when he read their words. Unreality, however, was fleeting, and the moment he closed a book the loneliness and the fears pressed back. He hoped the rain would stop soon.

Dampness. Surrounding him, the cold walls and the chill and the dampness. The unending gurgle and drip of water, the hollow, tapping splash of the falling drops. Even in his cot, wrapped in thick blankets, the dampness seemed to permeate his body. Sounds . . . Thin screams, pipings, chatterings, reedy whisperings above his head. They were dragging something along the street, something they'd killed, no doubt: an animal—a cat or a dog, perhaps . . . Lewis Stillman shifted, pulling the blankets closer about his body. He kept his eyes tightly shut, listening to the sharp, scuffling sounds on the pavement, and swore bitterly.

'Damn you,' he said. 'Damn all of you!'

Lewis Stillman was running, running down the long tunnels. Behind him, a tide of midget shadows washed from wall to wall; high, keening cries, doubled and tripled by echoes, rang in his ears. Claws reached for him; he felt panting breath, like hot smoke, on the back of his neck. His lungs were bursting, his entire body aflame.

He looked down at his fast-pumping legs, doing their job with pistoned precision. He listened to the sharp slap of his heels against the floor of the tunnel, and he thought: I might die at any moment, but my *legs* will escape! They will run on, down the endless drains, and never be caught. They move so fast, while my heavy, awkward upper body rocks and sways above them, slowing them down, tiring them—making them angry. How my legs must hate me! I must be clever and humour them, beg them to take me along to safety. How well they run, how sleek and fine!

Then he felt himself coming apart. His legs were detaching themselves from his upper body. He cried out in horror, flailing the air, beseeching them not to leave him behind. But the legs cruelly continued to unfasten themselves. In a cold surge of terror, Lewis Stillman felt himself tipping, falling towards the damp floor—while his legs raced on with a wild animal life of their own. He opened his mouth, high above those insane legs, and screamed, ending the nightmare.

He sat up stiffly in his cot, gasping, drenched in sweat. He drew in a long, shuddering breath and reached for a cigarette, lighting it with a trembling hand.

The nightmares were getting worse. He realized that his mind was rebelling as he slept, spilling forth the bottled-up fears of the day during the night hours.

He thought once more about the beginning, six years ago— about why he was still alive. The alien ships had struck Earth suddenly, without warning. Their attack had been thorough and deadly. In a matter of hours, the aliens had accomplished their clever mission—and the men and women of Earth were destroyed. A few survived, he was certain. He had never seen any of them, but he was convinced they existed. Los Angeles was not the world, after all, and since he had escaped, so must have others around the globe. He'd been working alone in the drains when the aliens struck, finishing a special job for the construction company on B tunnel. He could still hear the weird sound of the mammoth ships and feel the intense heat of their passage.

Hunger had forced him out, and overnight he had become a curiosity. The last man alive. For three years, he was not harmed. He worked with them, taught them many things, and tried to win their confidence. But, eventually, certain ones came to hate him, to be jealous of his relationship with the others. Luckily, he had been able to escape to the drains. That was three years ago, and now they had forgotten him.

His subsequent excursions to the upper level of the city had been made under cover of darkness—and he never ventured out unless his food supply dwindled. He had built his one-room structure directly to the side of an overhead grating—not close enough to risk their seeing it, but close enough for light to seep in during the sunlight hours. He missed the warm feel of open sun on his body almost as much as he missed human companionship, but he dare not risk himself above the drains by day.

When the rain ceased, he crouched beneath the street gratings to absorb as much as possible of the filtered sunlight. But the rays were weak, and their small warmth only served to heighten his desire to feel direct sunlight upon his naked shoulders.

The dreams . . . always the dreams.

'Are you cold, Lewis?'

'Yes. Yes, cold.'

'Then go out, dearest. Into the sun.'

'I can't. Can't go out.'

'But Los Angeles is your world, Lewis! You are the last man in it. The last man in the world.'

'Yes, but they own it all. Every street belongs to them, every building. They wouldn't let me come out. I'd die. They'd kill me.'

'Go out, Lewis.' The liquid dream-voice faded, faded. 'Out into the sun, my darling. Don't be afraid.'

That night, he watched the moon through the street gratings for almost an hour. It was round and full, like a huge yellow floodlamp in the dark sky, and he thought, for the first time in years, of night baseball at Blues Stadium in Kansas City. He used to love watching the games with his father under the mammoth stadium lights when the field was like a pond, frosted with white illumination, and the players dream-spawned and unreal. Night baseball was always a magic game to him when he was a boy.

Sometimes he got insane thoughts. Sometimes, on a night like this, when the loneliness closed in like a crushing fist and he could no longer stand it, he would think of bringing one of them down with him, into the drains. One at a time, they might be handled. Then he'd remember their sharp, savage eyes, their animal ferocity, and he would realize that the idea was impossible. If one of their kind disappeared, suddenly and without trace, others would certainly become suspicious, begin to search for him—and it would all be over.

Lewis Stillman settled back into his pillow; he closed his eyes and tried not to listen to the distant screams, pipings, and reedy cries filtering down from the street above his head.

Finally, he slept.

He spent the afternoon with paper women. He lingered over the pages of some yellowed fashion magazines, looking at all the beautifully photographed models in their fine clothes. Slim and enchanting, these page-women, with their cool enticing eyes and perfect smiles, all grace and softness and glitter and swirled cloth. He touched their images with gentle fingers, stroking the tawny paper hair, as though, by some magic formula, he might imbue them with life. Yet, it was easy to imagine that these women had never *really* lived at all—that they were simply painted, in microscopic detail, by sly artists to give the illusion of photos.

He didn't like to think about these women and how they died.

More and more, Lewis Stillman found his thoughts turning to the memory of his father and of long hikes through the moonlit Missouri countryside, of hunting trips and warm campfires, of the deep woods, rich and green in summer. He thought of his father's hopes for his future, and the words of that tall, grey-haired figure often came back to him.

'You'll be a fine doctor, Lewis. Study and work hard, and you'll succeed. I know you will.'

He remembered the long winter evenings of study at his father's great mahogany desk, poring over medical books and journals, taking notes, sifting and resifting facts. He remembered one set of books in particular—Erickson's monumental three-volume text on surgery, richly bound and stamped in gold. He had always loved those books, above all others.

What had gone wrong along the way? Somehow, the dream had faded; the bright goal vanished and was lost. After a year of pre-med at the University of California, he had given up medicine; he had become discouraged and quit college to take a labourer's job with a construction company. How ironic that this move should have saved his life! He'd wanted to work with his hands, to sweat and labour with the muscles of his body. He'd wanted to earn enough to marry Joan and then, later perhaps, he would have returned to finish his courses. It seemed so far away now, his reason for quitting, for letting his father down.

Now, at this moment, an overwhelming desire gripped him, a desire to pore over Erickson's pages once again, to recreate, even for a brief moment, the comfort and happiness of his childhood.

He'd once seen a duplicate set on the second floor of Pickwick's bookstore in Hollywood, in their used book department, and now he knew he must go after it, bring the books back with him to the drains. It was a dangerous and foolish desire, but he knew he would obey it. Despite the risk of death, he would go after the books tonight. *Tonight.*

One corner of Lewis Stillman's room was reserved for weapons. His prize, a Thompson submachine gun, had been procured from the Los Angeles police arsenal. Supplementing the Thompson were two automatic rifles, a Lüger, a Colt .45, and a .22 calibre Hornet pistol equipped with a silencer. He always kept the smallest gun in a spring-clip holster beneath his armpit, but it was not his habit to carry any of the larger weapons with him into the city. On this night, however, things were different.

The drains ended two miles short of Hollywood—which meant he would be forced to cover a long and particularly hazardous stretch of ground in order to reach the bookstore. He therefore decided to take along the .30 calibre Savage rifle in addition to the small hand weapon.

You're a fool, Lewis, he told himself as he slid the oiled Savage from its leather case, risking your life for a set of books. Are they *that* important? Yes, a part of him replied, they are that important. You want these books, then go *after* what you want. If fear keeps you from seeking that which you truly want, if fear holds you like a rat in the dark, then you are worse than a coward. You are a traitor, betraying yourself and the civilization you represent. If a man wants a thing and the thing is good, he must go after it, no matter what the cost, or relinquish the right to be called a man. It is better to die with courage than to live with cowardice.

Slinging the heavy rifle over one shoulder, Lewis Stillman set off down the tunnels.

Running in the chill night wind. Grass, now pavement, now grass beneath his feet. Ducking into shadows, moving stealthily past shops and theatres, rushing under the cold, high moon. Santa Monica Boulevard, then Highland, then Hollywood Boulevard, and finally—after an eternity of heartbeats—Pickwick's.

Lewis Stillman, his rifle over one shoulder, the small automatic gleaming in his hand, edged silently into the store.

A paper battleground met his eyes.

In filtered moonlight, a white blanket of broken-backed volumes spilled across the entire lower floor. Stillman shuddered; he could envision them, shrieking, scrabbling at the shelves, throwing books wildly across the room at one another. Screaming, ripping, destroying.

What of the other floors? *What of the medical section?*

He crossed to the stairs, spilled pages crackling like a fall of dry autumn leaves under his step, and sprinted up the first short flight to the mezzanine. Similar chaos!

He hurried up to the second floor, stumbling, terribly afraid of what he might find. Reaching the top, heart thudding, he squinted into the dimness.

The books were undisturbed. Apparently they had tired of their game before reaching these.

He slipped the rifle from his shoulder and placed it near the stairs. Dust lay thick all around him, powdering up and swirling as he moved down the narrow aisles; a damp, leathery mustiness lived in the air, an odour of mould and neglect.

Lewis Stillman paused before a dim, hand-lettered sign: MEDICAL SECTION. It was just as he remembered it. Holstering the small automatic, he struck a match, shading the flame with a cupped hand as he moved it along the rows of faded titles. Carter . . . Davidson . . . Enright . . . *Erickson.* He drew in his breath sharply. All three volumes, their gold stamping dust-dulled but legible, stood in tall and perfect order on the shelf.

In the darkness, Lewis Stillman carefully removed each volume, blowing it free of dust. At last, all three books were clean and solid in his hands.

Well, you've done it. You've reached the books and now they belong to you.

He smiled, thinking of the moment when he would be able to sit down at the table with his treasure and linger again over the wondrous pages.

He found an empty carton at the rear of the store and placed the books inside. Returning to the stairs, he shouldered the rifle and began his descent to the lower floor.

So far, he told himself, my luck is still holding.

But as Lewis Stillman's foot touched the final stair, his luck ran out.

The entire lower floor was alive with them!

Rustling like a mass of giant insects, gliding towards him, eyes gleaming in the half-light, they converged upon the stairs. They'd been waiting for him.

Now, suddenly the books no longer mattered. Now only his life mattered and nothing else. He moved back against the hard wood of the stair-rail, the carton of books sliding from his hands. They had stopped at the foot of the stairs; they were silent, looking up at him with hate in their eyes.

If you can reach the street, Stillman told himself, then you've still got half a chance. That means you've got to get through them to the door. All right then, *move*.

Lewis Stillman squeezed the trigger of the automatic. Two of them fell as Stillman rushed into their midst.

He felt sharp nails claw at his shirt, heard the cloth ripping away in their grasp. He kept firing the small automatic into them, and three more dropped under his bullets, shrieking in pain and surprise. The others spilled back, screaming, from the door.

The pistol was empty. He tossed it away, swinging the heavy Savage free from his shoulder as he reached the street. The night air, crisp and cool in his lungs, gave him instant hope.

I can still make it, thought Stillman, as he leaped the kerb and plunged across the pavement. If those shots weren't heard, then I've still got the edge. My legs are strong; I can outdistance them.

Luck, however, had failed him completely on this night. Near the intersection of Hollywood Boulevard and Highland, a fresh pack of them swarmed towards him.

He dropped to one knee and fired into their ranks, the Savage jerking in his hands. They scattered to either side.

He began to run steadily down the middle of Hollywood Boulevard, using the butt of the heavy rifle like a battering ram as they came at him. As he neared Highland, three of them darted directly into his path. Stillman fired. One doubled over, lurching crazily into a jagged plate glass store front. Another clawed at him as he swept around the corner to Highland, but he managed to shake free.

The street ahead of him was clear. Now his superior leg power would count heavily in his favour. Two miles. Could he make it before others cut him off?

Running, reloading, firing. Sweat soaking his shirt, rivering down his face, stinging his eyes. A mile covered. Halfway to the drains. They had fallen back behind his swift stride.

But more of them were coming, drawn by the rifle shots, pouring in from side streets, from stores and houses.

His heart jarred in his body, his breath was ragged. How many of them around him? A hundred? Two hundred? More coming. God!

He bit down on his lower lip until the salt taste of blood was on his tongue. You can't make it, a voice inside him shouted. They'll have you in another block and you know it!

He fitted the rifle to his shoulder, adjusted his aim, and fired. The long rolling crack of the big weapon filled the night. Again and again he fired, the butt jerking into the flesh of his shoulder, the bitter smell of burnt powder in his nostrils.

It was no use. Too many of them. He could not clear a path.

Lewis Stillman knew that he was going to die.

The rifle was empty at last; the final bullet had been fired. He had no place to run because they were all around him, in a slowly closing circle.

He looked at the ring of small cruel faces and thought, The aliens did their job perfectly; they stopped Earth before she could reach the age of the rocket, before she could threaten planets beyond her own moon. What an immensely clever plan it had been! To destroy every human being on Earth above the age of six—and then to leave as quickly as they had come, allowing our civilization to continue on a primitive level, knowing that Earth's back had been broken, that her survivors would revert to savagery as they grew into adulthood.

Lewis Stillman dropped the empty rifle at his feet and threw out his hands. 'Listen,' he pleaded, 'I'm really one of you. You'll *all* be like me soon. Please, *listen* to me.'

But the circle tightened relentlessly around him.

Lewis Stillman was screaming when the children closed in.

To Serve Man

DAMON KNIGHT

The Kanamit were not very pretty, it's true. They looked
something like pigs and something like people, and that
is not an attractive combination. Seeing them for the first
time shocked you; that was their handicap. When a thing with
the countenance of a fiend comes from the stars and offers a gift,
you are disinclined to accept.

I don't know what we expected interstellar visitors to look
like—those who thought about it at all, that is. Angels, perhaps,
or something too alien to be really awful. Maybe that's why we
were all so horrified and repelled when they landed in their great
ships and we saw what they really were like.

The Kanamit were short and very hairy—thick, bristly,
brown-grey hair all over their abominably plump bodies. Their
noses were snoutlike and their eyes small, and they had thick
hands of three fingers each. They wore green leather harness
and green shorts, but I think the shorts were a concession to our
notions of public decency. The garments were quite modishly
cut, with slash pockets and half-belts in the back. The Kanamit
had a sense of humour, anyhow.

There were three of them at this session of the UN, and, lord,
I can't tell you how queer it looked to see them there in the
middle of a solemn plenary session—three fat piglike creatures
in green harness and shorts, sitting at the long table below the
podium, surrounded by the packed arcs of delegates from
every nation. They sat correctly upright, politely watching each
speaker. Their flat ears drooped over the earphones. Later on, I
believe, they learned every human language, but at this time
they knew only French and English.

They seemed perfectly at ease—and that, along with their humour, was a thing that tended to make me like them. I was in the minority; I didn't think they were trying to put anything over.

The delegate from Argentina got up and said that his government was interested in the demonstration of a new cheap power source, which the Kanamit had made at the previous session, but that the Argentine government could not commit itself as to its future policy without a much more thorough examination.

It was what all the delegates were saying, but I had to pay particular attention to Señor Valdes, because he tended to sputter and his diction was bad. I got through the translation all right, with only one or two momentary hesitations, and then switched to the Polish–English line to hear how Grigori was doing with Janciewicz. Janciewicz was the cross Grigori had to bear, just as Valdes was mine.

Janciewicz repeated the previous remarks with a few ideological variations, and then the secretary-general recognized the delegate from France, who introduced Dr Denis Lévêque, the criminologist, and a great deal of complicated equipment was wheeled in.

Dr Lévêque remarked that the question in many people's minds had been aptly expressed by the delegate from the USSR at the preceding session, when he demanded, 'What is the motive of the Kanamit? What is their purpose in offering us these unprecedented gifts, while asking nothing in return?'

The doctor then said, 'At the request of several delegates and with the full consent of our guests, the Kanamit, my associates and I have made a series of tests upon the Kanamit with the equipment which you see before you. These tests will now be repeated.'

A murmur ran through the chamber. There was a fusillade of flashbulbs, and one of the TV cameras moved up to focus on the instrument board of the doctor's equipment. At the same time, the huge television screen behind the podium lighted up, and we saw the blank faces of two dials, each with its pointer resting at zero, and a strip of paper tape with a stylus point resting against it.

The doctor's assistants were fastening wires to the temples of one of the Kanamit, wrapping a canvas-covered rubber tube around his forearm, and taping something to the palm of his right hand.

In the screen, we saw the paper tape begin to move while the stylus traced a slow zigzag pattern along it. One of the needles began to jump rhythmically; the other flipped halfway over and stayed there, wavering slightly.

'These are the standard instruments for testing the truth of a statement,' said Dr Lévêque. 'Our first object, since the physiology of the Kanamit is unknown to us, was to determine whether or not they react to these tests as human beings do. We will now repeat one of the many experiments which were made in the endeavour to discover this.'

He pointed to the first dial. 'This instrument registers the subject's heartbeat. This shows the electrical conductivity of the skin in the palm of his hand, a measure of perspiration, which increases under stress. And this'—pointing to the tape-and-stylus device—'shows the pattern and intensity of the electrical waves emanating from his brain. It has been shown, with human subjects, that all these readings vary markedly depending upon whether the subject is speaking the truth.'

He picked up two large pieces of cardboard, one red and one black. The red one was a square about three feet on a side; the black was a rectangle three and a half feet long. He addressed himself to the Kanama.

'Which of these is longer than the other?'

'The red,' said the Kanama.

Both needles leaped wildly, and so did the line of the unrolling tape.

'I shall repeat the question,' said the doctor. 'Which of these is longer than the other?'

'The black,' said the creature.

This time the instruments continued in their normal rhythm.

'How did you come to this planet?' asked the doctor.

'Walked,' replied the Kanama.

Again the instruments responded, and there was a subdued ripple of laughter in the chamber.

'Once more,' said the doctor. 'How did you come to this planet?'

'In a spaceship,' said the Kanama, and the instruments did not jump.

The doctor again faced the delegates. 'Many such experiments were made,' he said, 'and my colleagues and myself are satisfied that the mechanisms are effective. Now'—he turned to the Kanama—'I shall ask our distinguished guest to reply to the question put at the last session by the delegate of the USSR— namely, what is the motive of the Kanamit people in offering these great gifts to the people of Earth?'

The Kanama rose. Speaking this time in English, he said, 'On my planet there is a saying, "There are more riddles in a stone than in a philosopher's head." The motives of intelligent beings, though they may at times appear obscure, are simple things compared to the complex workings of the natural universe. Therefore I hope that the people of Earth will understand, and believe, when I tell you that our mission upon your planet is simply this—to bring to you the peace and plenty which we ourselves enjoy, and which we have in the past brought to other races throughout the galaxy. When your world has no more hunger, no more war, no more needless suffering, that will be our reward.'

And the needles had not jumped once.

The delegate from the Ukraine jumped to his feet, asking to be recognized, but the time was up and the secretary-general closed the session.

I met Grigori as we were leaving the chamber. His face was red with excitement. 'Who promoted that circus?' he demanded.

'The tests looked genuine to me,' I told him.

'A circus!' he said vehemently. 'A second-rate farce! If they were genuine, Peter, why was debate stifled?'

'There'll be time for debate tomorrow, surely.'

'Tomorrow the doctor and his instruments will be back in Paris. Plenty of things can happen before tomorrow. In the name of sanity, man, how can anybody trust a thing that looks as if it ate the baby?'

I was a little annoyed. I said, 'Are you sure you're not more worried about their politics than their appearance?'

He said, 'Bah,' and went away.

The next day reports began to come in from government laboratories all over the world where the Kanamit's power source was being tested. They were wildly enthusiastic. I don't understand such things myself, but it seemed that those little metal boxes would give more electrical power than an atomic pile, for next to nothing and nearly forever. And it was said that they were so cheap to manufacture that everybody in the world could have one of his own. In the early afternoon there were reports that seventeen countries had already begun to set up factories to turn them out.

The next day the Kanamit turned up with plans and specimens of a gadget that would increase the fertility of any arable land by 60 to 100 per cent. It speeded the formation of nitrates in the soil, or something. There was nothing in the newscasts any more but stories about the Kanamit. The day after that, they dropped their bombshell.

'You now have potentially unlimited power and increased food supply,' said one of them. He pointed with his three-fingered hand to an instrument that stood on the table before him. It was a box on a tripod, with a parabolic reflector on the front of it. 'We offer you today a third gift which is at least as important as the first two.'

He beckoned to the TV men to roll their cameras into close-up position. Then he picked up a large sheet of cardboard covered with drawings and English lettering. We saw it on the large screen above the podium; it was all clearly legible.

'We are informed that this broadcast is being relayed throughout your world,' said the Kanama. 'I wish that everyone who has equipment for taking photographs from television screens would use it now.'

The secretary-general leaned forward and asked a question sharply, but the Kanama ignored him.

'This device,' he said, 'generates a field in which no explosive, of whatever nature, can detonate.'

There was an uncomprehending silence.

The Kanama said, 'It cannot now be suppressed. If one nation has it, all must have it.' When nobody seemed to understand, he explained bluntly, 'There will be no more war.'

That was the biggest news of the millennium, and it was perfectly true. It turned out that the explosions the Kanama was talking about included gasoline and diesel explosions. They had simply made it impossible for anybody to mount or equip a modern army.

We could have gone back to bows and arrows, of course, but that wouldn't have satisfied the military. Besides, there wouldn't be any reason to make war. Every nation would soon have everything.

Nobody ever gave another thought to those lie-detector experiments, or asked the Kanamit what their politics were. Grigori was put out; he had nothing to prove his suspicions.

I quit my job with the UN a few months later, because I foresaw that it was going to die under me anyhow. UN business was booming at the time, but after a year or so there was going to be nothing for it to do. Every nation on Earth was well on the way to being completely self-supporting; they weren't going to need much arbitration.

I accepted a position as translator with the Kanamit Embassy, and it was there that I ran into Grigori again. I was glad to see him, but I couldn't imagine what he was doing there.

'I thought you were on the opposition,' I said. 'Don't tell me you're convinced the Kanamit are all right.'

He looked rather shamefaced. 'They're not what they look, anyhow,' he said.

It was as much of a concession as he could decently make, and I invited him down to the embassy lounge for a drink. It was an intimate kind of place, and he grew confidential over the second daiquiri.

'They fascinate me,' he said. 'I hate them instinctively still—that hasn't changed—but I can evaluate it. You were right, obviously; they mean us nothing but good. But do you know'—he leaned across the table—'the question of the Soviet delegate was never answered.'

I am afraid I snorted.

'No, really,' he said. 'They told us what they wanted to do—"to bring to you peace and plenty which we ourselves enjoy." But they didn't say *why*.'

'Why do missionaries—'

'Missionaries be damned!' he said angrily. 'Missionaries have a religious motive. If these creatures have a religion, they haven't once mentioned it. What's more, they didn't send a missionary group; they sent a diplomatic delegation—a group representing the will and policy of their whole people. Now just what have the Kanamit, as a people or a nation, got to gain from our welfare?'

I said, 'Cultural—'

'Cultural cabbage soup! No, it's something less obvious than that, something obscure that belongs to their psychology and not to ours. But trust me, Peter, there is no such thing as a completely disinterested altruism. In one way or another, they have something to gain.'

'And that's why you're here,' I said. 'To try to find out what it is.'

'Correct. I wanted to get on one of the ten-year exchange groups to their home planet, but I couldn't; the quota was filled a week after they made the announcement. This is the next best thing. I'm studying their language, and you know that language reflects the basic assumptions of the people who use it. I've got a fair command of the spoken lingo already. It's not hard, really, and there are hints in it. Some of the idioms are quite similar to English. I'm sure I'll get the answer eventually.'

'More power,' I said, and we went back to work.

I saw Grigori frequently from then on, and he kept me posted about his progress. He was highly excited about a month after that first meeting; said he'd got hold of a book of the Kanamit's and was trying to puzzle it out. They wrote in ideographs, worse than Chinese, but he was determined to fathom it if it took him years. He wanted my help.

Well, I was interested in spite of myself, for I knew it would be a long job. We spent some evenings together, working with material from Kanamit bulletin boards and so forth, and with the extremely limited English–Kanamit dictionary they issued to the staff. My conscience bothered me about the stolen book, but gradually I became absorbed by the problem. Languages are my field, after all. I couldn't help being fascinated.

We got the title worked out in a few weeks. It was *How to Serve Man*, evidently a handbook they were giving out to new Kanamit members of the embassy staff. They had new ones in, all the time now, a shipload about once a month; they were opening all kinds of research laboratories, clinics, and so on. If there was anybody on Earth besides Grigori who still distrusted those people, he must have been somewhere in the middle of Tibet.

It was astonishing to see the changes that had been wrought in less than a year. There were no more standing armies, no more shortages, no unemployment. When you picked up a newspaper you didn't see H-BOMB or SATELLITE leaping out at you; the news was always good. It was a hard thing to get used to. The Kanamit were working on human biochemistry, and it was known around the embassy that they were nearly ready to announce methods of making our race taller and stronger and healthier—practically a race of supermen—and they had a potential cure for heart disease and cancer.

I didn't see Grigori for a fortnight after we finished working out the title of the book; I was on a long-overdue vacation in Canada. When I got back, I was shocked by the change in his appearance.

'What on earth is wrong, Grigori?' I asked. 'You look like the very devil.'

'Come on down to the lounge.'

I went with him, and he gulped a stiff scotch as if he needed it.

'Come on, man, what's the matter?' I urged.

'The Kanamit have put me on the passenger list for the next exchange ship,' he said. 'You, too, otherwise I wouldn't be talking to you.'

'Well,' I said, 'but—'

'They're not altruists.'

I tried to reason with him. I pointed out they'd made Earth a paradise compared to what it was before. He only shook his head.

Then I said, 'Well, what about those lie-detector tests?'

'A farce,' he replied, without heat. 'I said so at the time, you fool. They told the truth, though, as far as it went.'

'And the book?' I demanded, annoyed. 'What about that— *How to Serve Man*? That wasn't put there for you to read. They do *mean* it. How do you explain that?'

'I've read the first paragraph of that book,' he said. 'Why do you suppose I haven't slept for a week?'

I said, 'Well?' and he smiled a curious, twisted smile.

'It's a cookbook,' he said.

The Bounty Hunter

AVRAM DAVIDSON

There was a whirring noise and a flurry and part of the snow-bank shot up at a 45-degree angle—or so it seemed—and vanished in the soft grey sky. Orel stopped and put out his arm, blocking his uncle's way.

'It's a bird . . . only a bird . . . *get* on, now, Orel,' Councillor Garth said, testily. He gave his nephew a light shove. 'They turn white in the winter-time. Or their feathers do. Anyway, that's what Trapper says.'

They plodded ahead, Orel, partly distracted by the pleasure of seeing his breath, laughed a bit. 'A bird outside of a cage . . .' The councillor let him get a few feet ahead, then he awkwardly compressed a handful of snow and tossed it at his nephew's face when he turned it back. The first startled cry gave way to laughter. And so they came to the trapper's door.

The old fellow peered at them, but it was only a thing he did because it was expected of him; there was nothing wrong with his eyes. Garth had known him for many years, and he was still not sure how many of his mannerisms were real, how many put on. Or for that matter, how much of the antique stuff cluttering up the cabin was actually part of the trapper's life, and how much only there for show. Not that he cared: the trapper's job was as much to be quaint and amusing as to do anything else.

Orel, even before the introductions were over, noticed the cup and saucer on the top shelf of the cabinet, but not till his two elders paused did he comment, 'Look, Uncle: earthenware!'

'You've got a sharp eye, young fellow,' the trapper said, approvingly. 'Yes, it's real pottery. Brought over by my who-knows-how-many-times-removed grandfather from the home planet . . . Yes, my family, they were pretty important people on the home planet,' he added, inconsequentially. He stood silent for a moment, warmed with pride, then made a series of amiable noises in his throat.

'Well, I'm glad to meet you, young fellow. Knew your uncle before he was councillor, before you were born.' He went to the tiny window, touched the defroster, looked out. 'Yes, your machine is safe enough.' He turned around. 'I'll get the fire started, if there's no objections? And put some meat on to grill? Hm?'

The councillor nodded with slow satisfaction; Orel grinned widely.

The trapper turned off the heating unit and set the fire going. The three men gazed into the flames. The meat turned slowly on the jack. Orel tried to analyse the unfamiliar smells crowding around him—the wood itself, and the fire: no, fire had no smell, it was *smoke*; the meat, the furs and hides . . . he couldn't even imagine what they all were. It was different from the cities, that was sure. He turned to ask something, but his Uncle Garth and Trapper weren't attending. Then he heard it—a long, drawn-out, faraway sort of noise. Then the trapper grunted and spat in the fire.

'What was it?' Orel asked.

The old fellow smiled. 'Never heard it before? Not even recorded, in a nature studies course? That's one of the big varmints—the kind your uncle and the other big sportsmen come out here to hunt—in season—the kind I trap in any season.' Abruptly, he turned to Councillor Garth. 'No talk of their dropping the bounty, is there?' Smilingly, the councillor shook his head. Reassured, the trapper turned his attention to the meat, poked it with a long-pronged fork.

Orel compared the interior of the cabin to pictures and 3-D plays he had observed. Things looked familiar, but less—smooth, if that was the word. There was more disorder, an absence of symmetry. Hides and pelts—not too well cured, if the smell was evidence—were scattered all around, not neatly tacked up or laid in neat heaps. Traps and parts of traps sat where the old man had evidently last worked at mending them.

'Council's not in session, I take it?' the trapper asked. Orel's uncle shook his head. 'But—don't tell me school's out, too? Thought they learned right through the winter.'

Garth said, 'I was able to persuade the Dean that our little trip was a genuine—if small—field expedition, and that Orel's absence wouldn't break the pattern of learning.'

The trapper grunted. *Pattern!* Orel thought. The mention of the word annoyed him. Everything was part of a pattern: Pattern of learning, pattern of earning, pattern of pleasure . . . Life in the city went by patterns, deviations were few; people didn't even *want* to break the patterns. They were afraid to.

But it was obvious that the trapper didn't live by patterns. This . . . disorder.

'Do you have any children, Trapper?' he asked. The old man said he didn't. 'Then who will carry on your work?'

The trapper waved his hand to the west. 'Fellow in the next valley has two sons. When I get too old—a long time from now,' he said, defiantly, 'one of them will move in with me. Help me out. Split the bounties with me.

'I was married once.' He gazed into the fire. 'City woman. She couldn't get used to it out here. The solitude. The dangers. So we moved to the cities. *I* never got used to *that*. Got to get up at a certain time. Got to do everything a certain way. Everything has to be put in its place, neatly. All the people would look at you otherwise. Breaking the patterns? They didn't like it. Well, she died. And I moved back here as fast as I could get permission. And here I've stayed.'

He took down plates, forks, knives, carved the meat. They ate with relish. 'Tastes better than something out of a factory lab, doesn't it?'

Orel's mind at once supplied him with an answer: that synthetics were seven times more nutritious than the foods they imitated. But his mouth was full and besides, it *did* taste better. Much better . . . After the meal there was a sort of lull. The trapper looked at Councillor Garth in an expectant sort of way. The councillor smiled. He reached over into the pocket of his hunting jacket and took out a flask. Orel, as he smelled it (even before: after all, everyone knew that the bounty-hunters drank —the flask was part of every 3-D play about them), framed a polite refusal. But none was offered him.

'The purpose of this two-man field expedition,' his uncle said, after wiping his mouth, 'is to prepare a term paper for Orel's school showing how, in the disciplined present, the bounty-hunters maintain the free and rugged traditions of the past, on the Home Planet . . . let me have another go at the flask, Trapper.'

Orel watched, somewhat disturbed. Surely his uncle knew how unhealthy . . .

'My family, they were pretty important people back on the Home Planet.' The Old Trapper, having had another drink, began to repeat himself. Outside—the dusk had begun to set in—that wild, rather frightening, sound came again. The old man put the flask down. 'Coming nearer,' he said, as if to himself. He got to his feet, took up his weapon. 'I won't be gone long . . . they don't generally come so near . . . but it's been a hard winter. This one sounds kind of hungry. But don't you be frightened, young fellow,' he said to Orel, from the door. 'There's no chance of its eating *me*.'

'Uncle . . .' Orel said, after a while. The councillor looked up. 'Don't be offended, but . . . does it ever strike you that we lead rather useless lives in the city—compared, I mean, to *him*?'

The councillor smiled. 'Oh, come now. Next you'll be want-ing to run away and join the fun. Because that's all it is, really: fun. These beasts—the big "varmints," as he calls them—are no menace to us any longer. Haven't been since we switched from meat to synthetics. So it's not a truly useful life the old man leads. It's only our traditional reluctance to admit things have changed which keeps us paying the bounty . . .' He got up and walked a few steps, stretched.

'We *could* get rid of these creatures once and for all, do it in one season's campaign. Drop poisoned bait every acre through the whole range. Wipe them out.'

Orel, puzzled, asked why they didn't.

'And I'll tell you something else—but don't put it in your report. The old fellow, like all the trappers, sometimes cheats. He often releases females and cubs. He takes no chance of having his valley trapped out. "Why don't we?" you ask—why don't we get rid of the beasts once and for all, instead of paying bounties year after year? Well, the present cost is small. And as for getting an appropriation for an all-out campaign—who'd vote for it? *I* wouldn't.

'No more hunting—no more 3-D plays about the exciting life in the wild country—no more trappers—why, it would just about take what spirit is left away from us. And we are dispirited enough—tired enough—as it is.'

Orel frowned. 'But why are we like that? We weren't always. A tired people could never have moved here from the Home Planet, could never have conquered this one. Why are we so—so played out?'

The councillor shrugged. 'Do you realize what a tremendous effort it was to move such a mass of people such a distance? The further effort required to subdue a wild, new world? The terrible cost of the struggle against colonialism—and finally, the Civil Wars? We don't even like to think about it—we create our myths instead out of the life out here in the wilds—and all the time, we retreated further and further, back into our cities. We are tired. We've spent our energies, we've mortgaged them, in fact. We eat synthetics because it's easier, not because it's healthier.'

A gust of cold wind blew in on them. They whirled around. The Old Trapper came in, dragging his kill by the forelimbs. He closed the door. The two city folk came up close. The beast was a huge male, gaunt from the poor hunting which winter meant to the wild creatures.

'See here—' the trapper pointed out. 'Lost two toes there. *Old* wound. Must've gnawed his way out of a trap one time.

There—got *these* scars battling over a mate, I suppose. This *here's* a burn. Bad one. When was the last big forest fire we had?—one too big to outrun—' He figured with moving lips. '*That* long ago? How the time does pass . . . Let me have that knife there, young fellow—' Orel glanced around, located the knife, handed it to him; gazed down in fascination and revulsion. The wild life did not seem so attractive at this moment.

'Watch close, now, and I'll show you how to skin and dress a big varmint,' the Old Trapper said. He made the initial incision. 'Dangerous creatures, but when you know their habits as well as *I* do . . . Can't expect to wipe them out altogether—' He looked at the two guests. Orel wondered how much he knew or guessed of what had been said in his absence. 'No. Keep their numbers down, is all you can expect to do.' He tugged, grunted. 'I *earn* my bounty, I can tell you.' He turned the creature on its back.

Orel, struck by something, turned to the councillor.

'You know, Uncle, if this beast were cleaned up and shaved and'—he laughed at the droll fancy—'and dressed in clothes, it—'

Councillor Garth finished the sentence for him. 'Would bear a faint, quaint resemblance to *us*? Hm, yes . . . in a way . . . of course, but their external ears and their having only five digits on each—' He clicked his tongue and stepped aside. The Old Trapper, who didn't care how much blood he got on things or people, worked away, but the Councillor took his nephew closer to the fire to finish what he had to say.

Eight O'Clock in the Morning

RAY NELSON

At the end of the show the hypnotist told his subjects, 'Awake.'

Something unusual happened.

One of the subjects awoke all the way. This had never happened before. His name was George Nada and he blinked out at the sea of faces in the theatre, at first unaware of anything out of the ordinary. Then he noticed, spotted here and there in the crowd, the nonhuman faces, the faces of the Fascinators. They had been there all along, of course, but only George was really awake, so only George recognized them for what they were. He understood everything in a flash, including the fact that if he were to give any outward sign, the Fascinators would instantly command him to return to his former state, and he would obey.

He left the theatre, pushing out into the neon night, carefully avoiding giving any indication that he saw the green, reptilian flesh or the multiple yellow eyes of the rulers of Earth. One of them asked him, 'Got a light, buddy?' George gave him a light, then moved on.

At intervals along the street George saw the posters hanging with photographs of the Fascinators' multiple eyes and various commands printed under them, such as, 'Work eight hours, play eight hours, sleep eight hours', and 'Marry and Reproduce'. A TV set in the window of a store caught George's eye, but he looked away in the nick of time. When he didn't look at the Fascinator in the screen, he could resist the command, 'Stay tuned to this station'.

George lived alone in a little sleeping room, and as soon as he got home, the first thing he did was to disconnect the TV set.

In other rooms he could hear the TV sets of his neighbours, though. Most of the time the voices were human, but now and then he heard the arrogant, strangely bird-like croaks of the aliens. 'Obey the government,' said one croak. 'We are the government,' said another. 'We are your friends, you'd do anything for a friend, wouldn't you?'

'Obey!'

'Work!'

Suddenly the phone rang.

George picked it up. It was one of the Fascinators.

'Hello,' it squawked. 'This is your control, Chief of Police Robinson. You are an old man, George Nada. Tomorrow morning at eight o'clock, your heart will stop. Please repeat.'

'I am an old man,' said George. 'Tomorrow morning at eight o'clock, my heart will stop.'

The control hung up.

'No it won't,' whispered George. He wondered why they wanted him dead. Did they suspect that he was awake? Probably. Someone might have spotted him, noticed that he didn't respond the way the others did. If George were alive at one minute after eight tomorrow morning, then they would be sure.

No use waiting here for the end, he thought.

He went out again. The posters, the TV, the occasional commands from passing aliens did not seem to have absolute power over him, though he still felt strongly tempted to obey, to see these things the way his master wanted him to see them. He passed an alley and stopped. One of the aliens was alone there, leaning against the wall. George walked up to him.

'Move on,' grunted the thing, focusing his deadly eyes on George.

George felt his grasp on awareness waver. For a moment the reptilian head dissolved into the face of a lovable old drunk. Of course the drunk would be lovable. George picked up a brick and smashed it down on the old drunk's head with all his strength. For a moment the image blurred, then the blue-green blood oozed out of the face and the lizard fell, twitching and writhing. After a moment it was dead.

George dragged the body into the shadows and searched it. There was a tiny radio in its pocket and a curiously shaped knife and fork in another. The tiny radio said something in an incomprehensible language. George put it down beside the body, but kept the eating utensils.

I can't possibly escape, thought George. Why fight them?

But maybe he could.

What if he could awaken others? That might be worth a try.

He walked twelve blocks to the apartment of his girlfriend, Lil, and knocked on her door. She came to the door in her bathrobe.

'I want you to wake up,' he said.

'I'm awake,' she said. 'Come on in.'

He went in. The TV was playing. He turned it off.

'No,' he said. 'I mean really wake up.' She looked at him without comprehension, so he snapped his fingers and shouted, '*Wake up!* The masters command that you wake up!'

'Are you off your rocker, George?' she asked suspiciously. 'You sure are acting funny.' He slapped her face. 'Cut that out!' she cried. 'What the hell are you up to anyway?'

'Nothing,' said George, defeated. 'I was just kidding around.'

'Slapping my face wasn't just kidding around!' she cried.

There was a knock at the door.

George opened it.

It was one of the aliens.

'Can't you keep the noise down to a dull roar?' it said.

The eyes and reptilian flesh faded a little and George saw the flickering image of a fat middle-aged man in shirt-sleeves. It was still a man when George slashed its throat with the eating knife, but it was an alien before it hit the floor. He dragged it into the apartment and kicked the door shut.

'What do you see there?' he asked Lil, pointing to the many-eyed snake thing on the floor.

'Mister . . . Mister Coney,' she whispered, her eyes wide with horror. 'You . . . just killed him, like it was nothing at all.'

'Don't scream,' warned George, advancing on her.

'I won't, George. I swear I won't, only please, for the love of God, put down that knife.' She backed away until she had her shoulder blades pressed to the wall.

George saw that it was no use.

'I'm going to tie you up,' said George. 'First tell me which room Mister Coney lived in.'

'The first door on your left as you go towards the stairs,' she said. 'George . . . Georgie. Don't torture me. If you're going to kill me, do it clean. Please, George, please.'

He tied her up with bedsheets and gagged her, then searched the body of the Fascinator. There was another one of the little radios that talked a foreign language, another set of eating utensils, and nothing else.

George went next door.

When he knocked, one of the snake things answered, 'Who is it?'

'Friend of Mister Coney. I wanna see him,' said George.

'He went out for a second, but he'll be right back.' The door opened a crack, and four yellow eyes peeped out. 'You wanna come in and wait?'

'OK,' said George, not looking at the eyes.

'You alone here?' he asked, as it closed the door, its back to George.

'Yeah, why?'

He slit its throat from behind, then searched the apartment.

He found human bones and skulls, a half-eaten hand.

He found tanks with huge fat slugs floating in them.

The children, he thought, and killed them all.

There were guns too, of a sort he had never seen before. He discharged one by accident, but fortunately it was noiseless. It seemed to fire little poisoned darts.

He pocketed the gun and as many boxes of darts as he could and went back to Lil's place. When she saw him she writhed in helpless terror.

'Relax, honey,' he said, opening her purse. 'I just want to borrow your car keys.'

He took the keys and went downstairs to the street.

Her car was still parked in the same general area in which she always parked it. He recognized it by the dent in the right fender. He got in, started it, and began driving aimlessly. He drove for hours, thinking—desperately searching for some way out. He turned on the car radio to see if he could get some music, but there was nothing but news and it was all about him, George Nada, the homicidal maniac. The announcer was one of the masters, but he sounded a little scared. Why should he be? What could one man do?

George wasn't surprised when he saw the roadblock, and he turned off on a side street before he reached it. No little trip to the country for you, Georgie boy, he thought to himself.

They had just discovered what he had done back at Lil's place, so they would probably be looking for Lil's car. He parked it in an alley and took the subway. There were no aliens on the subway, for some reason. Maybe they were too good for such things, or maybe it was just because it was so late at night.

When one finally did get on, George got off.

He went up to the street and went into a bar. One of the Fascinators was on the TV, saying over and over again, 'We are your friends. We are your friends. We are your friends.' The stupid lizard sounded scared. Why? What could one man do against all of them?

George ordered a beer, then it suddenly struck him that the Fascinator on the TV no longer seemed to have any power over him. He looked at it again and thought, It has to believe it can master me to do it. The slightest hint of fear on its part and the power to hypnotize is lost. They flashed George's picture on the TV screen and George retreated to the phone booth. He called his control, the Chief of Police.

'Hello, Robinson?' he asked.

'Speaking.'

'This is George Nada. I've figured out how to wake people up.'

'What? George, hang on. Where are you?' Robinson sounded almost hysterical.

He hung up and paid and left the bar. They would probably trace his call.

He caught another subway and went downtown.

It was dawn when he entered the building housing the biggest of the city's TV studios. He consulted the building directory and then went up in the elevator. The cop in front of the studio entrance recognized him. 'Why, you're Nada!' he gasped.

George didn't like to shoot him with the poison dart gun, but he had to.

He had to kill several more before he got into the studio itself, including all the engineers on duty. There were a lot of police sirens outside, excited shouts, and running footsteps on the stairs. The alien was sitting before the TV camera saying, 'We are your friends. We are your friends,' and didn't see George come in. When George shot him with the needle gun he simply stopped in mid-sentence and sat there dead. George stood near him and said, imitating the alien croak, 'Wake up. Wake up. See us as we are and kill us!'

It was George's voice the city heard that morning, but it was the Fascinator's image, and the city did awake for the very first time and the war began.

George did not live to see the victory that finally came. He died of a heart attack at exactly eight o'clock.

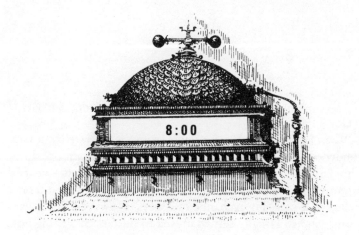

Dear Pen Pal

A. E. VAN VOGT

Planet Aurigae II

DEAR PEN PAL:

When I first received your letter from the interstellar correspondence club, my impulse was to ignore it. The mood of one who has spent the last seventy planetary periods—years I suppose you would call them—in an Aurigaen prison, does not make for a pleasant exchange of letters. However, life is very boring, and so I finally settled myself to the task of writing you.

Your description of Earth sounds exciting. I would like to live there for a while, and I have a suggestion in this connection, but I won't mention it till I have developed it further.

You will have noticed the material on which this letter is written. It is a highly sensitive metal, very thin, very flexible, and I have enclosed several sheets of it for your use. Tungsten dipped in any strong acid makes an excellent mark on it. It is important to me that you do write on it, as my fingers are too hot—literally—to hold your paper without damaging it.

I'll say no more just now. It is possible you will not care to correspond with a convicted criminal, and therefore I shall leave the next move up to you. Thank you for your letter. Though you did not know its destination, it brought a moment of cheer into my drab life.

SKANDER

Aurigae II

DEAR PEN PAL:

Your prompt reply to my letter made me happy. I am sorry your doctor thought it excited you too much, and sorry, also, if I have described my predicament in such a way as to make you feel badly. I welcome your many questions, and I shall try to answer them all.

You say the international correspondence club has no record of having sent any letters to Aurigae. That, according to them, the temperature on the second planet of the Aurigae sun is more than 500 degrees Fahrenheit. And that life is not known to exist there. Your club is right about the temperature and the letters. We have what your people would call a hot climate, but then we are not a hydrocarbon form of life, and find 500 degrees very pleasant.

I must apologize for deceiving you about the way your first letter was sent to me. I didn't want to frighten you away by telling you too much at once. After all, I could not be expected to know that you would be enthusiastic to hear from me.

The truth is that I am a scientist, and, along with the other members of my race, I have known for some centuries that there were other inhabited systems in the galaxy. Since I am allowed to experiment in my spare hours, I amused myself in attempts at communication. I have developed several simple systems for breaking in on galactic communication operations, but it was not until I developed a subspacewave control that I was able to draw your letter (along with several others, which I did not answer) into a cold chamber.

I use the cold chamber as both sending and receiving centre, and since you were kind enough to use the material which I sent you, it was easy for me to locate your second letter among the mass of mail that accumulated at the nearest headquarters of the interstellar correspondence club.

How did I learn your language? After all, it is a simple one, particularly the written language seems easy. I had no difficulty with it. If you are still interested in writing me, I shall be happy to continue the correspondence.

SKANDER

Aurigae II

DEAR PEN PAL:

Your enthusiasm is refreshing. You say that I failed to answer your question about how I expected to visit Earth. I confess I deliberately ignored the question, as my experiment had not yet proceeded far enough. I want you to bear with me a short time longer, and then I will be able to give you the details. You are right in saying that it would be difficult for a being who lives at a temperature of 500 degrees Fahrenheit to mingle freely with the people of Earth. This was never my intention, so please relieve your mind. However, let us drop that subject for the time being.

I appreciate the delicate way in which you approach the subject of my imprisonment. But it is quite unnecessary. I performed forbidden experiments upon my body in a way that was deemed to be dangerous to the public welfare. For instance, among other things, I once lowered my surface temperature to 150 degrees Fahrenheit, and so shortened the radio-active cycle-time of my surroundings. This caused an unexpected break in the normal person to person energy flow in the city where I lived, and so charges were laid against me. I have thirty more years to serve. It would be pleasant to leave my body behind and tour the universe—but as I said I'll discuss that later.

I wouldn't say that we're a superior race. We have certain qualities which apparently your people do not have. We live longer, not because of any discoveries we've made about ourselves, but because our bodies are built of a more enduring element—I don't know your name for it, but the atomic weight is 52.9??*

Our scientific discoveries are of the kind that would normally be made by a race with our kind of physical structure. The fact that we can work with temperatures of as high as—I don't know just how to put that—has been very helpful in the development of the subspace energies which are extremely hot, and require delicate adjustments. In the later stages these adjustments can be made by machinery, but in the development the work must be done by 'hand'—I put the word in quotes, because we have no hands in the same way that you have.

---

*A radioactive isotope of chromium.—Author's Note.

I am enclosing a photographic plate, properly cooled and chemicalized for your climate. I wonder if you would set it up and take a picture of yourself. All you have to do is arrange it properly on the basis of the laws of light—that is, light travels in straight lines, so stand in front of it—and when you are ready *think* 'Ready!' The picture will be automatically taken.

Would you do this for me? If you are interested, I will also send you a picture of myself, though I must warn you. My appearance will probably shock you.

Sincerely,

SKANDER

Aurigae II

DEAR PEN PAL:

Just a brief note in answer to your question. It is not necessary to put the plate into a camera. You describe this as a dark box. The plate will take the picture when you think, 'Ready!' I assure you it will be flooded with light.

SKANDER

Aurigae II

DEAR PEN PAL:

You say that while you were waiting for the answer to my last letter you showed the photographic plate to one of the doctors at the hospital—I cannot picture what you mean by doctor or hospital, but let that pass—and he took the problem up with government authorities. Problem? I don't understand. I thought we were having a pleasant correspondence, private and personal.

I shall certainly appreciate your sending that picture of yourself.

SKANDER

Aurigae II

DEAR PEN PAL:

I assure you I am not annoyed at your action. It merely puzzled me, and I am sorry the plate has not been returned to you. Knowing what governments are, I can imagine that it will not be returned to you for some time, so I am taking the liberty of enclosing another plate.

I cannot imagine why you should have been warned against continuing this correspondence. What do they expect me to do?—eat you up at long distance? I'm sorry but I don't like hydrogen in my diet.

In any event, I would like your picture as a memento of our friendship, and I will send mine as soon as I have received yours. You may keep it or throw it away, or give it to your governmental authorities—but at least I will have the knowledge that I've given a fair exchange.

With all best wishes,
SKANDER

Aurigae II

DEAR PEN PAL:

Your last letter was so slow in coming that I thought you had decided to break off the correspondence. I was sorry to notice that you failed to enclose the photograph, puzzled by your reference to having a relapse, and cheered by your statement that you would send it along as soon as you felt better—whatever that means. However, the important thing is that you did write, and I respect the philosophy of your club which asks its members not to write of pessimistic matters. We all have our own problems which we regard as overshadowing the problems of others. Here I am in prison, doomed to spend the next 30 years tucked away from the main stream of life. Even the thought is hard on my restless spirit, though I know I have a long life ahead of me after my release.

In spite of your friendly letter, I won't feel that you have completely re-established contact with me until you send the photograph.

Yours in expectation,
SKANDER

Aurigae II

DEAR PEN PAL:

The photograph arrived. As you suggest, your appearance startled me. From your description I thought I had mentally reconstructed your body. It just goes to show that words cannot really describe an object which has never been seen.

You'll notice that I've enclosed a photograph of myself, as I promised I would. Chunky, metallic-looking chap, am I not, very different, I'll wager, than you expected? The various races with whom we have communicated become wary of us when they discover we are highly radio-active, and that literally we are a radio-active form of life, the only such (that we know of) in the universe. It's been very trying to be so isolated and, as you know, I have occasionally mentioned that I had hopes of escaping not only the deadly imprisonment to which I am being subjected but also the body which cannot escape.

Perhaps you'll be interested in hearing how far this idea has developed. The problem involved is one of exchange of personalities with someone else. Actually, it is not really an exchange in the accepted meaning of the word. It is necessary to get an impression of both individuals, of their mind and of their thoughts as well as their bodies. Since this phase is purely mechanical, it is simply a matter of taking complete photographs and of exchanging them. By complete I mean of course every vibration must be registered.

The next step is to make sure the two photographs are exchanged, that is, that each party has somewhere near him a complete photograph of the other. (It is already too late, Pen Pal. I have set in motion the subspace energy interflow between the two plates, so you might as well read on.) As I have said it is not exactly an exchange of personalities. The original personality in each individual is suppressed, literally pushed back out of consciousness, and the image personality from the 'photographic' plate replaces it.

You will take with you a complete memory of your life on Earth, and I will take along memory of my life on Aurigae. Simultaneously, the memory of the receiving body will be blurrily at our disposal. A part of us will always be pushing up, striving to regain consciousness, but always lacking the strength to succeed.

As soon as I grow tired of Earth, I will exchange bodies in the same way with a member of some other race. Thirty years hence, I will be happy to reclaim my body, and you can then have whatever body I last happened to occupy.

This should be a very happy arrangement for us both. You, with your short life expectancy, will have outlived all your contemporaries and will have had an interesting experience. I admit I expect to have the better of the exchange—but now, enough of explanation. By the time you reach this part of the letter it will be me reading it, not you. But if any part of you is still aware, so long for now, Pen Pal. It's been nice having all those letters from you. I shall write you from time to time to let you know how things are going with my tour.

SKANDER

Aurigae II

DEAR PEN PAL:

Thanks a lot for forcing the issue. For a long time I hesitated about letting you play such a trick on yourself. You see, the government scientists analysed the nature of that first photographic plate you sent me, and so the final decision was really up to me. I decided that anyone as eager as you were to put one over should be allowed to succeed.

Now I know I don't have to feel sorry for you. Your plan to conquer Earth wouldn't have got anywhere, but the fact that you had the idea ends the need for sympathy.

By this time you will have realized for yourself that a man who has been paralysed since birth, and is subject to heart attacks, cannot expect a long life span. I am happy to tell you that your once lonely pen pal is enjoying himself, and I am happy to sign myself with a name to which I expect to become accustomed.

With best wishes,

SKANDER

Sweets from a Stranger

NICHOLAS FISK

First, the girl.

Tina Halliday, age eleven, almost black hair, waving at the ends. Brown eyes, tall for her age, quite pretty (but a nail-biter), good enough at most school subjects, very good at badminton (three trophies—and, if she won tonight, possibly a fourth soon to come).

Next, the car. Black Jaguar saloon, recent model, fawn leather upholstery, paintwork shining in the drizzly evening light.

And last, the driver of the car—

No, but wait. We will meet him a little later.

The black Jaguar was being driven slowly and badly. It lurched along the suburban street seeming to catch its breath, sneeze, then accelerate to all of fifteen miles an hour—then slow again. It came to a corner and took it in bites and nibbles, uncertainly, inexpertly.

Tina saw the car. She thought, That driver could be drunk. She moved closer to a low brick wall with a hedge. If the worst came to the worst—if the driver lost control—she could easily hop over the wall and be safe.

The car slowed. Now it seemed to be aiming at her: following her. Tina gripped her badminton racket tightly. She felt the first flutter of fear. The street was deserted. She thought, That car is coming for *me*.

The car almost stopped, right beside her, grating one wheel rim against the kerb. Panic jumped into Tina's throat. When the car's window slid down, she thought, Shall I run? But her knees and legs felt weak.

A high-pitched voice, a man's voice, came through the open window. 'Little girl! Little girl! Do you want a ride in my car?'

Very loudly and distinctly, Tina said, 'No! I do not!' She thought, I'll give him 'little girl' if he tries anything on. 'Badminton Builds Bionic Biceps,' she murmured, and tried to smile.

The voice said, 'But—but it's a nice car. Wouldn't you like a ride?'

Tina said—almost shouted, 'No! Go away!'

The panic was leaving her. A part of her mind was almost giggling. If only Mum could see this! A classic scene! The thing she had been warned against even when she was tiny! 'Bad Stranger Man trying to get Nice Little Girl into Big Wicked Car!' Next thing, he'd be offering her a sweetie . . .

The Jaguar wheezed as the driver over-revved the engine. It lurched and bumbled along beside her. The man inside—she could not see his face—said, 'Little girl! Wouldn't you like a sweetie? I've got some sweeties!'

At this, Tina began laughing. She laughed so much that she bent over in the middle. 'You're too much!' she choked. 'Really you are! Sweeties! A nice ride, and you've got some *sweeties*, too!'

The man said something that stopped her laughing. '*Please*,' he said. '*Please!*'

There was complete despair in his voice.

'Don't go away!' he said. She could see a sort of agony in the way his body stretched towards her. 'Don't go away! I don't *understand* anything . . . I don't know what to *do* . . .'

Tina, knowing she was behaving foolishly, went closer to the car, bent down and looked through the window. Even now she could not see the man. The instrument lights showed her only that he was small. Nothing else.

'They told me girls and boys liked sweets,' the man said, hopelessly. 'Crystallized fruits . . .' His voice was high and husky. 'They told me all sorts of things, but nothing helps. If only *you* would help . . .'

Tina told herself: You must be mad!—and got into the car.

Now she could see the man's head. It was turned away from her, bowed. Small man, small head.

'I don't know,' the man said. He made a gesture, a defeated throwing-out of his arm and hand. Tina saw the hand.

It was like a claw. It had only three fingers. There was skin that was not skin. There was dark, glossy hairiness.

The panic came back—leapt into her throat—choked her, froze her, numbed her.

'Nothing's working, nothing's going right,' the man said, in his high, rustling, despairing voice. Tina could not speak. She could only look at the hand, the dreadful hand.

He must have seen the whites of her eyes or the terrified O of her mouth, for he snatched his hand away, produced a glove and clumsily put it on. The glove had five fingers. Tina thought, Two of them must be padded. Still she could not move or speak. She made a gasping sound.

'I'm an invader,' the man said, as if replying to her sound. 'An invader. Come to conquer you. But it's not working.'

Tina coughed and forced her voice to work. 'An invader?' she said.

'Invading Earth,' the man said, dully. 'Your planet.'

'Where do you come from?' Tina said.

'Out there.' He waved his gloved hand vaguely upwards. 'Not from a planet: our home planet was finished thousands of years ago. We made our own world. We're having trouble with it. Not enough fuel, not enough ores and minerals, not enough of anything. Your planet has the things we need, so we're invading . . . But I don't know, I don't know . . .'

I'm not dreaming, Tina thought. This is real. It is happening. Escape! Run away! But she did not want to go.

'Look,' the man said. 'All I want to do is to stop being an invader. To go home. They told me things—told me what to do, what to say—but nothing fits, nothing goes right.'

'I don't see how I can help,' Tina said. 'I mean, what can *I* do?'

'Take me to a telephone. Get me a number, a particular number, I have it here—'

'But there's a telephone box just down the road, you passed it—'

'I couldn't make it work. They told me to use it, they told me how to use it; I did everything right, but it wouldn't work.'

'Come with me,' Tina said. Now she was no longer frightened, just very curious. 'Get out of the car. No, you must switch off the engine—that's right. And don't leave the keys in. Stop shaking, there's nothing to be afraid of. No, get out *your* side, there's no need to climb over the seats. Now close the door. Try again. Give it a good slam. Good. Take my arm. Come on.'

They reached the telephone box. The man walked as if his legs made him uneasy. He shook and trembled. Tina had to hold him up. He was not as tall as she.

The telephone would not work. 'Out of order,' Tina said, with a shrug.

'What does that mean?' the man said.

'Only that it doesn't work.'

'They never told us about "Out of Order",' the man said, dully.

'Wait a second!' Tina saw there was a coin jammed in the little slot. She managed to force the jammed coin in. Now the telephone worked. She dialled the number the man gave her. A high-pitched voice answered. The man took the handset—he held it the wrong way round at first—and spoke.

'Mission completed,' he said. Then, 'What? Oh. Oh. Well, I *can't* complete it any more than I *have* completed it, I can't go on *any longer*... What? No, no, I don't care, it's no good telling me that. Completed or uncompleted, I'm going home.'

He put the receiver back on the hook, sighed, and said, 'Well, I'm not the only one. Several others have failed too and *they're* going home.'

Now Tina could see his face, for the first time, by the light of a street lamp. It was a horrible face, a waxwork mask—a face no more human than one of those plastic, jointed dolls. Though the mouth had lips, it was really only a movable hole. The skin— but it was not skin—was too tight over the cheek-bones, too loose at the ears. And the ears were waxen, unreal. The hair began and ended too sharply. It did not grow from the scalp; it was fitted to it. A wig.

She shuddered. '*Why?*' she demanded. 'Why did they dress you up like this? I mean, if you're an invader, why couldn't you look like an invader—someone frightening and threatening and, what's the word, indomitable? You're just a—a mess. I'm sorry, but you are.'

'They—my masters—wanted us to be friendly invaders,' the man explained. 'Not monsters: people like yourselves. People who use telephones and drive cars and wear clothes. But it went wrong, of course. Everything's gone wrong.'

'What are you really like?' Tina said.

The man shifted uneasily. 'Probably you'd think us hideous,' he said. 'You might hate us if you saw us as we really are.'

'But you don't think *me* hideous?' Tina said, smiling. She knew she had a nice smile. Her smile faded as she saw the man's eyes (too big to fit the false eyelids) change, grow cautious and look away.

'Well . . .' he said. 'Well . . .'

'You *do* think me hideous?' Tina said, amazed.

'You're so different, that's what it is. So very different from us. Your eyes are so small and pale, and your skin so white, and your hair grows in the wrong places—'

'I see,' Tina said, pursing her lips.

'I hope I haven't given offence?'

'Not at all. Do go on,' she said, stiffly.

'Different,' the man said. 'Things are so different where I come from! Perhaps a bit better. A lot better in some ways.' He began to speak enthusiastically. 'We don't need to use telephones when we want to speak to each other: we just tune into minds. We don't need these complicated great machines, these cars, to travel in. We don't cover ourselves with layers of fabric to keep the weather out—'

'You go naked, I suppose?' Tina said, acidly.

'Well, we don't find it necessary to wrap ourselves in coloured rags! But perhaps you do it because you'd be so ugly if you didn't—Oh, I beg your pardon—'

'Don't mind *me*,' Tina said, coldly. 'A pity, though, that you can't seem to cope in your superior world! Pity you have to go round invading people! Or', she added spitefully, '*attempting* to invade them!'

'Our world must survive,' the man said, quietly. 'It's a beautiful and wonderful world. It must be saved!'

Tina said, 'Hmm.'

'The most beautiful! The most wonderful!' the man insisted. 'If only you could see it for yourself! Then you'd understand!'

'I'm sure you're right,' Tina said, distantly. She looked at her watch. 'Lord! I'm late! I must go! The time!'

'On our world, we control time,' the man told her. 'We always have time . . .' A thought struck him. 'Come with me! See my world! Don't worry about time—stay as long as you like and I promise you'll be back here only a minute or so from now! Come with me!'

His dark eyes blazed at her from the mask of his face. The mask was stupid: the eyes were not.

For the second time Tina told herself: You must be mad! Out loud, she said, 'All right, then. Show me your world.'

She felt herself twisted, racked, stretched, flung apart and thought, This is the journey, then.

'This is my face,' he said. The mock-human mask was gone. Huge, dark, liquid eyes looked at her from the furred face—the face of a cat, but not a cat, not a seal, not an otter, not any Earth animal. She saw the neat, flowing body, covered in dense fur, dark grey and tipped with silver. She saw the high forehead, the mobile mouth (He's smiling! she thought. So that's how they look when they smile!). No tail. Useful three-fingered hands. A mobile, businesslike thumb.

'There is my world,' he said. Through the glassy bubble of nothingness that separated them from the stars, a world gleamed and glittered in the blackness, coming closer and closer impossibly fast—a huge, complicated globe, jewelled with a million tiny lights, sprinkled with clouds—

'Shana,' he said. 'That is Shana. I am a Shanad. In the heart of the world, there is a city called Ro-yil. Can you say those words?'

She found that she could. Her mouth spoke them for her in a tongue her brain did not know. She tried out this new gift. 'What is your name?'

'Talis,' he said.

'Rhymes with Palace,' Tina said, vaguely. There was so much to look at, the glittering world was rushing at them—

'There,' said Talis. 'We have landed. Get out. I will show you the city first.'

He hurried her to the edge of a vast square shaft, took her hand, and made her fall, endlessly, through a tunnel of lights and textures, fleeting shapes and sounds. She wanted to scream; but Talis's calm face was beside her, his hand held hers, his voice spoke to her.

They seemed to meet some sort of invisible cushion. The sensation was like that of being in a lift, slowing violently.

And then they were in the city of Ro-yil.

The city hung, a sphere within a sphere, from glistening filaments, pulsing with light. ('They are avenues', Talis explained, matter-of-factly, 'rather like the one we are standing in.') Towers soared, glassy and magnificent. Plants taller than Earth trees sang softly. There were Shanads everywhere, many in glassy bubbles like that which had carried Tina and Talis from Earth. The bubbles seemed to move instantly from place to place. 'Hoverflies . . . fireflies,' Tina murmured.

'What?' Talis said.

'Beautiful,' she replied. 'Wonderful, beautiful, magnificent!'

A crystal bubble drifted by. It was empty. 'Tsa!' said Talis; the bubble stopped by them. 'Ata-al!' he said and the side of the bubble split open. 'Get in,' he said. 'I'll take you to my home.'

Tina memorized the words and tried to understand how Talis drove the bubble. There was no time. The city hurtled for a split-second, then gently slowed. Tina gasped. Talis smiled. 'You like my city, then?' His voice had changed. Now it was confident, laughing, sure.

Tina could only reply, 'Marvellous!' Then, 'This bubble,' she said. 'It's the same as the one that brought us here, isn't it?'

'The same. It can take you anywhere! Anywhere in the universe! But who would want to leave *this*?' He swept his arm at the jewelled city, the crystalline towers of pearl and jet, aquamarine and turquoise, strung together with luminous silver threads . . .

'Home,' he said. 'Come.'

A door opened in a glassy golden wall.

She entered and saw humans.

The door closed and Talis was gone.

There were perhaps twenty of them. The room was not big enough. They stared at her, silently. Then a raggedly dressed woman with a tired face came to Tina and said, 'Oh dear. Poor you. And so young.'

'But Talis said—Talis promised—'

'Oh, I dare say he did. I dare say he told you he can control time and all that . . . And you fell for it. Felt sorry for him, didn't you? Felt you had to help? Those big dark eyes of theirs . . . And you fell for it. So did I, years ago. I was a District Nurse. Do you know Hove? And Brighton? That was where I was—'

A young man, his clothes falling to pieces, snorted, 'Never mind about Hove and Brighton. We've had enough of them.' He turned his back on the District Nurse and said, 'What's your name, then? Tina? Tina. You're right in it now. Up to the neck. Like the rest of us. There's lots of us, you know. Not just this room: the whole building.' He shrugged despairingly. To the District Nurse he said, 'You explain to her.'

'You're a hostage, dear,' the woman said. 'At least, that's the way we work it out. I mean, they want to invade Earth, but they can't. You see, they want metals and minerals and I-don't-know-what from Earth; but their weapons won't work *without* the metals and minerals and I-don't-know-whats. So they're stuck, aren't they?'

'What do you mean, hostages?' Tina said.

Another man joined the group and answered. 'They're going to use us instead of weapons,' he said. 'They'll tell Earth they've got us. If Earth won't give them the things they want, they'll threaten to kill us, you see? They'll *barter* us! When they've got enough of us.'

Tina said, 'But—but they can't! I've got to go home!'

The young man told Tina, 'Cheer up, you're not dead yet. No good crying.'

Tina swallowed her sobs and said, 'How long have you been here?'

'He's been here longest,' the nurse said, pointing to a man huddled in a corner. 'Seven years. Old misery, he is. You won't get anything out of him. Given up speaking to anyone years ago.'

'Why don't you escape?' Tina said.

'Might be difficult, don't you think?' the young man said, cynically. 'I mean, we don't *look* much like them, do we? We'd be a bit *noticeable* outside, wouldn't we? Anyhow, if you think you can get out, have a go. Ah, food!'

A door in the wall opened: a gleaming box slid in. Immediately everyone—even the crouched man—came to life. They grabbed and gobbled, crammed their mouths, bargained noisily over swaps.

Tina thought, You're a shabby lot. She ate the food. It looked strange but tasted good. The things that looked like crystallized fruits were best of all. She saved some, hiding them in her pocket. She thought, They've given in; I won't. I'll learn everything I can, and hoard food and wait for the right moment: then I'll escape . . .

Nobody showed much interest when, three days later, Tina emptied the food box, climbed into it, and escaped the room.

Now she was at large in the city. The Shanad words she had learned from Talis were still in her mind. She had practised them and knew them well. But that was about all she knew.

Soon, she did not even know what she had hoped to gain by escaping. The Shanads thronging the city of Ro-yil neither helped nor hindered her. No sirens screamed, no vehicles dashed, no hard-faced law-enforcers pounced. The Shanads (to Tina, they all looked the same) ignored her. Their large, dark, intelligent eyes looked at her—then, deliberately, looked away.

'A bubble . . .' she said to herself. 'That's what I must have.' A bubble drifted beside her. 'Tsa!' she said. 'Ata-al!' She sat in the bubble, trying to find a knob or a lever or anything at all that would make it go. Shanads passed by, not looking or caring. She began to cry. She got out of the bubble and walked blindly, endlessly, through the gorgeous city.

She reached the shafts by accident. One shaft had brought her down from the surface of the world to the city; now she saw a twin shaft. Shanads walked into its entrance and went up. Up to the surface! 'One step nearer home,' Tina said, entered the shaft, and flew to the surface.

She found herself looking at white clouds in a green sky. Beyond, she saw darkness and in the darkness, stars and planets. 'One of you is Earth,' she said. She looked for a bubble. This time, she would not give up. This time, she would go home.

She saw a bubble. It was stationary. In front of it, two furry little things, charming, fat and jolly, rolled on the ground. They were smaller than Shanads, much smaller—

'Ah!' said Tina. '*Children!*'

'Tsa!' she hissed; and got into the bubble. The child Shanads rolled and squeaked, pounced and wrestled, outside. 'Ata-al!'

she said. The magic word once again failed to have any effect. She knocked on the wall of the bubble to attract the children's attention. They looked up at her. Their eyes were beautiful.

Tina said—her mind and voice struggling for the words, 'I'm a friend. I need your help. I'm a friend! Help me!'

The children stared. One made a gurgling noise that must have been giggling.

'Look,' Tina said, 'I've got this lovely bubble, but I can't seem to work it. Wouldn't you like to show me how to work it?'

Both children giggled. Neither moved.

'Look, suppose you get in with me, and show me what to do, then we can go for a ride!'

The Shanad children linked paws and stared at her, still giggling.

Tina remembered the crystallized fruits in her pocket. 'I'll give you these!' she cried. 'One for each of you! *Two* each!'

And suddenly the Shanad children were running away, running very fast. They ran until they reached an adult Shanad, then stopped and pointed at Tina. She could hear what they were saying.

'. . . wanted to take us for a *ride*!' one said.

'In a nice bubble!' said the other.

'Offered us *sweets*!' said the first. 'Us! As if we'd take sweets from strangers!'

They pointed their fingers and giggled, loudly and scornfully. They jumped up and down, delighted with themselves.

And then Talis was there, with many other Shanads.

They took Tina back to the room.

One day, perhaps, the Shanads will make contact with Earth. Until then, Tina will at least be fed. The things that look like crystallized fruits are delicious, at first.

Later, you grow tired of them.

The Chase

STEPHEN BOWKETT

We crested the hill and came upon the valley in the late afternoon. The setting sun was huge beyond the Sowelu mountains, casting a red light across the face of the moon rising behind us: I saw it reflected in Berkana's green eyes as she surveyed the scene and decided on the best plan of action.

'It is an hour ahead of us—no more than that,' Berkana declared. 'My instincts say we should go in and take it now—'

'In the dark!' Kano's voice was sharp and cynical, pitched high in critical disbelief. Like several of the males of our Cluster, Kano had been outraged by Berkana's election to leadership—that she was female and younger than he being a double blow to his pride.

Kano glanced round at the others in the hunting pack, looking for their support. His smirking face glowed with anger and disrespect. One or two of Kano's supporters nodded, but nervously in light of their defiance.

Berkana shrugged and remained calm. It made me smile to see her deal so coolly with her opponents.

'The creature's night vision is no better than ours. Its technology is no better than ours—'

'Its weapons are appalling!' Kano challenged. 'Think back to the huge destruction these monsters have caused to our cities!'

'Yes . . .' Berkana's eyes filled up with memories. 'But we fought back and we beat them. Now just one of these animals remains—and it is there in the woodland valley. It has only the weapons it could carry from its downed ship; and it is but one creature, and we are many.'

Berkana hefted her slingbag more securely across her shapely back.

'Our commission is to hunt down the last of these invaders. I want to see an end to them. You and your supporters stay here if you like, Kano, but I'm going on—'

'I'm with you, Berkana,' I chirped up, filled with admiration for her. She smiled at me.

'Thank you, Isa . . . You see, Kano, even the youngest among us is keen to continue.'

'The youngest and stupidest—'

Berkana's features froze at that. She turned away from Kano and began moving down off the crest of the hill into the trees. I followed, along with the others who were loyal. Glancing back moments later from the shadows, I saw Kano's advocates straggling after us . . . And then Kano himself, no doubt feeling a little insecure out in the open alone.

The war, if such it could be called, had been brief. The invaders came in three vast ships from the outer fringes of the galaxy. They seemed to have been explorers rather than conquerors, but they were heavily armed for all that, and their natures were destructive. Scout ships deployed from orbit surveyed our world and scanned our civilization, measuring our strength. Our scientists attempted to communicate, but without success; the aliens were not listening, or perhaps chose not to understand.

When they landed, our people came out to greet them; nervous of the aliens' great grey machines, but wishing to be seen as hosts rather than enemies. Despite that, we were never gullible; even as a delegation of our people moved out into the prairie-lands to meet the visitors, our droneships hovered nearby, anticipating trouble.

It came before we even saw their faces; it came with fire and smoke and beams of light too painfully dazzling to look upon. The delegation was wiped out instantly, their bodies shrivelled and twisted by flame and left lying. Without pausing, the invaders' machines rolled onwards, over the remains of the elders, towards the heartlands and our cities. Meanwhile, their motherships blazed at us from orbit.

The hoverdrones retaliated swiftly, piercing the armour of the enemy tanks and turning each into an enormous expanding fireball. Simultaneously—since the aliens had refused to acknowledge both our pleas and our warnings—ground-to-orbit missiles streaked upwards like needles into the night to breach the defences of the motherships . . .

I can remember watching them drifting through the late evening sky like shadowy birds beyond the clouds: then, all in a second, turning into papery streamers of fire and sparks and downward-spiralling fragments of glowing metal littering the heavens.

Whatever dreams of conquest the otherworlders had brought with them were incinerated that night. The alien landing-parties scattered, some of the creatures escaping immediate destruction. Hunting packs were gathered to track them down. I joined Berkana's, because I loved and admired her, and because in my heart I felt outraged for what had been done to our world; and I wanted the thirst of it satisfied.

Ours had long since ceased to be a dangerous planet. Over the centuries the larger predatory creatures had been confined to reservations bounded by field-fences. The alien had broken through this barrier of energies to reach the wooded valley. Such was its size that I doubted whether our most ferocious beasts would be able to harm it. The opposite was likely to be true! Berkana had shown us an image of what the stranger looked like . . . Such deformity in its bones and features, but such size and massive strength! The tallest of our people barely reached to its knees. The one we chased was bulked out further with body armour and its packs and pouches of provisions: a huge thing, terrifying and powerful—but running from us now. Running for its life.

'It could hide in here for months,' I muttered, speaking my thoughts aloud. The sunlight was fading quickly, its deep red giving way to blue shadows. And the air had grown still as daytime animals found their roosts and burrows, and the night-things came quietly out of hiding.

'Don't forget we have the hoverdrones,' Berkana reminded me. 'They can overview the valley and spot our quarry if it moves into a clearing or disturbs the undergrowth too much.'

Even as she said this, I looked up and saw the drones beyond the tree canopy, spreading out like silver moths flickering through the twilight. One lifted straight up and became a star, the others swooping low along the cardinal points.

'We'll be all right,' Berkana added for the benefit of the others. 'We have the motion trackers. Just stay alert and together. Now let's move on . . .'

We fanned out with Berkana as the arrowhead of our formation. The motion trackers we wore registered our bodies in green, moving quickly and efficiently through the faintly glowing landscape of light which was the undergrowth. Occasional blips and sparkles of red appeared on the screens; these were the night animals, birds and tree-crawlers, that posed no threat to us.

As we penetrated deeper into the woodland, I looked ahead and to my right at Berkana. She was setting a rapid pace, but one which would not tire us even if we kept it up all night—not that we could, for as the woods became denser our pattern would be broken and we would be forced to slow down. In my ears came the soft murmuring of the others in the group, communicating through their headsets. Even though we were on a mission of danger, I felt safe and comfortable among my people, pleased and proud to have been chosen for this important work.

We continued for an hour, coming occasionally upon traces of the alien's passing; broken twigs, crumpled bracken, the prints of its huge boots in the soft loam which spoke of its frightening size and weight. Berkana's voice gently reassured us, keeping us together in our minds, even as we struggled a little now to maintain our inverted-V formation.

'There's the river up ahead,' Kano declared. 'The trees fall away into a deep channel.'

Berkana thanked him, her tone telling him she hadn't needed reminding. It was our first real obstacle—not just physically, since it might not be easy to tell which way the alien had gone; left, right, or down into the gorge.

Ahead the ground tilted towards a rocky lip, where it became almost sheer. I could hear the rush of the river, and the air stirred now with the first chilly breath of the night wind off the high mountains.

Berkana stopped and we halted behind her.

'Let the drones do their work,' she told us. 'Rest awhile.'

Above, the hoverdrones pitched into the dark, sweeping out over the canyon. I glimpsed the bluish moonlight glinting momentarily on the wing surfaces of one of them as they swept away to deep-scan the area.

Moments later came a bleep from the motion trackers, indicating something big in the dense foliage of the trees fringing the edge of the gorge. I felt my body tightening with anticipation. Berkana unslung her pulse rifle, the rest of us swiftly following her wisdom.

She sent two of the machines closer to the target, keying-in a few adjustments on the drone-remote to obtain the best hi-definition images possible. We watched our tracker screens nervously as the blue smudge grew brighter and larger, sprouting powerful grasping limbs and the long prehensile tail of the jera-sloth.

I heard Kano chuckling wryly, and we all I think let out a sigh of grateful relief.

Berkana waved us forward—

And in that second the night lit up in a flash. A beam of brilliance streaked upwards, striking the nearest drone dead centre. The lenslike machine wobbled in the air, glowing as it seemed to inflate like a cloud of white light. Then it exploded, showering bits of itself down in a pattering rain.

Before the moment of confusion was over, there came the *boom* of a grenade close by and a wave of fire rushed towards us.

Berkana called a warning, but we were already diving for the ground . . . All except poor Thurisaz, whose reactions were an instant too slow: the tide of flame engulfed him, lit him like a torch and withered his body as we watched.

The heat swept by, luckily dissipated by the trees before it could do any more harm. But scores of little crackling fires had been set burning in the undergrowth, lighting up the area and making us easier targets.

Kano roared his outrage at the death of Thurisaz, and began to scramble up with his weapon drawn.

Berkana's order was sharp and clear—'Get down now!'

Her instincts were sound, for immediately afterwards came the deafening *chuddaddaddadda* of a powerful machine rifle blasting bullets through the underbrush. They came so rapidly and with such force that bushes and small trees were chewed up and spat aside as though by invisible jaws; and the air was filled with splinters and dust and sparks, and the endless whining of the shells.

We were pinned down helplessly by this fierce onslaught, and I realized that the first spraying was a suppressing fire, designed simply to terrify and disorient us, keep us hugging the ground. Very soon afterwards, the alien would begin taking a more careful aim to destroy us as we lay there.

Trembling all over, I dared to lift my face from the dirt and realized that the cascade of bullets was coming from the left and at a downward angle. I spoke hurriedly into my throat-mike.

'Berkana, the creature is up in the trees. Over to the left.'

There was a moment's pause, then:

'Yes, Isa, you're right. I see the discharge of its weapon. I think we must—'

She was interrupted by a sudden shriek, and not far away Algiz thrashed as a bullet struck him, and he died. The slaughter, I knew, had begun.

Even as the massive pounding of the alien's machine rifle continued automatically, there came the sharper *crack—crack* as the monster sought to pick us off with a secondary weapon. A high-impact bullet smashed into a tree not a body length from where Kano lay. He yelped and rolled frantically under a bush for cover.

'Help us, Berkana!' That was Perth starting to panic. 'What do we do!'

Berkana answered with action. She lay close to a section of bracken that was burning busily, and by its light I saw her manoeuvre her rifle round to the front of her, pointing ahead. Then, oddly, she seemed to be fiddling with the drone-remote, bringing a couple of the remaining machines closer—closer to the alien, until they were hovering silently above it on their invisible energy fields.

Berkana switched attention to her rifle and loosed a brief burst of glittering particles that flared and hissed among the leaves and branches.

The alien retaliated immediately—

And while its concentration was diverted, Berkana jabbed the remote and sent the drones crashing into the tree.

The shock more than the impact dislodged it. The machine-rifle tumbled first, smashing down from branch to branch, its devastating spatter of bullets flying wide. When it hit the ground, some part of the mechanism jammed and it stopped with a grinding howl of metal on metal, inert now and useless.

Berkana called for us to move, but we needed no telling. She opened out her delicate green wings and soared into the air, putting two shots through the alien's chest armour as it lost its balance and fell. Briefly it grabbed for a branch and clung there, but Kano and Perth and Raido were upon it, fluttering down to sink the long blades of their teeth into its wrists and neck.

The creature bellowed in pain and horror before its strength failed. As it dropped, its attackers sprang away and circled as it hit the ground with a thud.

We fired at it, not because it was a danger now but—I admit—in fury at what it and its kind had done to us. We fired until its breathing had all but stopped and its armour was pitted by a hundred needle-thin holes, melting around the rim.

Kano landed on the monster's forehead and let out a shriek of triumph that echoed shrilly through the forest. The alien tried to lift its hand to brush Kano away, but even that simple feat was beyond it. We gathered about the creature and waited. It took some minutes for the life to leave it fully; and all the while it looked at us with a gaze that was filled with questions and wonder. But in the end that gaze became clouded and distant, and the eyes closed.

We buried the warrior where it lay, with no remorse. Until that time the aliens had been an almost total mystery to us: only later as we searched through the creature's belongings were we provided with any clues—a simple identity tag bearing the strange message—

Corporal Benjamin Leech
Alliance Frontline Marine Corps
Earth >>>

The Pair

JOE L. HENSLEY

They tell the story differently in the history stereos and maybe they are right. But for me the way the great peace came about, the thing that started us on our way to understanding, was a small thing, a human thing—and also a Knau thing.

In the late days of the hundred-year war that engulfed two galaxies we took a planet that lay on the fringe of the Knau empire. In the many years of the war this particular planet had passed into our hands twice before, had been colonized, and the colonies wiped out when the Knau empire retook the spot—as we, in turn, wiped out the colonies they had planted there—for it was a war of horror with no quarter asked, expected, or given. The last attempt to negotiate a peace had been made ten years after the war began and for the past forty years neither side had even bothered to take prisoners, except a few for the purposes of information. We were too far apart, too ideologically different, and yet we each wanted the same things, and we were each growing and spreading through the galaxies in the pattern of empire.

The name of this particular planet was Pasman and, as usual, disabled veterans had first choice of the land there. One of the men who was granted a patent to a large tract of land was Michael Dargan.

Dargan stood on a slight rise and looked with some small pride at the curved furrow lines in the dark earth. All of his tillable land had been ploughed and made ready for the planting. The feeling of pride was something he had not experienced for a long time and he savoured it until it soured within him. Even then he continued to stare out over his land for a long time, for when he was standing motionless he could almost forget.

The mechanical legs worked very well. At first they had been tiring to use, but in the four years since his ship had been hit he had learned to use them adequately. The scars on his body had been cut away by the plastic surgeons and his face looked almost human now, if he could trust his mirror. But any disablement leaves deeper scars than the physical ones.

He sighed and began to move towards the house in his awkward yet powerful way. Martha would have lunch ready.

The house was in sight when it happened. Some sixth sense, acquired in battle, warned him that someone was following and he turned as quickly as possible and surveyed the land behind him. He caught the glint of sunlight on metal. He let himself fall to the earth as the air flamed red around him and for a long time he lay still. His clothes smouldered in a few spots and he beat the flames out with cautious hands.

Twice more, nearby, the ground flamed red and he lay crowded into the furrow which hid him.

Martha must have heard or seen what was happening from the house for she began shooting his heavy projectile 'varmint' gun from one of the windows and, by raising his head, Dargan

could see the projectiles picking at the top of a small rise a hundred yards or so from him. He hoped then that she would not kill the thing that had attacked, for if it was what he thought, he wanted the pleasure for himself.

There was silence for a little while and then Martha began to shoot again from the window. He raised his head again and caught a glimpse of his attacker as it scuttled up a hill. *It was a Knau.* He felt the blood begin to race in him, the wild hate.

'Martha!' he yelled. 'Stop shooting.'

He got his mechanical legs underneath him and went on down to the house. She was standing in the doorway, crying.

'I thought it had gotten you.'

He smiled at her, feeling a small exhilaration. 'I'm all right,' he said. 'Give me the pro gun.' He took it from her and went to the small window, but it was too late. The Knau had vanished over the hill.

'Fix me some food,' he said to her. 'I'm going after it.'

'It was a Knau, wasn't it?' She closed her eyes and shuddered, not waiting for his answer. 'I've never seen one before—only the pictures. It was horrible. I think I hit it.'

Dargan stared at her. 'Fix me some food, I said. I'm going after it.'

She opened her eyes. 'Not by yourself. I'll call the village. They'll send some men up.'

'By that time it will be long gone.' He watched her silently for a moment, knowing she was trying to read something in him. He kept his face impassive. 'Fix me some food or I will go without it,' he said softly.

'You want to kill it for yourself, don't you? You don't want anyone to help you. That's why you yelled at me to stop shooting.'

'Yes,' he admitted. 'I want to kill it myself. I don't want you to call the village after I am gone.' He made his voice heavy with emphasis. 'If you call the village I won't come back to you, Martha.' He closed his eyes and stood swaying softly as the tension built within him. 'Those things killed my parents and they have killed me. This is the first chance I've ever had to get close to one.' He smiled without humour and looked down at his ruined legs. 'It will be a long time dying.'

The trail was easy to follow at first. She had wounded it, but he doubted if the wound were serious after he had trailed awhile. Occasionally on the bushes it had crashed through were droplets of bright, orange-red blood.

Away from the cleared area of the farm the land was heavily rolling, timbered with great trees that shut away the light of the distant, double blue suns. There was growth under the trees, plants that struggled for breathing room. The earth was soft and took tracks well.

Dargan followed slowly, with time for thought.

He remembered when his ship had been hit. He had been standing in a passageway and the space battle had flamed all around him. A young officer in his first engagement. It was a small battle—known only by the co-ordinates where it had happened and worth only a line or two in the official reports of the day. But it would always be etched in Dargan's brain. His ship had taken the first hit.

If he had been a little further out in the passageway he would surely have died. As it was he only half died.

He remembered catching at the bulkhead with his hands and falling sideways. There was a feeling of horrible burning and then there was nothing for a long time.

But now there was something.

He felt anticipation take hold of his mind and he breathed strongly of the warm air.

He came to a tree where it had rested, holding on with its arms. A few drops of bright blood had begun to dry on the tree and he estimated from their height on the tree that the Knau had been wounded in the shoulder. The ground underneath the tree was wrong somehow. There should be four deep indentations where its legs had dug in, but there were only three, and one of the three was shaped wrong and shallower than the others.

Though he had followed for the better part of half the day, Dargan estimated that he was not far from his farm. The Knau seemed to be following some great curving path that bordered Dargan's land.

It was beginning to grow dark enough to make the trail difficult to read. He would have to make cold camp, for to start a fire might draw the Knau back on him.

He ate the sandwiches that Martha had fixed for him and washed them down with warm, brackish water from his canteen. For a long time he was unable to go to sleep because of the excitement that still gripped him. But finally sleep came and with it—dreams . . .

He was back on the ship again and he relived the time of fire and terror. He heard the screams around him. His father and mother were there too and the flames burned them while he watched. Then a pair of cruel, mechanical legs chased him through metal corridors, always only a step behind. He tore the mechanical legs to bits finally and threw them at Knau ships. The Knau ships fired back and there was flame again, burning, burning . . .

Then he was in the hospital and they were bringing the others in. And he cried unashamedly when they brought in another man whose legs were gone. And he felt a pity for the man, and a pity for himself . . .

He awoke and it was early morning. A light, misty rain had begun to fall and his face was damp and he was cold. He got up and began to move sluggishly down the trail that the Knau had left, fearing that the mist would wash it out. But it was still readable. After a while he came to a stream and drank there and refilled his canteen.

For a time he lost the trail and had to search frantically until he found it again.

By mid-suns he had located the Knau's cave hideaway and he lay below it, hidden in a clump of tall vegetation. The hideaway lay on the hill above him, a small black opening which was shielded at all angles except directly in front. The cave in the hillside was less than a mile from Dargan's home.

Several times he thought he could detect movement in the blackness that marked the cave opening. He knew that the Knau must be lying up there watching to see if it had been followed and he intended to give it ample time to think that it had gotten away without pursuit or had thrown that pursuit off.

The heat of the day passed after a long, bitter time filled with itches that could not be scratched and nonexistent insects that crawled all over Dargan's motionless body. He consoled himself with thoughts of what he would do when he had the upper hand. He hoped, with all hope, that the Knau would not resist and that he could take it unawares. That would make it even better.

He saw it for certain at the moment when dusk became night. It came out of the cave, partially hidden by the outcropping of rock that formed the shelf of the cave. Dargan lay, his body unmoving, his half-seeing eyes fascinated, while the Knau inspected the surrounding terrain for what seemed a very long time.

They're not so ugly, he told himself. *They told us in training that they were the ugliest things alive—but they have a kind of grace to them. I wonder what makes them move so stiffly?*

He watched the Knau move about the ledge of the cave. A crude bandage bound its shoulder and two of the four arms hung limply.

Now. You think you're safe.

He waited for a good hour after it had gone back inside the cave. Then he checked his projectile weapon and began the crawl up the hillside. He went slowly. Time had lost its meaning. *After this is done you have lost the best thing.*

He could see the light when he got around the first bend of the cave. It flickered on the rock walls of the cave. Dargan edged forward very carefully, clearing the way of tiny rocks so that his progress would be noiseless. The mechanical legs dragged soundlessly behind him, muffled in the trousers that covered them.

There was a fire and the Knau lay next to it. Dargan could see its chest move up and down as it gulped for air, its face tightened with pain. Another Knau, a female, was tending the wound, and Dargan felt exultation.

Two!

He swung the gun on target and it made a small noise against the cave floor. Both of the Knau turned to face him and there was a moment of no movement as they stared at him and he stared back. His hands were wet with perspiration. He knew, in that instant, that they were not going to try to do anything—to fight. They were only waiting for him to pull the trigger.

The fire flickered and his eyes became more used to the light. For the first time he saw the male Knau's legs and knew the reason for the strangeness of the tracks. The legs were twisted, and two of the four were missing. A steel aid was belted around the Knau's body, to give it balance, making a tripod for walking. The two legs that were left were cross-hatched with the scars of imperfect plastic surgery.

Dargan pulled himself to his feet, still not taking the gun off the two by the fire. He saw the male glance at the metallic limbs revealed beneath his pants cuff. And he saw the same look come into the Knau's eyes that he knew was in his own.

Then carefully Dargan let the safety down on the pro gun and went to help the female in treating the male.

It should have ended there, of course. For what does one single act, a single forgiveness by two, mean in a war of a hundred years? And it would have ended if the Knau empire had not taken that particular small planet back again and if the particular Knau that Dargan had tracked and spared had not been one of the mighty ones—who make decisions, or at least influence them.

But that Knau was.

But before the Knau empire retook Pasman it meant something too. It meant a small offering of flowers on Dargan's doorstep the morning following the tracking and, in the year before they came again, a friendship. It meant waking without hate in the mornings and it meant the light that came into Martha's eyes.

And Dargan's peace became our peace.

/S/ Samuel Cardings,
Gen. (Ret.) TA
Ambassador to Knau Empire

Star Daughter

SUE WELFORD

enn knew the girl was not of his planet the minute she came in. She was dressed like a native but the way she walked gave her away. She had the lightness of step, the grace of movement that only someone born in low grav could possibly have.

He was sitting in the dim and murky corner of the café, sucking his drink noisily through a straw when the door opened and in she came. He looked up and saw her. He was dazzled for a minute by the beams of the outside lamp carving a pathway of light across the dusty floor. She stepped forward and seemed to emerge from a circle of brightness. Small, long pale hair only half covered by the dark hood of her ankle length cape. The soft folds fell back as she walked towards the bar and he could see she wore something at her belt. It could have been an ornament of some kind, a communicator . . . a weapon?

The café was full. A few locals, a group of traders in the corner stopped off for a rest on their way to some market or other. Benn had seen their fourwheelers parked under the ramshackle awning at the top of the café steps. Machines, like people, needed shade from the merciless glare of the noonday suns.

A group of Skins was sitting at the bar. One of them had his face stuck in that day's news-sheet. The others looked up when the girl came in. Benn couldn't help it but his stomach turned with fear. Most Skins didn't like strangers. For some reason they felt threatened although Benn could never figure out why. Their leader looked the newcomer up and down with a sneer. Benn's stomach lurched again. This group *definitely* didn't like strangers. You didn't need to be a telepath to know that. The leader ran his hand over the tattooed sand-dragon on his scalp, turned away, and ordered another can of drink. A consignment had arrived that morning and the Skins seemed intent on guzzling the lot before anyone else got the chance.

The only seat available was at Benn's table for two so it was there that the girl headed. She reached him and stood for a minute staring. He eyed her from under his brows. His hunch had been right. She definitely wasn't of this planet. Now she was closer he could see her skin. Pale as moonslight, smooth. Her eyes. Green, yet within their depths were amber spirals, staircases of light and shade . . . knowledge that went far beyond *his* horizon.

'Is this anyone's seat?'

She spoke the language perfectly yet there was just a trace of an accent. There was a strange exotic softness to her voice, a kind of lisp that was both attractive and odd at the same time.

He shrugged. 'No.'

'Is it all right if I sit here, then?'

He shrugged again. 'Sure.'

She went to get a drink first. It was then that the Skins *really* noticed her. Benn saw them nudge one another and curl up their lips. Warning bells sounded in his head.

Sand-dragon shifted his stool away as if she had a bad smell. Benn saw her turn and gaze at him. Fearlessly. Maybe they didn't have those kind of people where she came from? Sand-dragon's eyes slid away and he shifted again, so far that he almost knocked one of his mates off his stool.

'Hey,' Sand-dragon growled, still eyeing the girl. 'Shove up, will you.'

His mate growled something back and returned to his news-sheet. The girl got her drink and came back to Benn's table. The Skins' eyes followed her, shifting beneath their lashes like something slithering through dunes. Silently.

The girl smiled at Benn as she sat down and the labyrinth in her eyes twisted and turned and he felt as if he was lost in a golden maze. She tilted her head to one side indicating the Skins at the bar.

'Do you know them?'

He shrugged. 'Sort of.'

He didn't actually *know* them. They just lived in the same settlement that was all. They had all turned and were watching the girl and Benn like toads watching flies. His heart beat like a drum. He had a horrible, sinking feeling that today was going to be a bad one.

The girl smiled. 'Don't look so worried.'

Benn shrugged for the third time. He reckoned she'd think he had some kind of nervous twitch. He swallowed. Her eyes were having a weird effect on him. He felt as if he was flying.

'It's just them,' he said in a low voice. 'They don't like people who are . . .'

She went on gazing at him. 'Different?' She finished the sentence for him.

He nodded. 'But not only that . . . it's people who . . .'

She gazed at him. 'Come from somewhere else?' Her stare seemed to be burning him so he dropped his eyes.

'Yes,' he mumbled.

It sounded crazy. It *was* crazy. How could he explain that some people felt threatened because of no more than that?

'Oh, I see,' she said thoughtfully although he wasn't sure she really did. 'By the way,' she went on. 'My name's Rea. What's yours?'

He told her.

'Bennnnnnn . . .' She rolled the word around then grinned. 'Don't worry about them. I can take care of myself.'

They sat in silence while she finished her drink. There were a million questions he wanted to ask her but something seemed to be stuck in his throat and sensible words wouldn't come out.

What her world was like. How long it had taken to get here. What was she doing in this subterranean hole of a place? Benn wasn't usually like this around girls. He never had any trouble talking to them before. They liked his long hair, his eyes the colour of a desert sky. At least that's what they'd told him in between rattling on about clothes and face paints and the latest music-bands. They usually ended up boring him silly. He'd got a feeling that if he had the chance to get to know Rea she wouldn't bore him silly. She would be able to tell him stories of other worlds, other galaxies, blue oceans and mountains of snow and rivers of ice. Things he had dreamed about for all of his sixteen years.

When she had finished she said, 'Fancy showing me around?'

Benn was fiddling with the table mat, tearing it into little shreds in his struggle to think of something to say that she might find interesting.

He shrugged. 'Show you around? There's not much to see.'

She leaned closer and touched his fingers. Against his, hers were slender and pale and smooth, nails white with little delicate half-moons. They didn't look like the hands of someone who could take care of herself.

'There's those old ruins,' she said.

He put his hood up over his head and stood up. 'All right,' he said. 'If you like.'

At the top of the steps, the noonday suns blazed. The desert, a sea of white sand beneath the yellow sky. The Skins' skim-bikes were parked at crazy angles next to the traders' four-wheelers. A green and red snizzard scurried up the side of the shelter and disappeared down the other side.

'Oh . . . !' Rea went round and scooped it up in her hands. She peered at it closely, examining its jewelled head, the barbed scales, the six clawed feet. She looked at Benn and he saw tiny beads of sweat breaking out on her brow. 'What is it?' she breathed.

He told her.

'It's beautiful . . . look at those colours.'

Benn looked and seemed to be seeing the creature for the very first time. It *was* beautiful. Vivid greens, violent reds catching the rays like fire.

Rea laughed when it jumped from her fingers and shot back up the side of the shelter. 'How does it run up like that without falling off?'

Benn had never really thought about it before. 'It's got special feet I guess,' he said.

Her eyes were shining and she looked thoughtful as she spoke. 'Umm . . . clever.' Then she looked at him. 'Where do you live?'

He indicated the city of mounds a kilometre or so in the distance. 'There.'

'What's it like?' she asked. 'Living under the ground.'

He shrugged. 'It's necessary,' he said.

'Is it nice?' she asked.

Nice? He'd never thought of the burrow as being nice. He shrugged again. 'It's cool,' he said.

'Where is everybody?' she asked, looking round.

'Indoors,' he said. 'You're supposed to be at this time of day.'

'Indoors? They must be mad.' She laughed and ran on ahead. Then she stopped by a step and bent to take off her boots. Then she ran again, sand oozing up between her toes. She held her face to the sky as if the suns' harsh rays wouldn't fry her delicate-looking skin to a frazzle in no time at all. Her hair flew about in the hot wind, whipping around her face like silk. Benn thought she was the most beautiful creature he had ever seen.

'Come on, Benn,' she called. 'You're supposed to be showing me around.'

He showed her the ruined square, the remains of the old school, the derelict fountain.

'Where's the water?' She had climbed over the wall and was swishing around in the sand-filled basin.

'There hasn't been any for years,' he told her.

'Oh,' she said. 'Of course. But why build it, then?' She was obviously puzzled.

'Because there used to be,' he explained. He was feeling better now, more accustomed to the spinning paradox of her eyes. 'Before greenhouse gases partly destroyed the ozone layer and the suns turned half the world to deserts.'

'Oh,' she said. She gazed at him. 'It's really strange, isn't it?'

'What is?' He gazed back at her, fascinated, hypnotized, hardly able to drag away his stare.

'How some worlds have too much water and some don't have enough.'

'Yes,' he said. Then at last he managed to ask her one of those questions he had been dying to ask. 'Where do you come from?'

Her eyes spiralled. 'Oh,' she said. 'You've probably never heard of it.' She lowered her voice. 'Actually I'm not supposed to be here.'

'Why not?'

'I'm *supposed* to . . .' Then she broke off. *They* had rounded the corner and were standing at the end of the street. The Skins. Shoulder to shoulder, legs apart, a few metres away from them. One held the news-sheet rolled loosely in his fingers.

Sand-dragon glared at Benn. 'Get lost or get hurt,' he snarled.

Out of the corner of his eye Benn saw Rea's hand go to her belt.

Suddenly brave, suddenly stupid, he said, 'Why should I?'

The one with the news-sheet stepped forward. 'Because we said so.'

In spite of his wildly beating heart and sweating palms Benn stayed where he was.

Sand-dragon moved so fast Benn didn't even see him coming. He knocked Benn to the ground, kicked his head then shoved his face into the sand. His ears echoed with the rumble of approaching bootsteps, their chant.

'A – lien, A – lien, A – lien.'

Benn struggled to get up but it was hopeless. Sand-dragon had his boot in the small of his back and he couldn't budge. All he could feel were needles of sand blasting his skin, the hard kiss of solid ground against his cheek. His vision darkened and he shut his eyes against the dizziness. He felt himself drift in and out of consciousness. Tears of frustration oozed from under his lids and made little pools on the ground beneath his face. For the first time in his life he had something to fight for and he hadn't been able to do a thing about it. He'd seen the result of Skin beatings. Broken limbs, cracked skulls, innocent strangers ferried out on the saddles of skim-bikes and left to die of dehydration in the desert.

Benn felt a terrible failure, a coward, even though in his heart he knew he would have fought for her if he'd been given the chance. Even if she *had* been able to look after herself.

And when the full force of the boot suddenly disappeared Benn still lay, face down. He felt giddy, disorientated. As if a week had gone by and he hadn't noticed. Even when his balance returned he still didn't dare to look up and see what they had done to her. All about him the silence was like the aftermath of a storm. Even the desert wind had dropped. He lay there, not counting the passing of time.

Eventually he got to his knees. Little pyramids of sand fell away, off his back, his legs, his neck. He rubbed his eyes free of grit and dust. He had expected to see Rea's body but there was nothing there. No one. No Skins. No alien. Nothing. Something fluttered past. The Skin's news-sheet, dancing on the wind like a white bird. He flung out his hand and caught it.

SAVED! was the banner headline. The story underneath read:

> The Government and the Antaran delegation have today announced a package of measures that could be our salvation.

Then in smaller letters:

> In a deal signed yesterday morning, the Antarans have agreed to ship millions of gallons of water through space. 'The desert will bloom again,' the Prime Governor said at an emotional press conference.

Benn scanned the story rapidly. There were pictures of the PG greeting the Antarans. Uncannily they all looked exactly the same as Rea. Female, long pale hair, long limbs. Almost the same as the native people of his planet . . . almost but not quite.

Then there was another headline.

CONCERN GROWS FOR MISSING STAR DAUGHTER

> It has been reported that Rea, the daughter of the leader of the Antaran delegation, has gone missing. 'Against my better judgement she went off to explore on her own,' her mother told our reporter. 'We know there are certain elements in your society who don't take kindly to strangers . . . metamorphs especially.'

Benn drew in his breath. Metamorphs! He'd heard there were some in the universe. He had often thought how great it would be if you could turn yourself into anything you liked.

Then he read the last line.

The Antaran leader stated. 'If anything has happened to my daughter then the deal is off.'

Benn groaned when he read that.

Stupid! Stupid! Stupid! Those stupid ignorant thugs . . . they'd really blown it. Bigotry, violence, hatred—it destroyed everything in the end.

Benn sat down and put his head in his hands. His skull throbbed where the Skin had kicked him.

'Hey, Benn, I'm here!'

Benn scrambled to his feet, spinning on his toes. She was there, on the wall of the fountain, grinning. He stumbled towards her.

'I thought . . . !'

'That they killed me?' She laughed. 'Not a hope.' She stretched out her arm and touched the sleeve of his cloak. 'Are you all right?' Her eyes washed over the bruise on his forehead, the graze on his cheek.

He shook his hair back from his eyes. 'I think so.' He winced and touched his face ruefully.

She frowned in sympathy. 'I'm sorry, it was my fault, I shouldn't have come here.'

He shook his head. 'No, it's all right, honestly.'

Then her eyes widened as he held the news-sheet out to her so she could see the story. 'You changed into something else,' he said, managing a grin. 'You flew away?'

She laughed again, the sound echoing round the empty streets like a bell. 'Not likely,' she said. 'Anyway, why should I? I'm all right as I am.'

She came closer, her eyes spiralling amusement into his face.

He shook his head. 'How did you do it then? There were five of them and one of you.'

'The sandstorm,' she said. 'You must have been out cold not to have noticed it.' She took the device from her belt and showed it to him. 'Disrupter,' she said. Then she grinned. 'I conjured it up. Good, don't you think?'

Benn's mouth fell open. 'Oh,' was all he could say.

'Then I simply walked away,' she went on. 'And they couldn't see where I had gone. Anyway, walking away is always the best thing to do.'

Hmm, Benn thought. He didn't know what life was like on

Antares but here . . . if you walked away from a Skin you were liable to get a blade in your back.

But a sandstorm . . . ? He stared at her. He'd been caught in several. Everything went black . . . sand blinded you, whipped your skin.

'But how could *you* see?' he asked, puzzled.

She blinked at him . . . a transparent membrane descended over her eyes before the outer lid momentarily hid them from his sight. He realized suddenly that was the first time she had closed her eyes since they had met.

She grinned. 'That's another good thing about being an alien, you can see in the dark.' Then her face grew serious. 'I'd better get back, my mum'll kill me.'

He caught her hand as she turned to leave. 'Will you ever come back?'

'Maybe,' she said. Then she laughed again. 'Look out for one of those snizzards. You never know, it just might be me.'

With that she turned and strode off down the street. At the corner she halted. Benn half expected her to turn herself into a bird or a fleet-footed desert cat or even a sandracer in her hurry to get back. But she didn't, she just glanced over her shoulder, waved, then spun on her heel and disappeared round the side of the derelict school building.

Back at the café, the owner was sweeping away the sand that had piled up on the stairs.

'That was short and sweet,' he commented as Benn went past. 'Thank goodness.'

Inside, the Skins were sitting at the counter looking the worse for wear. They hardly gave Benn a glance as he passed them on the way to his table. He could see they were furious, talking in low, hissing voices. Planning their revenge, he imagined. He chuckled to himself as he ordered another drink and sat down.

It hadn't turned out to be such a bad day after all.

Keyhole

MURRAY LEINSTER

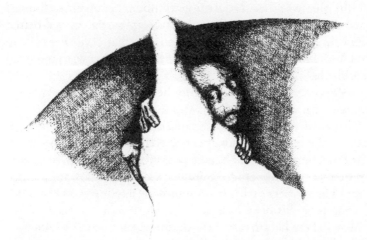

When they brought Butch into the station in Tycho Crater he seemed to shrivel as the gravity coils in the air lock went on. He was impossible to begin with. He was all big eyes and skinny arms and legs, and he was very young and he didn't need air to breathe. Worden saw him as a limp bundle of bristly fur and terrified eyes as his captors handed him over.

'Are you crazy?' demanded Worden angrily. 'Bringing him in like this? Would you take a human baby into eight gravities? Get out of the way!'

He rushed for the nursery that had been made ready for somebody like Butch. There was a rebuilt dwelling-cave on one side. The other side was a human schoolroom. And under the nursery the gravity coils had been turned off so that in that room things had only the weight that was proper to them on the Moon.

The rest of the station had coils to bring everything up to normal weight for Earth. Otherwise the staff of the station would be seasick most of the time. Butch was in the Earth-gravity part of the station when he was delivered, and he couldn't lift a furry spindly paw.

In the nursery, though, it was different. Worden put him on the floor. Worden was the uncomfortable one there—his weight only twenty pounds instead of a normal hundred and sixty. He swayed and reeled as a man does on the Moon without gravity coils to steady him.

But that was the normal thing to Butch. He uncurled himself and suddenly flashed across the nursery to the reconstructed dwelling-cave. It was a pretty good job, that cave. There were the five-foot chipped rocks shaped like dunce caps, found in all residences of Butch's race. There was the rocking stone on its base of other flattened rocks. But the spear stones were fastened down with wire in case Butch got ideas.

Butch streaked in to these familiar objects. He swarmed up one of the dunce-cap stones and locked his arms and legs about its top, clinging close. Then he was still. Worden regarded him. Butch was motionless for minutes, seeming to take in as much as possible of his surroundings without moving even his eyes.

Suddenly his head moved. He took in more of his environment. Then he stirred a third time and seemed to look at Worden with an extraordinary intensity—whether of fear or pleading Worden could not tell.

'Hmm,' said Worden, 'so that's what those stones are for! Perches or beds or roosts, eh? I'm your nurse, fella. We're playing a dirty trick on you but we can't help it.'

He knew Butch couldn't understand, but he talked to him as a man does talk to a dog or a baby. It isn't sensible, but it's necessary.

'We're going to raise you up to be a traitor to your kinfolk,' he said with some grimness. 'I don't like it, but it has to be done. So I'm going to be very kind to you as part of the conspiracy. Real kindness would suggest that I kill you instead—but I can't do that.'

Butch stared at him, unblinking and motionless. He looked something like an Earth monkey but not too much so. He was completely impossible but he looked pathetic.

Worden said bitterly, 'You're in your nursery, Butch. Make yourself at home!'

He went out and closed the door behind him. Outside he glanced at the video screens that showed the interior of the nursery from four different angles. Butch remained still for a long time. Then he slipped down to the floor. This time he ignored the dwelling-cave of the nursery.

He went interestedly to the human-culture part. He examined everything there with his oversized soft eyes. He touched everything with his incredibly handlike tiny paws. But his touches were tentative. Nothing was actually disturbed when he finished his examination.

He went swiftly back to the dunce-cap rock, swarmed up it, locked his arms and legs about it again, blinked rapidly, and seemed to go to sleep. He remained motionless with closed eyes until Worden grew tired of watching him and moved away.

The whole affair was preposterous and infuriating. The first men to land on the Moon knew that it was a dead world. The astronomers had been saying so for a hundred years, and the first and second expeditions to reach Luna from Earth found nothing to contradict the theory.

But a man from the third expedition saw something moving among the upflung rocks of the Moon's landscape and he shot it and the existence of Butch's kind was discovered. It was inconceivable, of course, that there should be living creatures where there was neither air nor water. But Butch's folk did live under exactly those conditions.

The dead body of the first living creature killed on the Moon was carried back to Earth and biologists grew indignant. Even with a specimen to dissect and study they were inclined to insist that there simply wasn't any such creature. So the fourth and fifth and sixth lunar expeditions hunted Butch's relatives very earnestly for further specimens for the advancement of science.

The sixth expedition lost two men whose spacesuits were punctured by what seemed to be weapons while they were hunting. The seventh expedition was wiped out to the last man. Butch's relatives evidently didn't like being shot as biological specimens.

It wasn't until the tenth expedition of four ships established a base in Tycho Crater that men had any assurance of being able to land on the Moon and get away again. Even then the staff of the station felt as if it were under permanent siege.

Worden made his report to Earth. A baby lunar creature had been captured by a tractor party and brought into Tycho Station. A nursery was ready and the infant was there now, alive. He seemed to be uninjured. He seemed not to mind an environment of breathable air for which he had no use. He was active and apparently curious and his intelligence was marked.

There was so far no clue to what he ate—if he ate at all— though he had a mouth like the other collected specimens and the toothlike concretions which might serve as teeth. Worden would, of course, continue to report in detail. At the moment he was allowing Butch to accustom himself to his new surroundings.

He settled down in the recreation room to scowl at his companion scientists and try to think, despite the programme beamed on radar frequency from Earth. He definitely didn't like his job, but he knew that it had to be done. Butch had to be domesticated. He had to be persuaded that he was a human being, so human beings could find out how to exterminate his kind.

It had been observed before, on Earth, that a kitten raised with a litter of puppies came to consider itself a dog and that even pet ducks came to prefer human society to that of their own species. Some talking birds of high intelligence appeared to be convinced that they were people and acted that way. If Butch reacted similarly he would become a traitor to his kind for the benefit of man. And it was necessary!

Men had to have the Moon, and that was all there was to it. Gravity on the Moon was one eighth that of gravity on Earth. A rocket ship could make the Moon voyage and carry a cargo, but no ship yet built could carry fuel for a trip to Mars or Venus if it started out from Earth.

With a fuelling stop on the Moon, though, the matter was simple. Eight drums of rocket fuel on the Moon weighed no more than one on Earth. A ship itself weighed only one eighth as much on Luna. So a rocket that took off from Earth with ten drums of fuel could stop at a fuel base on the Moon and soar away again with two hundred, and sometimes more.

With the Moon as a fuelling base men could conquer the solar system. Without the Moon, mankind was earthbound. Men had to have the Moon!

But Butch's relatives prevented it. By normal experience there could not be life on an airless desert with such monstrous extremes of heat and cold as the Moon's surface experienced. But there was life there. Butch's kinfolk did not breathe oxygen. Apparently they ate it in some mineral combination and it interacted with other minerals in their bodies to yield heat and energy.

Men thought squids peculiar because their bloodstream used copper in place of iron, but Butch and his kindred seemed to have complex carbon compounds in place of both. They were intelligent in some fashion, it was clear. They used tools, they chipped stone, and they had long, needlelike stone crystals which they threw as weapons.

No metals, of course, for lack of fire to smelt them. There couldn't be fire without air. But Worden reflected that in ancient days some experimenters had melted metals and set wood ablaze with mirrors concentrating the heat of the sun. With the naked sunlight of the Moon's surface, not tempered by air and clouds, Butch's folk could have metals if they only contrived mirrors and curved them properly like the mirrors of telescopes on Earth.

Worden had an odd sensation just then. He looked around sharply as if somebody had made a sudden movement. But the video screen merely displayed a comedian back on Earth, wearing a funny hat. Everybody looked at the screen.

As Worden watched, the comedian was smothered in a mass of soapsuds and the studio audience two hundred and thirty thousand miles away squealed and applauded the exquisite humour of the scene. In the Moon station in Tycho Crater somehow it was less than comical.

Worden got up and shook himself. He went to look again at the screens that showed the interior of the nursery. Butch was motionless on the absurd cone-shaped stone. His eyes were closed. He was simply a furry, pathetic little bundle, stolen from the airless wastes outside to be bred into a traitor to his race.

Worden went to his cabin and turned in. Before he slept, though, he reflected that there was still some hope for Butch.

Nobody understood his metabolism. Nobody could guess at what he ate. Butch might starve to death. If he did, he would be lucky. But it was Worden's job to prevent it.

Butch's relatives were at war with men. The tractors that crawled away from the station—they went amazingly fast on the Moon—were watched by big-eyed furry creatures from rock crevices and from behind the boulders that dotted the lunar landscape.

Needle-sharp throwing stones flicked through emptiness. They splintered on the tractor bodies and on the tractor ports, but sometimes they jammed or broke a tread and then the tractor had to stop. Somebody had to go out and clear things or make repairs. And then a storm of throwing stones poured upon him.

A needle-pointed stone, travelling a hundred feet a second, hit just as hard on Luna as it did on Earth—and it travelled further. Spacesuits were punctured. Men died. Now tractor treads were being armoured and special repair-suits were under construction, made of hardened steel plates. Men who reached the Moon in rocket ships were having to wear armour like medieval knights and men-at-arms! There was a war on. A traitor was needed. And Butch was elected to be that traitor.

When Worden went into the nursery again—the days and nights on the Moon are two weeks long apiece, so men ignored such matters inside the station—Butch leaped for the dunce-cap stone and clung to its top. He had been fumbling around the rocking stone. It still swayed back and forth on its plate. Now he seemed to try to squeeze himself to unity with the stone spire, his eyes staring enigmatically at Worden.

'I don't know whether we'll get anywhere or not,' said Worden conversationally. 'Maybe you'll put up a fight if I touch you. But we'll see.'

He reached out his hand. The small furry body—neither hot nor cold but the temperature of the air in the station—resisted desperately. But Butch was very young. Worden peeled him loose and carried him across the room to the human school-room equipment. Butch curled up, staring fearfully.

'I'm playing dirty', said Worden, 'by being nice to you, Butch. Here's a toy.'

Butch stirred in his grasp. His eyes blinked rapidly. Worden put him down and wound up a tiny mechanical toy. It moved. Butch watched intently. When it stopped he looked back at Worden. Worden wound it up again. Again Butch watched. When it ran down a second time the tiny handlike paw reached out.

With an odd tentativeness, Butch tried to turn the winding key. He was not strong enough. After an instant he went loping across to the dwelling-cave. The winding key was a metal ring. Butch fitted that over a throw-stone point, and twisted the toy about. He wound it up. He put the toy on the floor and watched it work. Worden's jaw dropped.

'Brains!' he said wryly. 'Too bad, Butch! You know the principle of the lever. At a guess you've an eight-year-old human brain! I'm sorry for you, fella!'

At the regular communication hour he made his report to Earth. Butch was teachable. He only had to see a thing done once—or at most twice—to be able to repeat the motions involved.

'And', said Worden, carefully detached, 'he isn't afraid of me now. He understands that I intend to be friendly. While I was carrying him I talked to him. He felt the vibration of my chest from my voice.

'Just before I left him I picked him up and talked to him again. He looked at my mouth as it moved and put his paw on my chest to feel the vibrations. I put his paw at my throat. The vibrations are clearer there. He seemed fascinated. I don't know how you'd rate his intelligence but it's above that of a human baby.'

Then he said with even greater detachment, 'I am disturbed. If you must know, I don't like the idea of exterminating his kind. They have tools, they have intelligence. I think we should try to communicate with them in some way—try to make friends—stop killing them for dissection.'

The communicator was silent for the second and a half it took his voice to travel to Earth and the second and a half it took to come back. Then the recording clerk's voice said briskly, 'Very good, Mr Worden! Your voice was very clear!'

Worden shrugged his shoulders. The lunar station in Tycho was a highly official enterprise. The staff on the Moon had to be competent—and besides, political appointees did not want to risk their precious lives—but the Earth end of the business of the Space Exploration Bureau was run by the sort of people who do get on official payrolls. Worden felt sorry for Butch—and for Butch's relatives.

In a later lesson session Worden took an empty coffee tin into the nursery. He showed Butch that its bottom vibrated when he spoke into it, just as his throat did. Butch experimented busily. He discovered for himself that it had to be pointed at Worden to catch the vibrations.

Worden was unhappy. He would have preferred Butch to be a little less rational. But for the next lesson he presented Butch with a really thin metal diaphragm stretched across a hoop. Butch caught the idea at once.

When Worden made his next report to Earth he felt angry.

'Butch has no experience of sound as we have, of course,' he said curtly. 'There's no air on the Moon. But sound travels through rocks. He's sensitive to vibrations in solid objects just as a deaf person can feel the vibrations of a dance floor if the music is loud enough.

'Maybe Butch's kind has a language or a code of sounds sent through the rock underfoot. They do communicate somehow! And if they've brains and a means of communication they aren't animals and shouldn't be exterminated for our convenience!'

He stopped. The chief biologist of the Space Exploration Bureau was at the other end of the communication beam then. After the necessary pause for distance his voice came blandly.

'Splendid, Worden! Splendid reasoning! But we have to take the longer view. Exploration of Mars and Venus is a very popular idea with the public. If we are to have funds—and the appropriations come up for a vote shortly—we have to make progress towards the nearer planets. The public demands it. Unless we can begin work on a refuelling base on the Moon, public interest will cease!'

Worden said urgently, 'Suppose I send some pictures of Butch? He's very human, sir! He's extraordinarily appealing! He has personality! A reel or two of Butch at his lessons ought to be popular!'

Again that irritating wait while his voice travelled a quarter-million miles at the speed of light and the wait for the reply.

'The—ah—lunar creatures, Worden,' said the chief biologist regretfully, 'have killed a number of men who have been publicized as martyrs to science. We cannot give favourable publicity to creatures that have killed men!' Then he added blandly, 'But you are progressing splendidly, Worden—*splendidly*! Carry on!'

His image faded from the video screen. Worden said naughty words as he turned away. He'd come to like Butch. Butch trusted him. Butch now slid down from that crazy perch of his and came rushing to his arms every time he entered the nursery.

Butch was ridiculously small—no more than eighteen inches high. He was preposterously light and fragile in his nursery, where only Moon gravity was obtained. And Butch was such an earnest little creature, so soberly absorbed in everything that Worden showed him!

He was still fascinated by the phenomena of sound. Humming or singing—even Worden's humming and singing—entranced him. When Worden's lips moved now Butch struck an attitude and held up the hoop diaphragm with a tiny finger pressed to it to catch the vibrations Worden's voice made.

Now, too, when he grasped an idea Worden tried to convey, he tended to swagger. He became more human in his actions with every session of human contact. Once, indeed, Worden looked at the video screens which spied on Butch and saw him—all alone—solemnly going through every gesture and every movement Worden had made. He was pretending to give a lesson to an imaginary still-tinier companion. He was pretending to be Worden, apparently for his own satisfaction!

Worden felt a lump in his throat. He was enormously fond of the little mite. It was painful that he had just left Butch to help in the construction of a vibrator-microphone device which would transfer his voice to rock vibrations and simultaneously pick up any other vibrations that might be made in return.

If the members of Butch's race did communicate by tapping on rocks, or the like, men could eavesdrop on them—could locate them, could detect ambushes in preparation, and apply mankind's deadly military countermeasures.

Worden hoped the gadget wouldn't work. But it did. When he put it on the floor of the nursery and spoke into the microphone, Butch did feel the vibrations underfoot. He recognized their identity with the vibrations he'd learned to detect in air.

He made a skipping, exultant hop and jump. It was plainly the uttermost expression of satisfaction. And then his tiny foot pattered and scratched furiously on the floor. It made a peculiar scratchy tapping noise which the microphone picked up. Butch watched Worden's face, making the sounds which were like highly elaborated footfalls.

'No dice, Butch,' said Worden unhappily. 'I can't understand it. But it looks as if you've started your treason already. This'll help wipe out some of your folks.'

He reported it reluctantly to the head of the station. Microphones were immediately set into the rocky crater floor outside the station and others were made ready for exploring parties to use for the detection of Moon creatures near them. Oddly enough, the microphones by the station yielded results right away.

It was near sunset. Butch had been captured near the middle of the three-hundred-and-thirty-four-hour lunar day. In all the hours between—a week by Earth time—he had had no nourishment of any sort. Worden had conscientiously offered him every edible and inedible substance in the station. Then at least one sample of every mineral in the station collection.

Butch regarded them all with interest but without appetite. Worden—liking Butch—expected him to die of starvation and thought it a good idea. Better than encompassing the death of all his race, anyhow. And it did seem to him that Butch was beginning to show a certain sluggishness, a certain lack of bounce and energy. He thought it was weakness from hunger.

Sunset progressed. Yard by yard, fathom by fathom, half mile by half mile, the shadows of the miles-high western walls of Tycho crept across the crater floor. There came a time when only the central hump had sunlight. Then the shadow began to creep up the eastern walls. Presently the last thin jagged line of light would vanish and the colossal cup of the crater would be filled to overflowing with the night.

Worden watched the incandescent sunlight growing even narrower on the cliffs. He would see no other sunlight for two weeks' Earth time. Then abruptly an alarm bell rang. It clanged stridently, furiously. Doors hissed shut, dividing the station into airtight sections.

Loudspeakers snapped, '*Noises in the rock outside! Sounds like Moon creatures talking nearby! They may plan an attack! Everybody into spacesuits and get guns ready!*'

At just that instant the last thin sliver of sunshine disappeared. Worden thought instantly of Butch. There was no spacesuit to fit him. Then he grimaced a little. Butch didn't need a spacesuit.

Worden got into the clumsy outfit. The lights dimmed. The harsh airless space outside the station was suddenly bathed in light. The multimillion-lumen beam, made to guide rocket ships to a landing even at night, was turned on to expose any creatures with designs on its owners. It was startling to see how little space was really lighted by the beam and how much of stark blackness spread beyond.

The loudspeaker snapped again, '*Two Moon creatures! Running away! They're zigzagging! Anybody who wants to take a shot—*' The voice paused. It didn't matter. Nobody is a crack shot in a spacesuit. '*They left something behind!*' said the voice in the loudspeaker. It was sharp and uneasy.

'I'll take a look at that,' said Worden. His own voice startled him but he was depressed. 'I've got a hunch what it is.'

Minutes later he went out through the air lock. He moved lightly despite the cumbrous suit he wore. There were two other staff members with him. All three were armed and the search-light beam stabbed here and there erratically to expose any relative of Butch who might try to approach them in the darkness.

With the light at his back Worden could see that trillions of stars looked down upon Luna. The zenith was filled with infinitesimal specks of light of every conceivable colour. The familiar constellations burned ten times as brightly as on Earth. And Earth itself hung nearly overhead. It was three-quarters full—a monstrous bluish giant in the sky, four times the Moon's diameter, its ice caps and continents mistily to be seen.

Worden went forebodingly to the object left behind by Butch's kin. He wasn't much surprised when he saw what it was. It was a rocking stone on its plate with a fine impalpable dust on the plate, as if something had been crushed under the egg-shaped upper stone acting as a mill.

Worden said sourly into his helmet microphone, 'It's a present for Butch. His kinfolk know he was captured alive. They suspect he's hungry. They've left some grub for him of the kind he wants or needs most.'

That was plainly what it was. It did not make Worden feel proud. A baby—Butch—had been kidnapped by the enemies of its race. That baby was a prisoner and its captors would have nothing with which to feed it. So someone, greatly daring— Worden wondered sombrely if it was Butch's father and mother—had risked their lives to leave food for him with a rocking stone to tag it for recognition as food.

'It's a dirty shame,' said Worden bitterly. 'All right! Let's carry it back. Careful not to spill the powdered stuff!'

His lack of pride was emphasized when Butch fell upon the unidentified powder with marked enthusiasm. Tiny pinch by tiny pinch Butch consumed it with an air of vast satisfaction. Worden felt ashamed.

'You're getting treated pretty rough, Butch,' said Worden. 'What I've already learned from you will cost a good many hundred of your folks' lives. And they're taking chances to feed you! I'm making you a traitor and myself a scoundrel.'

Butch thoughtfully held up the hoop diaphragm to catch the voice vibrations in the air. He was small and furry and absorbed. He decided that he could pick up sounds better from the rock underfoot. He pressed the communicator microphone on Worden. He waited.

'*No!*' said Worden roughly. 'Your people are too human. Don't let me find out any more, Butch. Be smart and play dumb!'

But Butch didn't. It wasn't very long before Worden was teaching him to read. Oddly, though, the rock microphones that had given the alarm at the station didn't help the tractor parties at all. Butch's kinfolk seemed to vanish from the neighbourhood of the station altogether. Of course if that kept up, the construction of a fuel base could be begun and the actual extermination of the species carried out later. But the reports on Butch were suggesting other possibilities.

'If your folks stay vanished,' Worden told Butch, 'it'll be all right for a while—and only for a while. I'm being urged to try to get you used to Earth gravity. If I succeed, they'll want you on Earth in a zoo. And if that works—why, they'll be sending other expeditions to get more of your kinfolk to put in other zoos.'

Butch watched Worden, motionless.

'And also'—Worden's tone was very grim—'there's some miniature mining machinery coming up by the next rocket. I'm supposed to see if you can learn to run it.'

Butch made scratching sounds on the floor. It was unintelligible of course, but it was an expression of interest at least. Butch seemed to enjoy the vibrations of Worden's voice, just as a dog likes to have his master talk to him. Worden grunted.

'We humans class you as an animal, Butch. We tell ourselves that all the animal world should be subject to us. Animals should work for us. If you act too smart we'll hunt down all your relatives and set them to work digging minerals for us. You'll be with them. But I don't want you to work your heart out in a mine, Butch! It's wrong!'

Butch remained quite still. Worden thought sickishly of small furry creatures like Butch driven to labour in airless mines in the Moon's frigid depths. With guards in spacesuits watching lest any try to escape to the freedom they'd known before the coming of men. With guns mounted against revolt. With punishments for rebellion or weariness.

It wouldn't be unprecedented. The Indians in Cuba when the Spanish came ... Black slavery in both Americas ... concentration camps ...

Butch moved. He put a small furry paw on Worden's knee. Worden scowled at him.

'Bad business,' he said harshly. 'I'd rather not get fond of you. You're a likeable little cuss but your race is doomed. The trouble is that you didn't bother to develop a civilization. And if you had, I suspect we'd have smashed it. We humans aren't what you'd call admirable.'

Butch went over to the blackboard. He took a piece of pastel chalk—ordinary chalk was too hard for his Moon-gravity muscles to use—and soberly began to make marks on the slate. The marks formed letters. The letters made words. The words made sense.

YOU, wrote Butch quite incredibly in neat pica lettering, GOOD FRIEND.

He turned his head to stare at Worden. Worden went white. 'I haven't taught you those words, Butch!' he said very quietly. 'What's up?'

He'd forgotten that his words, to Butch, were merely vibrations in the air or in the floor. He'd forgotten they had no meaning. But Butch seemed to have forgotten it too. He marked soberly:

MY FRIEND GET SPACESUIT. He looked at Worden and marked once more. TAKE ME OUT. I COME BACK WITH YOU.

He looked at Worden with large incongruously soft and appealing eyes. And Worden's brain seemed to spin inside his skull. After a long time Butch printed again—YES.

Then Worden sat very still indeed. There was only Moon gravity in the nursery and he weighed only one eighth as much as on Earth. But he felt very weak. Then he felt grim.

'Not much else to do, I suppose,' he said slowly. 'But I'll have to carry you through Earth gravity to the air lock.'

He got to his feet. Butch made a little leap into his arms. He curled up there, staring at Worden's face. Just before Worden stepped through the door Butch reached up a skinny paw and caressed Worden's cheek tentatively.

'Here we go!' said Worden. 'The idea was for you to be a traitor. I wonder—'

But with Butch a furry ball, suffering in the multiplied weight Earth gravity imposed upon him, Worden made his way to the air lock. He donned a spacesuit. He went out.

It was near sunrise then. A long time had passed and Earth was now in its last quarter, and the very highest peak of all that made up the crater wall glowed incandescent in the sunshine. But the stars were still quite visible and very bright. Worden walked away from the station, guided by the Earth-shine on the ground underfoot.

Three hours later he came back. Butch skipped and hopped beside his spacesuited figure. Behind them came two other figures. They were smaller than Worden but much larger than Butch. They were skinny and furry and they carried a burden. A mile from the station he switched on his suit radio. He called. A startled voice answered in his earphones.

'It's Worden,' he said drily. 'I've been out for a walk with Butch. We visited his family and I've a couple of his cousins with me. They want to pay a visit and present some gifts. Will you let us in without shooting?'

There were exclamations. There was confusion. But Worden went on steadily towards the station while another high peak glowed in sunrise light and a third seemed to burst into incandescence. Dawn was definitely on the way.

The air-lock door opened. The party from the airless Moon went in. When the air-lock filled, though, and the gravity coils went on, Butch and his relatives became helpless. They had to be carried to the nursery. There they uncurled themselves and blinked enigmatically at the men who crowded into the room where gravity was normal for the Moon and at the other men who stared in the door.

'I've got a sort of message,' said Worden. 'Butch and his relatives want to make a deal with us. You'll notice that they've put themselves at our mercy. We can kill all three of them. But they want to make a deal.'

The head of the station said uncomfortably, 'You've managed two-way communication, Worden?'

'*I* haven't,' Worden told him. '*They* have. They've proved to me that they've brains equal to ours. They've been treated as animals and shot as specimens. They've fought back—naturally! But they want to make friends. They say that we can never use the Moon except in spacesuits and in stations like this, and they could never take Earth's gravity. So there's no need for us to be enemies. We can help each other.'

The head of the station said drily, 'Plausible enough, but we have to act under orders, Worden. Did you explain that?'

'They know,' said Worden. 'So they've got set to defend themselves if necessary. They've set up smelters to handle metals. They get the heat by sun mirrors, concentrating sunlight. They've even begun to work with gases held in containers. They're not far along with electronics yet, but they've got the theoretic knowledge and they don't need vacuum tubes. They live in a vacuum. They can defend themselves from now on.'

The head said mildly, 'I've watched Butch, you know, Worden. And you don't look crazy. But if this sort of thing is sprung on the armed forces on Earth there'll be trouble. They've been arguing for armed rocket ships. If your friends start a real war for defence—if they can—maybe rocket warships will be the answer.'

Worden nodded.

'Right. But our rockets aren't so good that they can fight this far from a fuel store, and there couldn't be one on the Moon with all of Butch's kinfolk civilized—as they nearly are now and as they certainly will be within the next few weeks. Smart people, these cousins and such of Butch!'

'I'm afraid they'll have to prove it,' said the head. 'Where'd they get this sudden surge in culture?'

'From us,' said Worden. 'Smelting from me, I think. Metallurgy and mechanical engineering from the tractor mechanics. Geology—call it lunology here—mostly from you.'

'How's that?' demanded the head.

'Think of something you'd like Butch to do,' said Worden grimly, 'and then watch him.'

The head stared and then looked at Butch. Butch—small and furry and swaggering—stood up and bowed profoundly from the waist. One paw was placed where his heart could be. The other made a grandiose sweeping gesture. He straightened up and strutted, then climbed swiftly into Worden's lap and put a skinny furry arm about his neck.

'That bow', said the head, very pale, 'is what I had in mind. You mean—'

'Just so,' said Worden. 'Butch's ancestors had no air to make noises in for speech. So they developed telepathy. In time, to be sure, they worked out something like music—sounds carried through rock. But like our music it doesn't carry meaning. They communicate directly from mind to mind. Only we can't pick up communications from them and they can from us.'

'They read our minds!' said the head. He licked his lips. 'And when we first shot them for specimens, they were trying to communicate. Now they fight.'

'Naturally,' said Worden. 'Wouldn't we? They've been picking our brains. They can put up a terrific battle now. They could wipe out this station without trouble. They let us stay so they could learn from us. Now they want to trade.'

'We have to report to Earth,' said the head slowly, 'but—'

'They brought along some samples,' said Worden. 'They'll swap diamonds, weight for weight, for records. They like our music. They'll trade emeralds for textbooks—they can read now! And they'll set up an atomic pile and swap plutonium for other things they'll think of later. Trading on that basis should be cheaper than a war!'

'Yes,' said the head. 'It should. That's the sort of argument men will listen to. But how—'

'Butch,' said Worden ironically. 'Just Butch! We didn't capture him—they planted him on us! He stayed in the station and picked our brains and relayed the stuff to his relatives. We wanted to learn about them, remember? It's like the story of the psychologist . . .'

There's a story about a psychologist who was studying the intelligence of a chimpanzee. He led the chimp into a room full of toys, went out, closed the door and put his eye to the keyhole to see what the chimp was doing. He found himself gazing into a glittering, interested brown eye only inches from his own. The chimp was looking through the keyhole to see what the psychologist was doing.

The Streets of Ashkelon

HARRY HARRISON

Somewhere above, hidden by the eternal clouds of Wesker's World, a thunder rumbled and grew. Trader John Garth stopped when he heard it, his boots sinking slowly into the muck, and cupped his good ear to catch the sound. It swelled and waned in the thick atmosphere, growing louder.

'That noise is the same as the noise of your sky-ship,' Itin said, with stolid Wesker logicality, slowly pulverizing the idea in his mind and turning over the bits one by one for closer examination. 'But your ship is still sitting where you landed it. It must be, even though we cannot see it, because you are the only one who can operate it. And even if anyone else could operate it we would have heard it rising into the sky. Since we did not, and if this sound is a sky-ship sound, then it must mean . . .'

'Yes, another ship,' Garth said, too absorbed in his own thoughts to wait for the laborious Weskerian chains of logic to clank their way through to the end. Of course it was another spacer, it had been only a matter of time before one appeared, and undoubtedly this one was homing on the S.S. radar reflector as he had done. His own ship would show up clearly on the newcomer's screen and they would probably set down as close to it as they could.

'You better go ahead, Itin,' he said. 'Use the water so you can get to the village quickly. Tell everyone to get back into the swamps, well clear of the hard ground. That ship is landing on instruments and anyone underneath at touchdown is going to be cooked.'

This immediate threat was clear enough to the little Wesker amphibian. Before Garth finished speaking Itin's ribbed ears had folded like a bat's wing and he slipped silently into the nearby canal. Garth squelched on through the mud, making as good time as he could over the clinging surface. He had just reached the fringes of the village clearing when the rumbling grew to a head-splitting roar and the spacer broke through the low-hanging layer of clouds above. Garth shielded his eyes from the down-reaching tongue of flame and examined the growing form of the grey-black ship with mixed feelings.

After almost a standard year on Wesker's World he had to fight down a longing for human companionship of any kind. While this buried fragment of herd-spirit chattered for the rest of the monkey tribe, his trader's mind was busily drawing a line under a column of figures and adding up the total. This could very well be another trader's ship, and if it were his monopoly of the Wesker trade was at an end. Then again, this might not be a trader at all, which was the reason he stayed in the shelter of the giant fern and loosened his gun in its holster.

The ship baked dry a hundred square metres of mud, the roaring blast died, and the landing feet crunched down through the crackling crust. Metal creaked and settled into place while the cloud of smoke and steam slowly drifted lower in the humid air.

'Garth—you native-cheating extortionist—where are you?' the ship's speaker boomed. The lines of the spacer had looked only slightly familiar, but there was no mistaking the rasping tones of that voice. Garth wore a smile when he stepped out into the open and whistled shrilly through two fingers. A directional microphone ground out of its casing on the ship's fin and turned in his direction.

'What are you doing here, Singh?' he shouted towards the mike. 'Too crooked to find a planet of your own and have to come here to steal an honest trader's profits?'

'Honest!' the amplified voice roared. 'This from the man who has been in more jails than cathouses—and that a goodly number in itself, I do declare. Sorry, friend of my youth, but I cannot join you in exploiting this aboriginal pesthole. I am on course to a more fairly atmosphered world where a fortune is waiting to be made. I only stopped here since an opportunity presented to turn an honest credit by running a taxi service. I bring you friendship, the perfect companionship, a man in a different line of business who might help you in yours. I'd come out and say hello myself, except I would have to decon for biologicals. I'm cycling the passenger through the lock so I hope you won't mind helping with his luggage.'

At least there would be no other trader on the planet now, that worry was gone. But Garth still wondered what sort of passenger would be taking one-way passage to an uninhabited world. And what was behind that concealed hint of merriment in Singh's voice? He walked around to the far side of the spacer where the ramp had dropped, and looked up at the man in the cargo lock who was wrestling ineffectually with a large crate. The man turned towards him and Garth saw the clerical dog-collar and knew just what it was Singh had been chuckling about.

'What are you doing here?' Garth asked; in spite of his attempt at self control he snapped the words. If the man noticed this he ignored it, because he was still smiling and putting out his hand as he came down the ramp.

'Father Mark,' he said, 'of the Missionary Society of Brothers. I'm very pleased to . . .'

'I said what are you doing here?' Garth's voice was under control now, quiet and cold. He knew what had to be done, and it must be done quickly or not at all.

'That should be obvious,' Father Mark said, his good nature still unruffled. 'Our missionary society has raised funds to send spiritual emissaries to alien worlds for the first time. I was lucky enough . . .'

'Take your luggage and get back into the ship. You're not wanted here and have no permission to land. You'll be a liability and there is no one on Wesker to take care of you. Get back into the ship.'

'I don't know who you are, sir, or why you are lying to me,' the priest said. He was still calm but the smile was gone. 'But I have studied galactic law and the history of this planet very well. There are no diseases or beasts here that I should have any particular fear of. It is also an open planet, and until the Space Survey changes that status I have as much right to be here as you do.'

The man was of course right, but Garth couldn't let him know that. He had been bluffing, hoping the priest didn't know his rights. But he did. There was only one distasteful course left for him, and he had better do it while there was still time.

'Get back in that ship,' he shouted, not hiding his anger now. With a smooth motion his gun was out of the holster and the pitted black muzzle only inches from the priest's stomach. The man's face turned white, but he did not move.

'What the hell are you doing, Garth!' Singh's shocked voice grated from the speaker. 'The guy paid his fare and you have no rights at all to throw him off the planet.'

'I have this right,' Garth said, raising his gun and sighting between the priest's eyes. 'I give him thirty seconds to get back aboard the ship or I pull the trigger.'

'Well I think you are either off your head or playing a joke,' Singh's exasperated voice rasped down at them. 'If a joke, it is in bad taste, and either way you're not getting away with it. Two can play at that game, only I can play it better.'

There was the rumble of heavy bearings and the remote-controlled four-gun turret on the ship's side rotated and pointed at Garth. 'Now—down gun and give Father Mark a hand with the luggage,' the speaker commanded, a trace of humour back in the voice now. 'As much as I would like to help, old friend, I cannot. I feel it is time you had a chance to talk to the father; after all, I have had the opportunity of speaking with him all the way from Earth.'

Garth jammed the gun back into the holster with an acute feeling of loss. Father Mark stepped forward, the winning smile back now and a Bible taken from a pocket of his robe, in his raised hand. 'My son,' he said.

'I'm not your son,' was all Garth could choke out as defeat welled up in him. His fist drew back as the anger rose, and the best he could do was open the fist so he struck only with the flat of his hand. Still the blow sent the priest crashing to the ground and fluttered the pages of the book splattering into the thick mud.

Itin and the other Weskers had watched everything with seemingly emotionless interest, and Garth made no attempt to answer their unspoken questions. He started towards his house, but turned back when he saw they were still unmoving.

'A new man has come,' he told them. 'He will need help with the things he has brought. If he doesn't have any place for them, you can put them in the big warehouse until he has a place of his own.'

He watched them waddle across the clearing towards the ship, then went inside and gained a certain satisfaction from slamming the door hard enough to crack one of the panes. There was an equal amount of painful pleasure in breaking out one of the remaining bottles of Irish whiskey that he had been saving for a special occasion. Well this was special enough, though not really what he had had in mind. The whiskey was good and burned away some of the bad taste in his mouth, but not all of it. If his tactics had worked, success would have justified everything. But he had failed and in addition to the pain of failure there was the acute feeling that he had made a horse's ass out of himself.

Singh had blasted off without any goodbyes. There was no telling what sense he had made of the whole matter, though he would surely carry some strange stories back to the traders' lodge. Well, that could be worried about the next time Garth signed in. Right now he had to go about setting things right with the missionary. Squinting out through the rain he saw the man struggling to erect a collapsible tent while the entire population of the village stood in ordered ranks and watched. Naturally none of them offered to help.

By the time the tent was up and the crates and boxes stowed inside it the rain had stopped. The level of fluid in the bottle was a good bit lower and Garth felt more like facing up to the unavoidable meeting. In truth, he was looking forward to talking to the man. This whole nasty business aside, after an entire solitary year any human companionship looked good.

Will you join me now for dinner. John Garth, he wrote on the back of an old invoice. But maybe the guy was too frightened to come? Which was no way to start any kind of relationship. Rummaging under the bunk, he found a box that was big enough and put his pistol inside. Itin was of course waiting outside the door when he opened it, since this was his tour as Knowledge Collector. He handed him the note and box.

'Would you take these to the new man,' he said.

'Is the new man's name New Man?' Itin asked.

'No, it's not!' Garth snapped. 'His name is Mark. But I'm only asking you to deliver this, not get involved in conversation.'

As always when he lost his temper, the literal minded Weskers won the round. 'You are not asking for conversation,' Itin said slowly, 'but Mark may ask for conversation. And others will ask me his name, if I do not know his na—'

The voice cut off as Garth slammed the door. This didn't work in the long run either because next time he saw Itin—a day, a week, or even a month later—the monologue would be picked up on the very word it had ended and the thought rambled out to its last frayed end. Garth cursed under his breath and poured water over a pair of the tastier concentrates that he had left.

'Come in,' he said when there was a quiet knock on the door. The priest entered and held out the box with the gun.

'Thank you for the loan, Mr Garth, I appreciate the spirit that made you send it. I have no idea of what caused the unhappy affair when I landed, but I think it would be best forgotten if we are going to be on this planet together for any length of time.'

'Drink?' Garth asked, taking the box and pointing to the bottle on the table. He poured two glasses full and handed one to the priest. 'That's about what I had in mind, but I still owe you an explanation of what happened out there.' He scowled into his glass for a second, then raised it to the other man. 'It's a big universe and I guess we have to make out as best we can. Here's to Sanity.'

'God be with you,' Father Mark said, and raised his glass as well.

'Not with me or with this planet,' Garth said firmly. 'And that's the crux of the matter.' He half-drained the glass and sighed.

'Do you say that to shock me?' the priest asked with a smile. 'I assure you it doesn't.'

'Not intended to shock. I meant it quite literally. I suppose I'm what you would call an atheist, so revealed religion is no concern of mine. While these natives, simple and unlettered stone-age types that they are, have managed to come this far with no superstitions or traces of deism whatsoever. I had hoped that they might continue that way.'

'What are you saying?' the priest frowned. 'Do you mean they have no gods, no belief in the hereafter? They must die . . . ?'

'Die they do, and to dust returneth like the rest of the animals. They have thunder, trees, and water without having thunder-gods, tree sprites, or water nymphs. They have no ugly little gods, taboos, or spells to hag-ride and limit their lives. They are the only primitive people I have ever encountered that are completely free of superstition and appear to be much happier and sane because of it. I just wanted to keep them that way.'

'You wanted to keep them from God—from salvation?' the priest's eyes widened and he recoiled slightly.

'No,' Garth said. 'I wanted to keep them from superstition until they knew more and could think about it realistically without being absorbed and perhaps destroyed by it.'

'You're being insulting to the Church, sir, to equate it with superstition . . .'

'Please,' Garth said, raising his hand. 'No theological arguments. I don't think your society footed the bill for this trip just to attempt a conversion on me. Just accept the fact that my beliefs have been arrived at through careful thought over a period of years, and no amount of undergraduate metaphysics will change them. I'll promise not to try and convert you—if you will do the same for me.'

'Agreed, Mr Garth. As you have reminded me, my mission here is to save these souls, and that is what I must do. But why should my work disturb you so much that you try and keep me from landing? Even threaten me with your gun, and—' the priest broke off and looked into his glass.

'And even slug you?' Garth asked, suddenly frowning. 'There was no excuse for that, and I would like to say that I'm sorry. Plain bad manners and an even worse temper. Live alone long enough and you find yourself doing that kind of thing.'

He brooded down at his big hands where they lay on the table, reading memories into the scars and callouses patterned there. 'Let's just call it frustration, for lack of a better word. In your business you must have had a lot of chance to peep into the darker places in men's minds and you should know a bit about motives and happiness. I have had too busy a life to ever consider settling down and raising a family, and right up until recently I never missed it. Maybe leakage radiation is softening up my brain, but I had begun to think of these furry and fishy Weskers as being a little like my own children, that I was somehow responsible to them.'

'We are all His children,' Father Mark said quietly.

'Well, here are some of His children that can't even imagine His existence,' Garth said, suddenly angry at himself for allowing gentler emotions to show through. Yet he forgot himself at once, leaning forward with the intensity of his feelings. 'Can't you realize the importance of this? Live with these Weskers awhile and you will discover a simple and happy life that matches the state of grace you people are always talking about. They get *pleasure* from their lives—and cause no one pain. By circumstance they have evolved on an almost barren world, so have never had a chance to grow out of a physical stone age culture. But mentally they are our match—or perhaps better. They have all learned my language so I can easily explain the many things they want to know. Knowledge and the gaining of knowledge gives them real satisfaction. They tend to be exasperating at times because every new fact must be related to the structure of all other things, but the more they learn the faster this process becomes. Someday they are going to be man's equal in every way, perhaps surpass us. If—would you do me a favour?'

'Whatever I can.'

'Leave them alone. Or teach them if you must—history and science, philosophy, law, anything that will help them face the realities of the greater universe they never even knew existed before. But don't confuse them with your hatreds and pain, guilt, sin, and punishment. Who knows the harm—'

'You are being insulting, sir!' the priest said, jumping to his feet. The top of his grey head barely came to the massive spaceman's chin, yet he showed no fear in defending what he believed. Garth, standing now himself, was no longer the penitent. They faced each other in anger, as men have always stood, unbending in the defence of that which they think right.

'Yours is the insult,' Garth shouted. 'The incredible egotism to feel that your derivative little mythology, differing only slightly from the thousands of others that still burden men, can do anything but confuse their still fresh minds! Don't you realize that they believe in truth—and have never heard of such a thing as a lie. They have not been trained yet to understand that other kinds of minds can think differently from theirs. Will you spare them this . . . ?'

'I will do my duty which is His will, Mr Garth. These are God's creatures here, and they have souls. I cannot shirk my duty, which is to bring them His word, so that they may be saved and enter into the kingdom of heaven.'

When the priest opened the door the wind caught it and blew it wide. He vanished into the stormswept darkness and the door swung back and forth and a splatter of raindrops blew in. Garth's boots left muddy footprints when he closed the door, shutting out the sight of Itin sitting patiently and uncomplaining in the storm, hoping only that Garth might stop for a moment and leave with him some of the wonderful knowledge of which he had so much.

By unspoken consent that first night was never mentioned again. After a few days of loneliness, made worse because each knew of the other's proximity, they found themselves talking on carefully neutral grounds.

Garth slowly packed and stowed away his stock and never admitted that his work was finished and he could leave at any time. He had a fair amount of interesting drugs and botanicals that would fetch a good price. And the Wesker Artefacts were sure to create a sensation in the sophisticated galactic market. Crafts on the planet here had been limited before his arrival, mostly pieces of carving painfully chipped into the hard wood with fragments of stone. He had supplied tools and a stock of raw metal from his own supplies, nothing more than that. In a few months the Weskers had not only learned to work with the new materials, but had translated their own designs and forms into the most alien—but most beautiful—artefacts that he had ever seen. All he had to do was release these on the market to create a primary demand, then return for a new supply. The Weskers wanted only books and tools and knowledge in return, and through their own efforts he knew they would pull themselves into the galactic union.

This is what Garth had hoped. But a wind of change was blowing through the settlement that had grown up around his ship. No longer was he the centre of attention and focal point of the village life. He had to grin when he thought of his fall from power; yet there was very little humour in the smile. Serious and attentive Weskers still took turns of duty as Knowledge Collectors, but their recording of dry facts was in sharp contrast to the intellectual hurricane that surrounded the priest.

Where Garth had made them work for each book and machine, the priest gave freely. Garth had tried to be progressive in his supply of knowledge, treating them as bright but unlettered children. He had wanted them to walk before they could run, to master one step before going on to the next.

Father Mark simply brought them the benefits of Christianity. The only physical work he required was the construction of a church, a place of worship and learning. More Weskers had appeared out of the limitless planetary swamps and within days the roof was up, supported on a framework of poles. Each morning the congregation worked a little while on the walls, then hurried inside to learn the all-promising, all-encompassing, all-important facts about the universe.

Garth never told the Weskers what he thought about their new interest, and this was mainly because they had never asked him. Pride or honour stood in the way of his grabbing a willing listener and pouring out his grievances. Perhaps it would have been different if Itin was on Collecting duty; he was the brightest of the lot; but Itin had been rotated the day after the priest had arrived and Garth had not talked to him since.

It was a surprise then when after seventeen of the trebly-long Wesker days, he found a delegation at his doorstep when he emerged after breakfast. Itin was their spokesman, and his mouth was open slightly. Many of the other Weskers had their mouths open as well, one even appearing to be yawning, clearly revealing the double row of sharp teeth and the purple-black throat. The mouths impressed Garth as to the seriousness of the meeting: this was the one Wesker expression he had learned to recognize. An open mouth indicated some strong emotion; happiness, sadness, anger, he could never really be sure which. The Weskers were normally placid and he had never seen enough open mouths to tell what was causing them. But he was surrounded by them now.

'Will you help us, John Garth,' Itin said. 'We have a question.'

'I'll answer any question you ask,' Garth said, with more than a hint of misgiving. 'What is it?'

'Is there a God?'

'What do you mean by "God"?' Garth asked in turn. What should he tell them?

'God is our Father in Heaven, who made us all and protects us. Whom we pray to for aid, and if we are Saved will find a place—'

'That's enough,' Garth said. 'There is no God.'

All of them had their mouths open now, even Itin, as they looked at Garth and thought about his answer. The rows of pink teeth would have been frightening if he hadn't known these creatures so well. For one instant he wondered if perhaps they had been already indoctrinated and looked upon him as a heretic, but he brushed the thought away.

'Thank you,' Itin said, and they turned and left.

Though the morning was still cool, Garth noticed that he was sweating and wondered why.

The reaction was not long in coming. Itin returned that same afternoon. 'Will you come to the church?' he asked. 'Many of the things that we study are difficult to learn, but none as difficult as this. We need your help because we must hear you and Father Mark talk together. This is because he says one thing is true and you say another is true and both cannot be true at the same time. We must find out what is true.'

'I'll come, of course,' Garth said, trying to hide the sudden feeling of elation. He had done nothing, but the Weskers had come to him anyway. There could still be grounds for hope that they might yet be free.

It was hot inside the church, and Garth was surprised at the number of Weskers who were there, more than he had seen gathered at any one time before. There were many open mouths. Father Mark sat at a table covered with books. He looked unhappy but didn't say anything when Garth came in. Garth spoke first.

'I hope you realize this is their idea—that they came to me of their own free will and asked me to come here?'

'I know that,' the priest said resignedly. 'At times they can be very difficult. But they are learning and want to believe, and that is what is important.'

'Father Mark, Trader Garth, we need your help,' Itin said. 'You both know many things that we do not know. You must help us come to religion which is not an easy thing to do.'

Garth started to say something, then changed his mind. Itin went on. 'We have read the Bibles and all the books that Father Mark gave us, and one thing is clear. We have discussed this and we are all agreed. These books are very different from the ones that Trader Garth gave us. In Trader Garth's books there is the universe which we have not seen, and it goes on without God, for he is mentioned nowhere; we have searched very carefully. In Father Mark's books He is everywhere and nothing can go without Him. One of these must be right and the other must be wrong. We do not know how this can be, but after we find out which is right then perhaps we will know. If God does not exist . . .'

'Of course He exists, my children,' Father Mark said in a voice of heartfelt intensity. 'He is our Father in Heaven who has created us all—'

'Who created God?' Itin asked and the murmur ceased and every one of the Weskers watched Father Mark intensely. He recoiled a bit under the impact of their eyes, then smiled.

'Nothing created God, since He is the Creator. He always was—'

'If He always was in existence—why cannot the universe have always been in existence? Without having had a creator?' Itin broke in with a rush of words. The importance of the question was obvious. The priest answered slowly, with infinite patience.

'Would that the answers were that simple, my children. But even the scientists do not agree about the creation of the universe.

While they doubt—we who have seen the light *know*. We can see the miracle of creation all about us. And how can there be a creation without a Creator? That is He, our Father, our God in Heaven. I know you have doubts; that is because you have souls and free will. Still, the answer is so simple. Have faith, that is all you need. Just believe.'

'How can we believe without proof?'

'If you cannot see that this world itself is proof of His existence, then I say to you that belief needs no proof—if you have faith!'

A babble of voices arose in the room and more of the Wesker mouths were open now as they tried to force their thoughts through the tangled skein of words and separate the thread of truth.

'Can you tell us, Garth?' Itin asked, and the sound of his voice quieted the hubbub.

'I can tell you to use the scientific method which can examine all things—including itself—and give you answers that can prove the truth or falsity of any statement.'

'That is what we must do,' Itin said, 'we had reached the same conclusion.' He held a thick book before him and a ripple of nods ran across the watchers. 'We have been studying the Bible as Father Mark told us to do, and we have found the answer. God will make a miracle for us, thereby proving that He is watching us. And by this sign we will know Him and go to Him.'

'That is the sin of false pride,' Father Mark said. 'God needs no miracles to prove His existence.'

'But *we* need a miracle!' Itin shouted, and though he wasn't human there was need in his voice. 'We have read here of many smaller miracles, loaves, fishes, wine, snakes—many of them, for much smaller reasons. Now all He need do is make a miracle and He will bring us all to Him—the wonder of an entire new world worshipping at His throne, as you have told us, Father Mark. And you have told us how important this is. We have discussed this and find that there is only one miracle that is best for this kind of thing.'

His boredom at the theological wrangling drained from Garth in an instant. He had not been really thinking or he would have realized where all this was leading. He could see the illustration in the Bible where Itin held it open, and knew in advance what picture it was. He rose slowly from his chair, as if stretching, and turned to the priest behind him.

'Get ready!' he whispered. 'Get out the back and get to the ship; I'll keep them busy here. I don't think they'll harm me.'

'What do you mean . . . ?' Father Mark asked, blinking in surprise.

'Get out, you fool!' Garth hissed. 'What miracle do you think they mean? What miracle is supposed to have converted the world to Christianity?'

'No!' Father Mark said. 'It cannot be. It just cannot be—!'

'GET MOVING!' Garth shouted, dragging the priest from the chair and hurling him towards the rear wall. Father Mark stumbled to a halt, turned back. Garth leaped for him, but it was already too late. The amphibians were small, but there were so many of them. Garth lashed out and his fist struck Itin, hurling him back into the crowd. The others came on as he fought his way towards the priest. He beat at them but it was like struggling against waves. The furry, musky bodies washed over and engulfed him. He fought until they tied him, and he still struggled until they beat on his head until he stopped. Then they pulled him outside where he could only lie in the rain and curse and watch.

Of course the Weskers were marvellous craftsmen, and everything had been constructed down to the last detail, following the illustration in the Bible. There was the cross, planted firmly on the top of a small hill, the gleaming metal spikes, the hammer. Father Mark was stripped and draped in a carefully pleated loincloth. They led him out of the church.

At the sight of the cross he almost fainted. After that he held his head high and determined to die as he had lived, with faith.

Yet this was hard. It was unbearable even for Garth, who only watched. It is one thing to talk of crucifixion and look at the gently carved bodies in the dim light of prayer. It is another to see a man naked, ropes cutting into his skin where he hangs from a bar of wood. And to see the needle-tipped spike raised and placed against the soft flesh of his palm, to see the hammer come back with the calm deliberation of an artisan's measured stroke. To hear the thick sound of metal penetrating flesh.

Then to hear the screams.

Few are born to be martyrs; Father Mark was not one of them. With the first blows, the blood ran from his lips where his clenched teeth met. Then his mouth was wide and his head strained back and the guttural horror of his screams sliced through the susuration of the falling rain. It resounded as a silent echo from the masses of watching Weskers, for whatever emotion opened their mouths was now tearing at their bodies with all its force, and row after row of gaping jaws reflected the crucified priest's agony.

Mercifully he fainted as the last nail was driven home. Blood ran from the raw wounds, mixing with the rain to drip faintly pink from his feet as the life ran out of him. At this time, somewhere at this time, sobbing and tearing at his own bonds, numbed from the blows on the head, Garth lost consciousness.

He awoke in his own warehouse and it was dark. Someone was cutting away the woven ropes they had bound him with. The rain still dripped and splashed outside.

'Itin,' he said. It could be no one else.

'Yes,' the alien voice whispered back. 'The others are all talking in the church. Lin died after you struck his head, and Inon is very sick. There are some that say you should be crucified too, and I think that is what will happen. Or perhaps killed by stoning on the head. They have found in the Bible where it says . . .'

'I know.' With infinite weariness. 'An eye for an eye. You'll find lots of things like that once you start looking. It's a wonderful book.' His head ached terribly.

'You must go, you can get to your ship without anyone seeing you. There has been enough killing.' Itin as well, spoke with a new-found weariness.

Garth experimented, pulling himself to his feet. He pressed his head to the rough wood of the wall until the nausea stopped. 'He's dead.' He said it as a statement, not a question.

'Yes, some time ago. Or I could not have come away to see you.'

'And buried of course, or they wouldn't be thinking about starting on me next.'

'And buried!' There was almost a ring of emotion in the alien's voice, an echo of the dead priest's. 'He is buried and he will rise on High. It is written and that is the way it will happen.

Father Mark will be so happy that it has happened like this.' The voice ended in a sound like a human sob.

Garth painfully worked his way towards the door, leaning against the wall so he wouldn't fall.

'We did the right thing, didn't we?' Itin asked. There was no answer. 'He will rise up, Garth, won't he rise?'

Garth was at the door and enough light came from the brightly lit church to show his torn and bloody hands clutching at the frame. Itin's face swam into sight close to his, and Garth felt the delicate, many-fingered hands with the sharp nails catch at his clothes.

'He will rise, won't he, Garth?'

'No,' Garth said, 'he is going to stay buried right where you put him. Nothing is going to happen because he is dead and he is going to stay dead.'

The rain runnelled through Itin's fur and his mouth was opened so wide that he seemed to be screaming into the night. Only with effort could he talk, squeezing out the alien thoughts in an alien language.

'Then we will not be saved? We will not become pure?'

'You were pure,' Garth said, in a voice somewhere between a sob and a laugh. 'That's the horrible ugly dirty part of it. You were pure. Now you are—'

'Murderers,' Itin said, and the water ran down from his lowered head and streamed away into the darkness.

Starbride

ANTHONY BOUCHER

I always knew, ever since we were in school together, that he'd love me some day; and I knew somehow too that I'd always be in second place. I didn't really care either, but I never guessed then what I'd come second to: a native girl from a conquered planet.

I couldn't guess because those school days were before the Conquest and the Empire, back in the days when we used to talk about a rocket to a moon and never dreamed how fast it would all happen after that rocket.

When it did all begin to happen I thought at first what I was going to come second to was Space itself. But that wasn't for long and now Space can never take him away from me and neither can she, not really, because she's dead.

But he sits there by the waters and talks and I can't even hate her, because she was a woman too, and she loved him too, and that was what she died of.

He doesn't talk about it as often as he used to, and I suppose that's something. It's only when the fever's bad, or he's tried to talk to the Federal Council again about a humane colonial policy. That's worse than the fever.

He sits there and he looks up at her star and he says, 'But damn it, they're *people*. Oh, I was like all the rest at first; I was expecting some kind of monster even after the reports from the Conquest troops. And when I saw that they looked almost like us, and after all those months in the space ship, with the old regulation against mixed crews . . .'

He has to tell it. The psychiatrist explained that to me very carefully. I'm only glad it doesn't come so often now.

'Everybody in Colonial Administration was doing it,' he says. 'They'd pick the girl that came the closest to somebody back home and they'd go through the Vlnian marriage rite—which of course isn't recognized legally under the C A, at least not where we're concerned.'

I've never asked him whether she came close to me.

'It's a beautiful rite, though,' he says. 'That's what I keep telling the Council: Vln had a much higher level of pre-Conquest civilization than we'll admit. She taught me poetry and music that . . .'

I know it all by heart now. All the poetry and all the music. It's strange and sad and like nothing you ever dreamed of . . . and like everything you ever dreamed.

'It was living with her that made me know,' he says. 'Being with her, part of her, knowing that there was nothing grotesque, nothing monstrous about green flesh and white in the same bed.'

No, that's what he used to say. He doesn't say that part any more. He does love me. 'They've got to understand!' he says, looking at her star.

The psychiatrist explained how he's transferring his guilt to the Council and the Colonial policy; but I still don't see why he has to have guilt. He couldn't help it. He wanted to come back. He meant to come back. Only that was the trip he got space fever, and of course after that he was planet-bound for life.

'She had a funny name,' he says. 'I never could pronounce it right—all vowels. So I called her Starbride, even though she said that was foolish—we both belonged to the same star, the sun, even if we were of different planets. Now is that a primitive reaction? I tell you the average level of Vlnian scientific culture . . .'

And I still think of it as her star when he sits there and looks at it. I can't keep things like that straight, and he does call her Starbride.

'I swore to come back before the child was born,' he said. 'I swore by her God and by mine and He heard me under both names. And she said very simply, "If you don't, I'll die." That's all, just "I'll die." And then we drank native wine and sang folksongs all night and went to bed in the dawn.'

And he doesn't need to tell me about his letter to her, but he does. He doesn't need to because I sent it myself. It was the first thing he thought of when he came out of the fever and saw the calendar and I wrote it down for him and sent it. And it came back with the C A stamp: *Deceased* and that was all.

'And I don't know how she died,' he says, 'or even whether the child was born. Try to find out anything about a native from a Colonial Administrator! They've got to be made to realize . . .'

Then he usually doesn't talk for a while. He just sits there by the waters and looks up at the blue star and sings their sad folksongs with the funny names: *Saint Louis Blues* and *Barbara Allen* and *Lover, Come Back To Me*.

And after a while I say, 'I'm not planet-bound. Some day when you're well enough for me to leave you I'll go to Vln—'

' "*Earth*," ' he says, almost as though it was a love-word and not just a funny noise. 'That's their name for Vln. She called herself an Earth woman, and she called me her Martian.'

'I'll go to Earth,' I say, only I never can pronounce it quite right and he always laughs a little, 'and I'll find your child and I'll bring it back to you.'

Then he turns and smiles at me and after a while we leave the waters of the canal and go inside again away from her blue star. Those are the times when I can almost endure the pain of being second in his heart, second to a white Starbride far away and dead on a planet called Earth.

Out of the Everywhere

MARIAN ABBEY

It came in the night. Suddenly there was another being in the house, and we caught our breath and stared. Silence at first, and then its closed face opened and it screamed. But not at us.

The sound was terrifying. I looked to the window, but there was nothing—no movement, no noise outside. Beyond the door, nothing stirred. Everywhere still and yet it was here. Its scream cut through the air, like no sound I had ever heard before. Certainly no human sound—cat-like if anything, but fuller and more eerie, more piercing. A scream of anger and rage, of pain and surprise, for where it found itself.

At the turn of the night, when dark blue thinned to a glimmer in the sky, it opened its eyes. It must have opened its eyes to the sky first because when finally it swivelled its head we saw the dark night-sky colour of its eyes gazing at us. Perhaps it brought nothing with it but took everything from this new world in which it had arrived.

So it looked at us with its night eyes, out of its wrinkled, wise face, and seemed to know everything there was to know.

Yet it needed help. It needed something to cover it against the coolness. When we brought a blanket, it quietened. And when we held it, it seemed content. It writhed for a while, then closed those strange deep eyes, and it was as though the shutters had come down. It didn't so much go to sleep as go away. Its body was still here, slumped and curled as a kitten, but its being was elsewhere.

I looked at it, lying like an island in the middle of my world, and wondered where it had gone to, when it would come back.

And although it couldn't hear me, or understand our language, I whispered into the whirl at the side of its head.

So what to do? We told our friends about it, of course, and soon a constant stream of people arrived, nosy and noisy, with their questions and comments. And cameras. They brought exclamations of surprise and amazement, and left with the efforts of trying to capture it on film. Because it was unique—the camera was the only way they had to take a part of it with them. The creature stared at them and bore the bright flashes calmly. If these strange people and their little machines didn't harm it, then they could be tolerated. Eventually it would close its eyes against the lights and drift off into another world inside its head where no one could reach it.

Sometimes at night I would wake, with no reason and no idea why I had done so. Some instinct, some calling perhaps that humans don't usually hear. And I would tiptoe down the hallway and into the end room. It slept there, so quietly. I would wet my fingers and hold them in front of the holes in its face, and feel the little winds blow in and out, and know that it was still with us. And beyond the window the sky was dark, and all the little dots of stars shone through the winter branches of the tree, and the great big obvious moon flooded light into the garden and I would wonder, why here? Why us?

It knew very little about us in some ways, and then I would look into those dark eyes and know, without doubt, that it knew everything. That it had arrived in our world knowing everything that was important.

But the basic, day-to-day things, the tasks to survive, we had to teach it ourselves. It would watch us and copy, its odd face mimicking our expressions, its dumpy body trying hopelessly to move in the way we did. It learnt to eat and drink, to force food into that moving hole in its face. It learnt to reach out for things, and examine them—to work out what different objects could do and what they were good for. It would taste them, sniff, turn them over and over, watching all the time.

Sometimes I thought it might even understand us. We had no idea of its own language, of course, so it taught us that at the same time as we taught it ours. We learnt a bit about what its different sounds meant, but a lot of its communication was done with body and face. Eventually we learnt when it was happy or sad, frightened or calm. It was all we could understand.

But it couldn't last. Nothing so strange ever does. Separate beings, distinct races, can never live together as such for long. One must triumph in the end. It is not human nature to allow separateness for ever. The old human instincts rose up: to destroy, to know, to make like us.

And in a way it lost. The little thing. It had to. After all, it had come to depend on us for food, for shelter, even for company. How do you subject another race? You make them dress like you, eat your food, obey your rules. And ultimately you teach them your language, and tell them that that is right, that is how they must communicate. And it was like that with this creature. It was the only way we could live with it, and so we went ahead and made it to be one of us.

Deep inside it, I know, there may still be a core that is other. Even now, sometimes, when I look at its eyes (which have changed, by the way—they are lighter and a normal blue-grey and no longer know everything), when I catch a look that I cannot understand, it occurs to me that I have not won. Not fully. But nearly. Nearly. Because eventually it gave in and acquiesced. It took time. The world had turned round to summer again. And the sun was bright and sharp the day it toddled towards me, having learnt human walking; and held out its arms, having been taught to need a human caress; and said 'Mummy'.

Acknowledgements

The editor wishes to thank Ken Cowley for his suggestions and his help in locating some of the stories in this collection.

Marian Abbey: 'Out of the Everywhere', Copyright © Marian Abbey 1998, first published in this collection by permission of the author. **Francis Beckett**: 'Judgement Day', Copyright © Francis Beckett 1998, first published in this collection by permission of the author. **Robert Bloch**: 'Space-Born', first published in Roger Elwood (ed.): *Children of Infinity* (Franklin Watts, 1973/Faber, 1974), Copyright © 1974 by Roger Elwood, reprinted by permission of the author's estate and its agents, Scott Meredith Literary Agency, L.P. **Stephen Bowkett**: 'The Chase', Copyright © Stephen Bowkett 1998, first published in this collection by permission of the author. **Anthony Boucher**: 'Starbride', first published in *Thrilling Wonder Stories*, Copyright © 1951 by Anthony Boucher. **Fredric Brown**: 'Not Yet the End' from *Nightmares and Geezenstacks* (Bantam, 1961). **Arthur C. Clarke**: 'Encounter at Dawn' from *Of Time and Stars* (Gollancz, 1972), reprinted by permission of the author and the author's agents, David Higham Associates and Scovil Chichak Galen Literary Agency, Inc. **Avram Davidson**: 'The Bounty Hunter' from *What Strange Stars and Skies* (Ace Books, 1965), first published in *Fantastic Universe*, March 1958, reprinted by permission of Grania Davis, proprietor of the Avram Davidson Estate. **Philip K. Dick**: 'The Father-Thing' from Isaac Asimov (ed.): *Tomorrow's Children* (Compton Russell, 1976), reprinted by permission of the author and the author's agents, Scovil Chichak Galen Literary Agency, Inc. **Nicholas Fisk**: 'Sweets from a Stranger' from *Horror Stories and Mystery Stories*, Copyright © Nicholas Fisk 1978, reprinted by permission of the author c/o the Laura Cecil Literary Agency. **Nicholas Stuart Gray**: 'The Star Beast' from *Mainly in Moonlight*, by permission of the publishers, Faber & Faber Ltd. **Harry Harrison**: 'The Streets of Ashkelon' from *Two Tales and Eight Tomorrows* (Gollancz, 1963), first published in *New World Science Fiction*, reprinted by permission of Sobel Weber Associates, Inc. **Joe L. Hensley**: 'The Pair', first published in *Fantastic Universe*. **Damon Knight**: 'To Serve Man' from *Far Out* (Gollancz, 1961), reprinted by permission of the author. **Murray Leinster**: 'Keyhole', Copyright © 1951 by Standard Magazines, first published in *Thrilling Wonder Stories*, Copyright © 1979 by the estate of William Fitzgerald Jenkins, reprinted by permission of the estate and its agents, Scott Meredith Literary Agency, L.P. **Roger Malisson**: 'The Holiday-Makers' from Mary Danby (ed.): *Nightmares* (Armada, 1983), reprinted by permission of the author. **Ray Nelson**: 'Eight O'Clock in the Morning' from R. Chetwynd-Hayes (ed.): *Tales of Terror from Outer Space* (Collins Fontana, 1975), reprinted by permission of the author. **William F. Nolan**: 'The Underdweller' from *Wonderworlds* (Gollancz, 1977), originally published in *Fantastic Universe*, Copyright © 1957 by Kingsize Publications, copyright renewed 1985 by William F. Nolan, reprinted by permission of the author. **Barbara Paul**: 'Earth Surrenders', Copyright © 1997 by Barbara Paul, first published in Martin H. Greenberg and Larry Segriff (eds.): *First Contact* (Daw, 1997), reprinted by permission of the author. **Theodore L. Thomas**: 'Day of Succession' from Damon Knight (ed.): *A Century of Science Fiction* (Gollancz). **A. E. van Vogt**: 'Dear Pen Pal' from *Destination: Universe!* by A. E. van Vogt (Pellegrini & Cudahy, 1952), first published in *Arkham Sampler*, 1949, reprinted by permission of the Ashley Grayson Literary Agency on behalf of the author. **Sue Welford**: 'Star Daughter', Copyright © Sue Welford 1998, first published in this collection by permission of Laurence Pollinger Ltd on behalf of the author.

Acknowledgements

The illustrations are by:

David Wyatt pp i, iii, 1, 12, 16, 79, 86, 115, 148-149, 153
Paul Fisher Johnson pp ii, 21, 47, 58, 116, 121, 161, 167, 189, 193, 204, 207
Helen Burr pp 25, 64, 78, 171, 181, 185
Brian Pedley pp 35, 94, 104
Ian Miller pp 38, 41, 127, 155, 160
Dave Hopkins p 144

EVERY NON-RESIDENT ALIEN
MUST FILE A UNITED STATES
INCOME TAX RETURN